............We distinguished

of flight or battle,

with those young

to the bad guys.

mountainous jung

recognizable civilization, are fighting NVA, of equal courage, under the most intolerable conditions. Our helicopters, the tools used to initiate these contacts, return during and after the heat of battle to replenish, to retrieve the wounded, and also the body bags. To know and feel destruction and death, and simply return home disaffected to the quiet of a flight line at the end of the day could not be shared with anyone but those who had experienced that same magnitude of life and death on a daily basis. A knowing look from crew member to crew member conveyed more than words could ever say.

To Tom

Warm regards

Frank

3-14

ISBN: 978-0-9791906-0-5

9 780979 190605

51399

GHOST RIDERS

A War Story

Frank Lampi

Sergei Publications

GHOST RIDERS...A WAR STORY

SERGEI PUBLICATIONS

Address for information: Sergei Publications,
23810 Overlook Circle, Bingham Farms, MI 48025

ISBN: 978-0-9791906-0-5

Printed in the United States of America
Library of Congress Control Number: 2007903755

Acknowledgements

My heartfelt thanks to those who helped make this a more "readable" story, but principally to Mary Beth Korte, who blew the dust off my manuscript and turned it into a book. I would also like to express my appreciation to BJ Barnett for the pictures he graciously provided for the front and back covers of this book.

This story is historical fiction. Although based on actual events, liberties have been taken to make the story more cohesive. Timelines and names have been altered or pseudonyms used to protect not only the living, but the families of the deceased.

For all my "brothers" who did make it back to the "World"... "Welcome home"...Not everyone fought the enemy directly. In fact, the statistics do show that of the 475,000 men in place in Viet Nam in 1969, only 62,000 were actual infantry combatants. But to "merely" have served your time "in-country" merits the same accolades any warrior would deserve. We all faced hardships in some form; whether it was the misery of the monsoon season, guard duty, sleep deprivation, the heat, lack of more than basic creature comforts, and let's not forget the rockets and mortars. Whether you were in a combat role, direct or indirect support, stand tall, we all did our job. For all those in uniform, I wish you peace.

This story is dedicated to 58,169 brothers who didn't make it home to tell their "stories" to friends and loved ones. But most particularly for John, Ralph, Bob, Dave, William, Bear, and especially Greg; who was a hero living in our midst. He was a man of conviction, who lived and died looking for nothing more than peace.

Foreword

Frank Lampi's account, "Ghost Riders" is a story of his experiences as gunner and later as crew chief and gunner on a Huey helicopter. Lampi served in the 101st Airborne Division twenty-five years after the end of World War II. It is a good example of how far the concept of airborne envelopment has come since the day of the parachute and glider being used for insertion.

In Lampi's year "in country," the helicopter was used to insert and extract the grunts who fought in the jungles, rice paddies and mountains of Viet Nam. As I read the accounts of the myriad tasks that the helicopter forces performed I marveled at the way this new breed of airborne soldier performed in battle day after day in support of the infantrymen who carried the battle to the Viet Cong and the North Vietnamese.

Lampi has a special way of describing the adventures. I found myself involved in the actions and several of his experiences found their way into my dreams during ensuing nights. During the first flights of their four-man crew they flew donut dollies with their goodies to forward bases. That was a moral booster to the troops. They extracted a USO group which was delayed by fog after a performance for front line troops. They were always welcomed in the forward areas when they brought in PX supplies.

The action picked up when the 158th Assault Helicopter Battalion moved forward to Camp Evans. Their first actions against the enemy involved moving elements of the First Battalion, First ARVN Division on a night time assault, inserting them on the beach on the South China Sea. They were to serve as a blocking force for a company of the 2nd Battalion of the 506th Infantry which was on a recon mission of a suspect VC village and bunker complex.

Company "A" of the 158th AHB was known as the Ghost Riders. The choppers of each unit or company had distinct markings so they could be recognized in the air and on the ground. Their chopper "644" had the Screaming Eagle logo painted on the tail boom. I was pleased to read of their work inserting and extracting the 1st of the 327th, the 1st of the 502nd and the 2nd of the 506th, all familiar and famous fighting units of the Screaming Eagles in World War II. I was also impressed with the teamwork and coordinated work of the Air Force and the airborne infantry.

Chopper 644 is eventually lost in combat and replaced. Several pilots, co-pilots and gunners are killed or wounded in various actions. Frank fills out his year in country always believing "it will be the other guy, not me." It was vital that each crew was close knit – a mistake by one could cost the life of some or even an entire crew.

This account is filled with heroics, vividly described by an author who credits his survival to others on his team or those who play a supporting role in the action.

George Koskimaki
Author of "D-Day" With The Screaming Eagles, The Battered Bastards of Bastogne, and Hell's Highway.
Northville, Michigan

Any member of the military, regardless of rank or vocational specialty, must first and foremost realize that in war their primary purpose, their job, before anything else, is to strategically disrupt and kill the enemy by any means or force available.

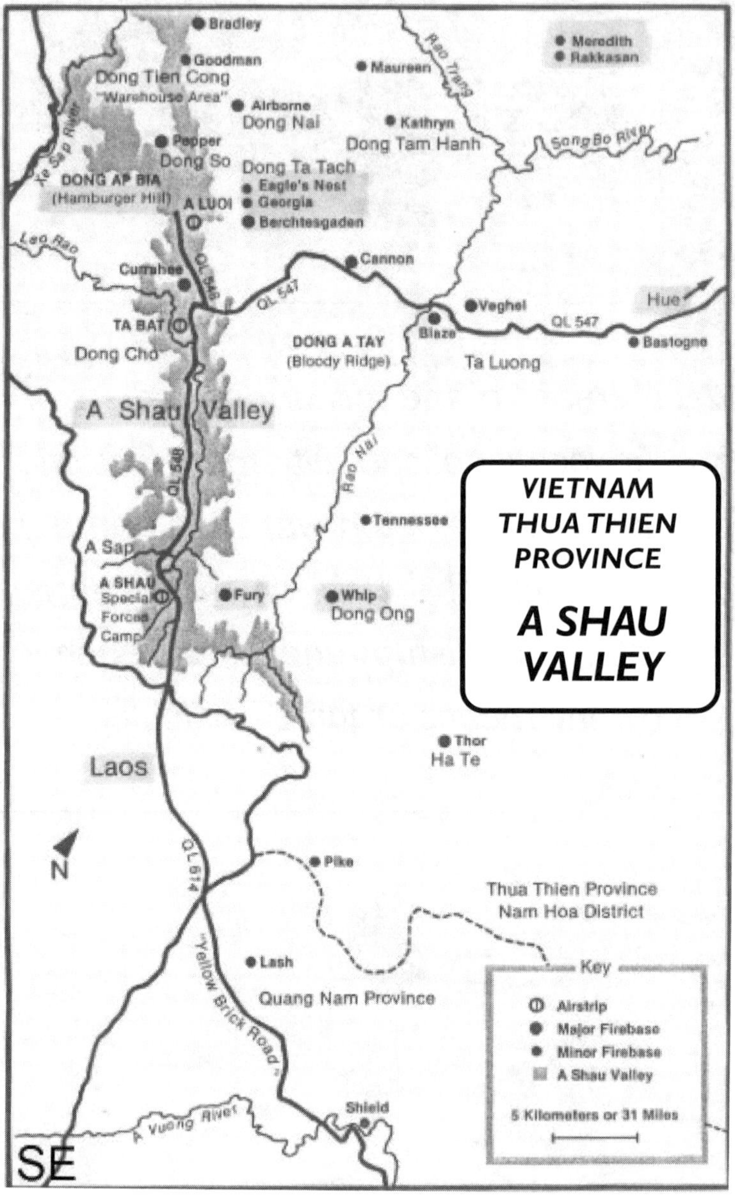
VIETNAM
THUA THIEN
PROVINCE
A SHAU
VALLEY
Bradley
Goodman
Meredith
Rakkasan
Maureen
Rao Trang
Dong Tien Cong
"Warehouse Area"
Airborne
Dong Nai
Kathryn
Dong Tam Hanh
Song Bo River
Pepper
Dong So
Dong Ta Tach
Eagle's Nest
Georgia
Berchtesgaden
Xe Sap River
DONG AP BIA
(Hamburger Hill)
A LUOI
Leo Rao
Currahee
QL 548
QL 547
Cannon
Veghel
Hue
Blaze
Bastogne
TA BAT
Dong Cho
DONG A TAY
(Bloody Ridge)
Ta Luong
A Shau Valley
Rao Nai
Tennessee
A Sap
A SHAU
Special
Forces
Camp
Fury
Whip
Dong Ong
Thor
Ha Te
Laos
N
QL 614
Pike
Thua Thien Province
Nam Hoa District
"Yellow Brick Road"
Lash
Quang Nam Province
Key
Airstrip
Major Firebase
Minor Firebase
A Shau Valley
5 Kilometers or 31 Miles
Shield
A Vuong River
SE

Chapter One

The DC-8 shook violently, as if being hammered by ack-ack, anti aircraft artillery fire, or "triple A." I closed my eyes and imagined how it would have been twenty-five years earlier, over German occupied Europe, World War II. The ominous black flak of the German 88's, as they mercilessly pounded the B-17's. But that was so long ago and now…Viet Nam, September 1968. Today it wasn't triple A, only the warm moist tropical air creating severe updrafts in the towering white cumulus clouds. As the big stretch jet was bounced and pummeled by the turbulent air, we descended toward the green jungle below. I was nineteen, with already one year of service with the U.S. Army, the "green machine" as a UH-1 Huey helicopter crew chief. A "rotor toter" helicopter mechanic getting ready to add a new occupational specialty to my military career, that of "door gunner." But that was yet to come… Now I concentrated on the landscape, wondering how many "bad guys," "gooks," "dinks," "zips," "VC," were down in that green mass of jungle waiting, just to kill me. I had always been a war buff. Anything I could get my hands on to read about war, whether it was the Indian wars and cavalry, World War I or II, Korea, anything, so long as it was action packed! Now I was going to find out what it's all about in *my* war.

I had volunteered for duty in Viet Nam, afraid the war would be over before I could get there. Now as I watched the countryside grow bigger and ever closer, the details of symmetry in the plantations and rice paddies were plain to see. Everything was checkerboard perfect. The water reflected off the rice paddies like jewels dancing on the ground. It was hard to believe conflict and death existed in such a beautiful panorama of lush greens, slivers of silver as light reflected off water, the deep blue of the ocean and the terracotta reds of Earth roads winding off into the small villages.

Beside me sat Scotty, a friend who had been with me since our training days on the Huey at Fort Rucker, Alabama. When we had departed from Milwaukee earlier that week after a thirty-day leave, Scotty had cried like a baby, he was scared shitless. He knew he wasn't coming home. I, on the other hand, had a smile on my face that was as big as all out doors. Like I said, I loved war, and I couldn't wait to get it on. Now, Scotty was crying for a different reason. Bright red blood was oozing from his right ear, and he was in extreme pain. I called for the stewardess thinking maybe she could help my buddy. She had him drink some water and start chewing gum, as she explained the Captain of our big jet had to make an extreme descent to dodge any potential ground fire. The end result was that the cabin pressure differential had equalized with the outside air, and as we continued to descend at an alarming rate, our ears were taking a beating for it. After that wonderful explanation from our lovely attendant (very little of which I understood), we began the approach to Tan Son Nhut airbase just outside of Saigon.

The city of Saigon was huge. I had not thought much about the city. More so, that Viet Nam was one vast jungle with rice paddies, and grass hut villages. But the city was teeming with activity. It was quite reminiscent of New York or Chicago at lunch hour. I couldn't believe that a war was going on below me.

As we touched down on the runway I breathed a sigh of relief. It had been a long trip, twenty six and a half hours with fuel stops in Anchorage, Alaska and Yokota, Japan. I was exhausted, and Scotty was still bleeding a little from his ear. The pain had subsided only a little. At least he wasn't crying anymore. The flight attendant had made arrangements to get Scotty off the aircraft first for medical attention. As we taxied into the reception area my face was plastered to the porthole window looking at all the activity around us. There were huge tractor like forklifts carrying the all too familiar steel conex in which all manner of equipment and supplies from the States was shipped to Viet Nam. All the buildings had corrugated steel roofs, four-foot plywood walls with screen extending to the eaves of the roof and sandbags stacked half way up the walls for blast protection from rockets and mortars. The revetments where the sleek F-4 Phantoms and the older F-105 Thunderchiefs were parked also had huge blast walls three feet thick packed with sand. There was so much activity it reminded me of a colony of ants all working in unison to some unknown end.

As the big aircraft pulled up to the waiting portable stairs, I become aware of the long line of familiar olive green busses waiting to take us to the replacement depot. What was not so familiar was the steel mesh welded over each of the windows of the bus. It seems that on occasion a local "VC" would attempt to lob a hand grenade through the window of the passing bus as the dinks sped by on their moped or motor scooters, and then disappear into the crowded Saigon streets. I then noticed something more sobering as we continued taxiing in to the ramp; hundreds of GI's sitting under corrugated steel roofed outdoor assembly area. Only these guys were waiting to go home. A handful were dressed in the same khaki uniforms we were wearing, but most had on new jungle fatigues. The only way to discern the veterans from someone new coming "in country" was by their jungle boots. The boots were weathered and colored the brownish red of the Vietnamese soil. They were a subdued and somber bunch, smoking cigarettes and most staring out at nothing. I would later learn that was called the thousand-yard stare. These were eyes that could see, but not speak the words that could ever tell of the graphic violence and trauma that war brings. The battle hardened boys, now men by the very nature of the horrors of war. There was none of the carrying on that is so symptomatic and symbolic of nineteen and twenty year old American boys. As I looked back at them, I wondered how many of their friends they had left behind. And then I wondered, how many will I leave behind, and, will I be one of the lucky ones sitting here one year from now?

As I stepped from the air-conditioned comfort of the aircraft I was greeted with a blast of extremely hot, humid air. Even hotter and more humid than I could ever remember experiencing while I had been stationed in southern Alabama. I immediately turned into a wet sponge and my fresh starched Army khakis wilted into a sticky, clammy mess pasted to my back and chest. As I walked down the air stair a sergeant kept repeating "if you hear the siren, immediately fall out and into the nearest bunker" as he pointed in the direction of huge pierced steel planking walls filled with sandbags covered by eight foot culverts that were also topped with sandbags.

As we walked by the GI's waiting for their "Freedom Bird" back to the "World," they started to fill our ears and heads with our new vocabulary of Vietnam slang. "Hey cherry boy" (someone who has never been shot at), "I'm going back to the 'world'" (the good old USA), "the land of the round eyes." "Round eyes" meant Caucasians, but when it was said with a soft and sensuous voice inflection, it became a more exclusive term to GI's referring to a beautiful American female, rather than Caucasians in general. The cat calling and whoops were interspersed with a well-intentioned "good luck" and some sincere voices saying "keep your head down," "be cool." So many sights and sounds were battering the senses it was hard to comprehend that there was any organization involved in this whole process.

Boarding the bus, I involuntarily looked back as we pulled away from the reception area and that big DC-8, my "freedom bird," my last reality check of civility and home, and I wondered....

Chapter Two

As the bus pulled into Long Binh replacement depot, our driver, a PFC, sarcastically welcomed us to the home of "LBJ." In this regard he was not speaking of our commander-in- chief, Lyndon Baines Johnson, but in reference to Long Binh Jail. LBJ was where all the truly "bad" boys of the U.S. military would end up for crimes committed in country. Anybody that had perpetrated a crime of any sort, drugs, murder, theft, would start their journey to prison here.

Two and a half days at the replacement depot, the "repot-depot" in Long Binh, only 362 days and a "wake up" to go. I'm already starting to think and speak the slang like the rest of these "old timers." Two and a half days of living out of a duffel bag, lousy food and endless bullshit details. The only bright spot was the return of Scotty from the dispensary. He had perforated his right eardrum during the approach into Saigon and was on the mend. His only concern was that it would affect his flying status, and whether or not he would be able to "crew" his own "bird."

There were formations three times a day for reassignment orders. Names were called alphabetically and then assigned a division or unit. Every MOS (military occupational specialty) you could think of was represented. Artillery, mortars, supply, communications, truck mechanics, tank mechanics, helicopter mechanics, motor pool, POL specialists (petroleum, oil, lubrication) cooks, clerks, combat engineers, medics, drivers for all and much more. But they were all "remfs"; rear echelon motherfuckers, when it came to the most important MOS of all... "eleven bravo," "eleven bush," "grunts" the infantry. THE MIGHTY INFANTRY. It was said it took ten remfs' to support and provide care for one infantryman. I was a "remf." But in my opinion, I was at least sitting on the edge of some of the action. After all, who would be taking these infantry grunts to the fun and games?

What I was seeing at the repot-depot confirmed all of the support needed for our guys. Guys were going to the "Big Red One" the 1st Infantry Division, 25th Infantry, "5th Mech" Fifth Mechanized Infantry, Ninth Infantry, "First Cav" First Air Cavalry, Eleventh Armored Cavalry, "Eighty Deuce" 82nd Airborne, 173rd Airborne, 101st Airborne, Fourth Infantry Division, the "Americal Division," 1st Aviation Brigade, "MACV" Military Assistance Command Vietnam, service support units, and many more.

As we stood for yet another formation, Scotty and I were standing side by side as they started calling names. "Scotini" (Scotty's surname) was called. As they continued through the alphabetical list and got to the Z's, I realized it would be a parting of the ways for Scotty and me. Scotty was heading south with the Ninth Infantry to an aviation unit down in the "Delta," or IV Corps as the Army called it. We shook hands; said "good luck" and he was gone, just that quick.

Forty-five minutes later, after waiting for two more unit assignments, the name I had been waiting three days to hear was finally called. "Lahti, Frank" my name, finally. I held my breath as I waited for my unit assignment. My chest swelled a little with pride. I was going to the 101st Airborne Division. Having finished parachute jump training the prior spring, I felt I almost had it in my pocket to pull an airborne outfit for my tour. The "Screaming Eagles," rich in the history of World War II, one of the units I had read so much about in my youth, was now a reality for me. Good-bye to Long Binh and LBJ, hello Bien Hoa, my new home, temporarily…

Chapter Three

Upon receiving orders for my new division assignment, the first order of business was to find out where the unit was in country. We, as newly arrived soldiers, were fast learning the lingo of Americans in Viet Nam.

Viet Nam had been split into four segments geographically by the South Vietnamese military and they called them “Corps.” I Corps pronounced “eye” or “First Corps” was located in the North. Its boundary was from the DMZ or demilitarized zone separating North and South Viet Nam to Chu Lai, which was south of Danang. Two and three Corps extended south through the country from Chu Lai to Saigon. IV Corps ran from South of Saigon to the delta region of South Viet Nam.

I found an old timer who could help with all my questions about the 101st. He was a staff sergeant, wearing the unit patch of the Ninth Infantry on his right shoulder signifying he had already served a combat tour in Viet Nam. I figured he would be a good source for information. “Hey do you know where the 101st is located?” I asked as I caught his eye. He didn’t let me down. “Oh man,” he said, “you’re going up North...I Corps” he pronounced it “eye” to the “street of no joy,” up on Highway One.

"They said the 'NVA,' the North Vietnamese Army is marching up and down that road at will." He continued, "they control large areas of the country up there, and I heard that the First Cav got their ass kicked real bad. So bad, that they decided to pull them out and put the 101st up there." "But I thought the 101st is at Bien Hoa" I said. "Yeah, that's their division rear" he said, "They only have a brigade down here. Everybody else is up North." So, I, being young, dumb, and naïve, took it hook, line, and sinker. As my brain tried to translate a simple matter of what "up North" meant, I knew I would definitely be where the action was. I figured if I was going north, and the "bad guys" were coming from the North, I was in deep shit... The bravado I had felt only minutes earlier had rapidly diminished to a degree of self-preservation. Now I felt like a lamb going to slaughter; especially if the NVA were marching down a road in broad daylight! As the depth of my maturity increased rapidly in the face of many and immediate challenges, I would soon realize that the rumor mill indeed was simply that...rumor. Although there was always a tidbit of truth to many rumors, the old military maxim of believing nothing of what you hear, and only half of what you see still held true. But now my mind raced, as I gathered up my gear and boarded yet another bus for the drive to Bien Hoa.

I arrived at the rear division headquarters of the 101st in Bien Hoa on Saturday. We were immediately hustled around being issued jungle fatigues, boots, towels, underwear and other assorted camouflage clothing including the most incredible nylon blanket they called a "poncho liner" that kept you cool when it was hot, and warm when you were cold. Along with our clothing issue, we had also been issued our weapons; the new M-16 or "black slack" as the grunts called it. I immediately memorized the serial number on my weapon. If it was lost (or stolen), I would be held responsible to pay for it, and I sure didn't make that kind of money in this mans' army. As my year progressed, I would learn to covet the simple, little pleasures in life, such as dry clothes, a good blanket and a clean weapon.

The 101st had established a policy of providing five days of "SERTS" (Screaming Eagle Replacement Training School), "primary training" or "P" training to acquaint all new division troopers on surviving the initial cherry months in a hostile environment. Although I could not know it at the time, I would later come to appreciate this P training and put it to good use. The infantry sergeants that were assigned to us for this training were called "cadre" and wore black baseball caps and black shirts. All had pulled at least one tour in the "bush" as infantry "eleven bravos" or grunts prior to returning to the rear.

Our "hooch" where we would spend the next week in P training is located on a gentle rise about a mile from the Bien Hoa air base. Throughout the day, I keep hearing "thumps" preceding the scream of jet engines roaring down the runway. I am getting accustomed to the boom of artillery, but I can't determine what the thumps are. Then as our duties end for the evening, I am standing by the side of my hooch and hear the now familiar thump followed moments later by another thump. As I look toward the airport, I notice huge flames extending from the tailpipes of two F-4's as they quickly accelerate down the runway. The jets are loaded with an incredible array of bombs filling every available space under the wing. I am totally amazed and in awe as the pilot smoothly points the nose of the jet fighter skyward. Lifting off, the jet continues to accelerate; the pilot pulling the nose of the jet up to near vertical. I automatically bend my head back to follow the aircraft in its steep ascent, my mouth open in disbelief. I have never seen an aircraft perform like that! "Hey sarge, what's that all about?" as I point to the F-4's now in a tight formation disappearing in the sky. The sergeant who has also stopped to watch explains, "They hustle outta here like that when our guys are in trouble out in the boonies," he explains. "The grunts that need his 'close air' support aren't very far away probably" as he continues to follow the disappearing smoke trail of the jets. "What makes you say that?" I ask, intrigued by the thought of battles brewing so close. As he responds, he lifts his arm simulating the jet and the steepness at which it climbed away from the runway. "He's probably in a hurry to get up to altitude so he can make that steep, diving, bomb run those jet jocks love to do" as he finishes his statement his hand comes diving down, simulating the arc of the jet. The Phantoms' take off was a most impressive demonstration of our air power, and in the coming year I would experience on several occasions my own close air support from a pair of those great Phantoms.

5:30 Sunday morning, I am woke from a sound sleep, lights blazing in my eyes, and a second tour cadre "buck" sergeant screaming at us to get up and get going. As I rolled over not believing my ears I said, "Hey man, its Sunday, what the hell's up?" He came over to my bunk and gave me a look that would have stopped me cold in my tracks if I were running at full speed. "Your in 'the Nam' man, every day is a work day, now you get moving before I decide to put you on an LP (listening post) by yourself tonight." Not really believing he could do it, but not disbelieving it either, I unassed my cot and got moving.

Along with classroom work, there were always practical exercises in honing our new skills. We went out to the division perimeter and fired every weapon that we could encounter in the infantry unit. This was great fun, as I had always had an arsenal of hunting weapons at home. But nothing that I had done previously, could compare to dropping a mortar round down the tube. Listening to the wumpf as it left the tube, you could actually watch its graceful but deadly arc through the sky, disappearing in a blur as it picked up speed hurtling towards the distant tree line. As the round crashed with a resounding boom in a flash of fire and black smoke on the trees and scrub, I had a creepy sensation of many "Mr. Charles" eyeballing us at that very same moment.

The .50 caliber machine gun I had read so much about left me in awe as I watched them "rock and roll" on a distant burned out two and a half-ton truck or "deuce and a half" as it was more commonly called. Coming from a small town in northern Michigan, I had led a sheltered life, and I wasn't afraid to admit it. I had never attended a military air show or many of the other "big city" events that could have prepared me more for the reality that struck me right between the eyes now. The might of so many different weapons designed for only one reason, to kill other human beings, was staggering to think of. As I would learn very soon, I had just scratched the surface of what killing machines are.

As the day wore on and darkness was fast approaching, we had one weapon left to fire. One of the black shirt sergeants asked if anyone had previously fired the M-60 machine gun. I quickly raised my hand anticipating the opportunity to do some rock and rolling of my own. Prior to leaving Fort Rucker we had practiced aerial gunnery with the M-60 flying in a "C" model Huey gun ship. While the new Warrant Officer pilots were honing their skills firing the 2.75-inch rockets, we practiced shooting the "sixty." However, as with any job you volunteer for in the Army, you usually get the shit end of the stick. Because of the approaching darkness, the black shirt cadre wanted to secure our perimeter. So another guy from our group who also had experience on the sixty took the opposite end of the firing line on high ground and we set up our M-60's for perimeter defense.

I swung open the spring-loaded supporting legs at the end of the barrel of the machine gun so it could rest at an angle pointing skyward as the butt plate rested on the ground. It had been six months since I had last fired the weapon, and I prayed to myself I could remember the finer points of its operation, like how to load the damn thing! I opened the feed cover of the M-60, grabbed a "belt" from the ammo can of 7.62-millimeter "ball" ammunition and laid it down on the feed tray of the gun. After I closed the feed cover, I pulled the arming lever back and slammed it forward as the 7.62 round chambered itself in the weapon. Well, that had gone smoothly enough, I thought to myself. Just like I had remembered. At least now I felt I was contributing to the safety of my fellow soldiers!

It was a great show watching the new guys shooting the sixties down range. Red tracers ricocheted off the twilight ground like roman candles spewing balls of fire. As the gunnery exercise was complete and the troops filed back through the gate into the secure perimeter, I stepped up my vigilance and scan of the now dark tree line. I anticipated at the very least a full-blown frontal assault by a VC sapper team while we were in an exposed, vulnerable, position. (We had just learned about "sappers" the previous day in P training.) I quickly was brought back to reality by one of our cadre sergeants. “You gonna stay out here all night cherry?” the sergeant asked as he walked up behind me. I gave him a stupid shrug of my shoulder and offered a lame excuse that I hadn’t been relieved of my duties at this post. The sergeant got in my face and said “well didn’t you see me pull the other guy off the south perimeter?” I had, but once again I felt stupid and continued to pack up the M-60 and ammo. The sergeant continued “you act stupid like this over here boy, and you go home in a body bag!” Another lesson learned, 358 days and a wake up to go.

Our fifth day of P training, and graduation day, or to be more exact, graduation night. Our test will be to navigate a trail through a maze of hedges and locate every booby trap, trip wire, punji pit, antipersonnel and “stick” mine that we have learned about during our stay with the black shirts. The bad guys, or “Charlie,” will take our unexploded ordinance, whether it’s an unexploded five hundred pound aerial bomb, artillery shell, claymore or anything they can use or extract explosive from to make their own nasty little antipersonnel mines.

At 2200 hours, twenty-nine troopers line up single file in preparation for entering the maze. It is a dark, moonless, starry night. The sky is so clear; it seems possible to see a million stars at a glance. The time difference between my girl in the states and me is twelve hours. I wonder if she looks at the stars and feels the same longing I have for her. It all seems so far away. Only a week in country and I feel so alone. In the distance you can hear the laughter and music coming from the “EM club” the enlisted men’s club as the boys drink and laugh away the day’s trials and tribulations.

Back in the maze, the “point” man, followed closely by one of our “black shirt cadre” has found the first booby trap. It is a thin trip wire, so thin; in the darkness it is invisible to the eye. It is strung chest high, across the trail, and is connected to the pin of a hand grenade. Our point man has found it only because we are moving at a snails pace. The test continues as the next new “point” man moves at a pace that is so slow, that by morning we would only be a hundred feet down the trail. Ten minutes later a trip flare ignites as we dive for the side of the trail. Our new point man has failed his walk in the woods, but no one is the worse for it as I move into point.

As I begin stepping forward on the trail, I can feel the breath of my cadre sergeant right behind me. He has the maze memorized, and knows where every booby trap is. His breathing seems loud in my ears as I strain to see the outline of the trail in the starlight. Now I know why the guy before me had moved so slowly. It is as black as the inside of a West Virginia coal mine at midnight. I wait for my eyes to readjust to the dark after the blinding white brilliance of the trip flare. By looking out of the corner of my eyes, I can more easily distinguish the lighter shade of the trail against the varied shades of gray, which makes up the outline of the thick hedge. Moving my free hand up and down, left and right feeling for trip wires or extended branches that don’t move freely; I bend at the knees going down to ankle level and lower searching for anything that seems out of place. My hand rubs the hard packed earth of the trail, searching for freshly turned earth or branches and leaves that could hide some form of trigger device.

My mind wanders; there are over thirty troops on this exercise, yet I can only hear the music from the enlisted men’s club. The troops at the club are singing along to “Leaving on a Jet Plane” as they try to harmonize through the song. The tune rises and falls as the soldiers try to out-do each other in emphasizing “leaving” and it turns into a cacophony of wailing and laughter.

Although the night is cool, and a gentle breeze dances across my face, I am sweating as if walking in the middle of the Sahara desert. It sure would be nice to be chugging a cold beer from the club about now.

After surveying two feet of the trail in front of me, I take another step and another, repeating the search process until I have traveled nearly twenty feet. Then as my hand moves across the ground, I feel a slight bump or protrusion on the ground; it could be just a small pebble or rock. I stand up, raise my left arm, fist clenched to signify a halt. The red filtered glow of my flashlight fills the trail at my feet where my suspicions are confirmed. There in the dirt no bigger than the head of a big matchstick is the shiny tip of a .50 caliber bullet, a "toe popper." Leaving the round in place, I motion to my black shirt what I have found. He is already acknowledging with thumbs up that I'm "good to go." I have survived point in the maze.

As I move back to the rear of the line, the sergeant is explaining to the troops once again how this little device works. The VC will file down the base or primer of the round until it is paper-thin. Then they stick a nail through a piece of wood to act as the firing pin. The nail is placed in the hole with the primer base of the .50 caliber round over the nail. When foot pressure pushes the round onto the nail, it fires taking the foot or toe with it. This is a war of attrition. When a man is wounded, it takes at least two others to carry and care for him. The dinks know that, and they are as good as we are at playing the attrition game. We continued our progress through the maze and lose only four point men that night. It had taken nearly four hours to progress a half mile. For some of us, it was time for the real thing.

Chapter Four

The C-130 Hercules we were flying north to our new assignments reminded me of jump school. It seemed like so long ago. But now instead of “sticks” of new paratroopers, we are a gaggle of young, and for the most part, cherry boys. Some of the guys on the C-130 are returning from rest and recreation, R&R, others are going back north for an extension of their tour. But for me it’s a new adventure, and for all the cherries, thinking about the unknown and what may lie ahead.

In the spirit of youth, death is a non-recognizable part of life. Somebody else will die, not me. We all had that spirit, somebody else, not me. I knew guys could die, and for sure would die, but not me. As I faced death in the coming months, I would not only see death in the faces of those young G.I.’s who would die, but also on the faces of our enemy. We were all of the same brotherhood. The look of disbelief on their face that this could happen to them! Not fear, just incredulous disbelief that their “number was up,” “zapped,” “greased,” “wasted,” “KIA,” killed in action. To cope with the sudden and often horrific manner in which men die, most will adopt a mental policy of “better him than me.” I didn’t give it a thought at the time, but would accept it later to maintain my own grip on some form of reality.

The trip took an hour and forty-five minutes to Phu Bai from Bien Hoa airbase. It was just another sixty or so miles up Highway One to the DMZ. We loaded on deuce and a half trucks for the trip to Camp Eagle, only a fifteen-minute ride. As the truck convoy proceeded up Highway One the "street of no joy," I saw no evidence of the rumored NVA dead or alive. So much for rumors! Traveling up the new two lane black top highway, I wondered how much the Vietnamese would appreciate this road built by U.S. Navy "Seabees" at U.S. taxpayer's expense.

The Vietnamese "Mama-sans," "Papa-sans," and children dressed in their black silk pajamas and woven bamboo conical shaped hats walked along the dirt shoulder on both sides of the road as we traveled south. Some of the old men, Papa-sans, wore white cotton or silk shirts, squinting at us as we stared back at them. We were as curious about them as they were of us. Little boys and girls in all states of dress, their hands held out as we passed them in a cloud of red dust, begging for anything we might throw down to them. There were cyclo cabs with middle age Vietnamese men pumping their bicycle pedals at a leisurely pace. The more affluent appearing young Vietnamese men wore black suit pants with white dress shirts and sandal shoes. On the back of there motor scooters were some of the prettiest French-Vietnamese beauties sitting sidesaddle. Their boyfriends wove in and out of traffic, as if it was their right, seemingly defying death, as their pretty cargo looked back at us with subdued curiosity.

The rice paddies stretched to the mountains on my right and the sea on my left. The rice paddies, well tended by the farmers, whose water buffalo even now walked on the dikes and sloshed through the water and mud, were oblivious to the noise of the big diesel engines in our two and a half-ton trucks. Occasionally we would pass a roadside stand selling big frosty sixteen ounce Coca-Cola, Marlboro and Winston cigarettes, the vendors waving to us with big smiles with black or missing teeth. I wondered where they got their hands on all of the American goods.

As we continued our drive south, I continued to take in the panorama of the Vietnamese countryside. This was my first unhindered opportunity to see the real country and its people. It was a warm, sunny day, with white wispy clouds stretched over the long blue sky. The mountains were covered in a gray veil of haze that made their features soft and blurry, the air was fresh and clean, and as I lifted my face to feel the warmth of the sun I drifted back to an early summer day in June back home. As I enjoyed the warmth of the sun and the wind blowing across my face, I thought about how I had gotten here.

I had volunteered to come here to fight, because I wanted to experience war. This was for me alone. A selfish act to be sure and I enjoyed the moment for what it was, and looked with anticipation to reaching my new unit. I had no preconceived ideas of who was right or wrong, nor did I care about ideology or politics. All I wanted was the opportunity to experience the drama and excitement of a pitched battle and all that combat and fighting entailed. It never did cross my mind about the dangerous aspect of my youthful follies. Life was to be lived!

Pulling into the company area, my new home, Company A, 101st Assault Helicopter Company, the "Commancheros," was an eye opener for all of us on the truck. On either side of the "headquarters" tent stretched rows of tents two deep, interspersed with the sand bagged pierced steel planking, culvert bunkers that had become all too familiar, but as of yet not utilized by me.

Fifteen cherry boys hopped off the deuce and a half followed by our duffle bags. As we milled around the sandy open area outside the headquarters tent, I began to take in all the activities that surrounded us.

"A" Company's company area was situated on the eastern edge of a small hill. Our company area made up the extreme eastern perimeter of Camp Eagle. Eagle extended a mile in circumference. The Army called it a Fire Support Base camp. It had everything you could think of, even that big old PX we all loved so much. The enlisted men's twelve man tents were located to the north of the company area in two rows. The officers and enlisted men of the two flight platoons were to the South of the company area with the flight line terraced in three tiers down the eastern edge of the hill in line with the flight platoons. Beyond the flight line were two maintenance tents capable of each holding one helicopter. Approximately one hundred yards east of the helicopter maintenance area was the company perimeter with its bunkers and guard towers.

The other side of our little hill was the "MARS" communication station for Camp Eagle. The MARS station was our direct line communication with not only everyone in Viet Nam, but also our girlfriends and family back home. Through a network of ham operators we could call home free. That is as long as we were willing to have as many as a half dozen ham and military operators listening to our conversation. Unlike a normal telephone conversation, the person talking would have to say "over" every time we were through with a sentence or comment. Then all the operators would flip a switch so the other person could respond. It was a clumsy way of communicating, especially for a civilian or non-military person. I never took advantage, as much as I would have loved to talk to my girl, I couldn't get into party line conversations.

For the most part, the soldiers in the immediate area ignored us as they went about their tasks. The air was filled with the noise of generators for electricity, helicopters approaching and departing the company area, trucks and jeeps plying their way around the roads of the firebase, and the sporadic distant wump of outgoing artillery. Helicopters filled the air in every quadrant of the sky. Big "Chinooks," CH-47 helicopters came and went with their sling loads of ammo, "C" rations, water and everything it takes to make an infantry unit operate in the field. The sleek, menacing "Cobra" its' pilots sitting in tandem, one behind the other, just newly arrived in Viet Nam, dazzled us as they sped along the perimeter. It was a true gun platform with the Gatling mini-gun protruding from the bottom nose of the aircraft and racks of rockets hung from the sides. Hueys, or "slicks" as we came to know them, (cargo carriers) flew from the respective company helipads around the firebase. With their doors wide open, the crew chief and right side door gunners would sit tucked back in the "well" just aft of the cargo bay area. It was exciting to think I would be riding a Huey very soon.

As we all stood taking in the sights and sounds of a military company at work, out of the headquarters tent came our new first sergeant or "top" as he was affectionately called. He cast a long shadow over our green gaggle. Top cast a long shadow in the sun because he was long, and he was tall. A smooth, full face, about thirty-five years old, he had a belly that was rapidly heading south, and hair so fine, it reminded me of a young child's hair as a light breeze tossed it about on his high forehead. "Alright give me a line," he said in a soft-spoken voice. We immediately formed a line and stood at a loose command of "attention" not really knowing how to respond to his command. He began with a subdued welcome and immediately began the "in-processing" so typical for every new arrival at a new command. Specialist Derrick, the company clerk took my travel orders assigning me to "A" company. "Until we get your MOS and orders sorted out" Top said, "were going to put you in the 'casual' tent behind our headquarters tent here" as he crooked his neck and turned his face to the right. A small collective groan came from our group as we faced yet another casual duty assignment. Top continued as he reacted to our groan of despair, "we'll have ya'll assigned in a few days" he said in a reassuring voice. "We need you working more than we need casual details" he said. At least he sounded sincere I thought.

I dumped my duffel bag onto an empty cot in my designated tent and went in search of the supply area to pick up my linens. I picked up my linens, which comprised one wool blanket, and that was it. Oh well, this is war I thought. But damn, I sure could have used a pillow. That was the moment I became a "scrounger." A scrounger could find just about anything if they put their mind to it.

I took the time to write my mom and girlfriend to give them my new mailing address. We had been issued post cards by company headquarters for the express purpose of letting the world know we had arrived alive. I sure was missing mail call and news from home. I thought it was pretty cool how all I had to do was write "free" on the upper right corner of anything, and Uncle Sam would get it to the recipient. (The insides of C ration cardboard boxes containing scribbled letters were sent home by the grunts in the field for lack of anything better to write on.)

As usual, the new guys are stuck with the details of mundane and boredom that few ever care to carry out, but in every case are required of any military unit in the field. In Viet Nam the "shit burning" detail was by far the most distasteful, and was usually assigned to men in the company who were receiving punishment for minor military infractions or a platoon sergeant's "discretionary" correction of an unruly trooper under his command.

Shit burning had become a necessary evil in the 101st because the local farmers wanted to use our outhouse waste as fertilizer in their rice paddies. So to circumvent that from happening, division headquarters had issued an order that all human waste would be disposed of "antiseptically" on a daily basis. Higher command deduced that by daily burning of the outhouse waste, the order could be satisfied. In essence, fifty-five gallon oil drums that were cut in half to collect the defecation were pulled out of the outhouse trap doors every morning. We would move them a safe distance from, and, always downwind of our mess tent and company area. Then we would dump five gallons of JP-4 jet fuel in the drum and light it on fire. As the JP-4 kerosene ignited, the flames would rapidly spread around the barrel. The small flame would quickly become a rolling undulating cauldron of yellow and orange flames. As it roiled up the sides of the barrel and leapt into the morning air, the now depleted hydro-carbon, its energy spent, was nothing more than a thick plume of black smoke. Keeping it burning through the day and giving it an occasional stir would reduce it to gray ash. Needless to say, it was a detail abhorred by all.

I digress to mention this shit burning not only because it was a “casual” or punishment duty, but because it was also a most pervasive sight and smell around every base camp that existed in Viet Nam. Along with the rising clouds of red dust created by helicopters lifting off from all points of the compass, the noise and black smoke of diesel engines from generators, trucks, bulldozers, tanks, armored personnel carriers “APC’s” and earthmovers, the long straight pall of black smoke rising into the early morning air meant only one thing to the GI’s who had experienced that “holy grail” of fire of another kind.

Not that burning shit was the only important detail the “lifers” could think of. We also enjoyed filling, tying and “humping” sand bags to some newly erected officer’s tent or bunker. Then there was the ever-present cigarette butt detail. Picking up all the filtered cigarette and non-“field stripped” cigarette butts and assorted trash that failed to make it to the other fifty-five gallon trash cans, which, by the way, needed to also be emptied on a regular basis.

I must have been living the clean life when the assignments where being issued out to our group of newly arrived. I was assigned to guard duty on a tower that overlooked our perimeter and flight line on the other side of the rice paddy from our company area. A Company’s perimeter area of responsibility was protected by four bunkers and two guard towers. The bunkers were spaced every fifty yards along the perimeter over a distance of two hundred yards. The guard towers, twenty five feet high were on each end of the four bunkers. During daylight hours, the perimeter was manned with one soldier in each tower with an M-60 and radio communication with A Company.

After chow the following morning, I drew my M-60 from the supply area and marched off to the tower. The view from the top of the tower gave a better view of my new home. From the perimeter of the firebase was an endless row of barbed wire. The wire was strung twenty feet vertically to a height of four feet. Horizontally, it was strung six inches off the ground in twelve-inch separations in a triangular pattern out horizontally every two feet. They called this wire configuration tangle foot. It was almost impossible to run through tangle foot. On either side of the barbed wire was concertina or razor wire stacked two coils wide with one coil on top to form a triangle. Trip flares were hung inside both the razor wire and barbed wire along with an assortment of anti-personnel mines throughout the field of wire.

In front of each bunker along the perimeter were four claymore mines. The mines were spread in an arc to provide interlocking coverage between bunkers. A claymore mine is a molded plastic convex shaped antipersonnel weapon filled with hundreds of steel buckshot. It is a tremendous weapon for use in ambush and perimeter defense because they can be quickly set up or retrieved if not used. The thirty-yard blast radius would kill anything in a fan shaped area from two inches off the ground up to a height of four feet. The claymore can be quickly set up on two wire legs that scissor open from the body of the mine. A blasting cap is inserted into the body of the weapon, and the firing wire is connected to a “clicker” type of self generating electric detonation device. The claymores could be fired independently or simultaneously.

On top of each bunker was a guard with an M-60 that provided interlocking fire with the bunker on either side of them. As I studied our perimeter defense, I felt pretty secure that we could deal with anything the gooks could throw at us. Soon it would be put to the test.

Beyond the perimeter of barbed wire was a cleared area that extended out a half mile to our base camp garbage dump. I would spend endless hours watching the local Vietnamese pick through our garbage for anything of use. They would salvage our discarded artillery ammunition boxes, which are made of pine. Then they would make foot lockers and sell them back to us for five bucks. They are very ingenious people leaving nothing go to waste. As we fought them in battle, I would find they were also very resourceful in leveraging our tactics to their advantage.

We are approaching the monsoon season and my wonderful guard tower becomes a miserable and dreary place to sit when the rain comes and the winds begin to blow. I have become more vigilant as the reduced visibility from the rain and fog only means more opportunity for a surprise visit from VC or NVA. The monsoon season starts with rain beginning during the night and ending early in the morning. As the sun burns away the fog and slowly peaks its bright rays of light around the edge of heavy, gray, rain-laden clouds, I look forward to the warmth it will bring. It will rain again at mid-morning and alternately rain and shine through the rest of the day. The ground is becoming saturated with water, and the once empty trenches surrounding the firebase are filling with water.

On my fourth day of guard tower duty as I am returning to the company area for evening chow, I am half way up the terraced flight line when I hear "crump," "wump-wump," "crump" in quick succession. As I quickly scan the flight line and maintenance area, there's not a soul in sight. This is a new and disturbing sound as the crumps continue to "walk" their way towards me in an erratic but ever increasing volume. As I make a running dive into the nearest ditch, I hear "incoming" being yelled from different areas of the camp as the wail of a siren announces "incoming." Well I thought, at least I don't look foolish diving in this ditch. The "old timers" love to laugh at cherry boys when they react to "normal" things, such as when they duck their heads when "outgoing" artillery booms. Well now at least I know what the bunkers are for! I have a terribly indescribable feeling of "nakedness" at being exposed in the open. As I lift my head to look for obvious signs of the impending blasts I look straight into the eyes of Mr. French. Mr. French, a CW4 chief warrant officer is from my old company at Hunter Air Field in Savannah. "Mr. French, what are you doing here?" I ask. Before he can respond, I continue, "I didn't even know you had left the company in Savannah. He responded, "I just got here yesterday." "This is my first experience with 'incoming'" I explained, "and I wasn't sure if it was or wasn't. But when I looked around and didn't see anybody I figured I'd better find some cover." Such as it is, the shallow ditch was better protection than being in the open. Mr.

French said in a grim manner "This is my second tour over here, and you just don't get used to this shit." We heard a few more rounds impact on the far side of camp, and then the "all clear" was sounded.

I waved to Mr. French as we got up and went our separate ways, I thought how strange it was to have "hit the ditch" and not noticed him laying immediately three feet in front of me at the moment I took the dive. I never saw Mr. French again after that day. I presume he had moved on to another assignment. As my maturity grew about reactions under hostile conditions, I'd learn that in time of war, there would be many unexplained events and circumstances that were more than chance, but never the less unexplainable as to why or how. I've now been under fire and I feel that I handled myself respectably, and I try to analyze how I might handle a real battle scenario. Three hundred forty-eight days and a wake up to go.

A week on the tower and I have been ordered to report to the command tent in the morning for assignment orders. As I enter the command tent the company clerk "specialist four Derrick" nods and without as much as a how-de-doo informs me that I am assigned to a maintenance platoon! "You'll be working with 'C' team, first maintenance platoon" he said. I was crushed! Without catching his breath he continued "your tent is the second to the left behind the mail room and bunker" as he motioned over his right shoulder with a jerk of his thumb pointing in the general direction of my new living quarters. "Hey, I'm a crew chief" I said as he threw my file on top of a growing stack of similar files. "I came here to fly." "You got 'orders' saying you're on flight status?" he asked. I knew something was going terribly wrong when he said that. "No" I said. "How many 67N's" my "MOS" "67N20", the military acronym meaning Military Occupational Specialty, or "Single rotor turbine helicopter specialist" "do you think we have in this company?" Derrick asked. He continued, "We have twenty one Hueys, two flight platoons of ten each and the maintenance bird. That's forty two flight slots for gunners and chiefs" he used the colloquial term for the enlisted flight crew. "If you don't come in here with flight orders, you go to the maintenance section" he said. "Well how do I get on flight status?" Without stopping to wait for an answer I continued, "I had aerial gunnery training at Rucker, and I flew maintenance test flights at Hunter," referring to Hunter Army Airfield in Savannah Georgia. "If you didn't have orders at Hunter, you get on a waiting list like everybody else and wait for a slot to open up" Derrick said. Top came from behind a canvas wall in the interior of the tent. He had obviously been listening to the conversation. "When we get an opening for crew either through 'DEROS' or 'attrition' we fill from the waiting list," he said. "DEROS" was a military acronym for "Date of Estimated Return from Overseas," or more exactly, the date we would leave Viet Nam. In my situation, a term of one year. "Attrition" was pretty self explanatory, either somebody left, or somebody got "wasted." "Well how long could it take to get pulled from the waiting list?" I asked. I asked a question that I knew would not have an acceptable answer for me. "It could take six months minimum depending on how long the list is and how other things go," Top said.

I left the tent with my name now on the "list." A beautiful sunny day had just turned into a foul and gloomy shit hole before my very eyes. I just knew that if I had to spend a year on the ground, I would figuratively blow my brains out. My mind began working overtime trying to figure my way out of a seemingly impossible dilemma. As I walked through the company area my mind was still focused on a way around getting into a flight platoon. As I searched for my new home, the "C" section maintenance tent, I heard someone call my name. I turned and saw a familiar face. It was Garcia, a guy I had known casually from my maintenance company at Hunter Airfield in Savannah. I gave him a smile and wave, and as we shook hands I said to him "When did you get here?" "Yeah, I got over here a month ago man" he said in that lazy Puerto Rican style of speech. I had liked Garcia; he was an easy going, go with the flow kind of guy. And he was smart and had his shit together.

I immediately started to throw questions at him about the company, how it worked, where things were and what he was doing. "Slow down man, slow down" he said in that unhurried,

Hispanic but definitely East Coast accent. “I’m ‘crewing’ a Huey in second flight platoon,” he said. “How the hell did you get a flight slot?” I asked as we continued walking. “Shit man, when I got here, they were so hard up for crew I didn’t ask, they just gave it to me.” I was disbelieving. I couldn’t believe what I had just heard. “You mean to tell me that a month ago they were hard up for crew chiefs, and now I can’t beg, borrow or steal a flight slot,” I said incredulously. “Yeah we’ve gotten a lot of new guys this past month” he said kind of half smiling. “That really sucks” I said. “Let me see what I can do about getting you into second flight platoon” Garcia said. “Would you be willing to just ‘gun’ if you could get in?” he asked. Being a gunner meant sitting on the right side of the helicopter. The only difference was that it was an E-4 pay slot, which I already was, and I had to clean both guns at the end of the day while the crew chief took care of the maintenance side of things. Without a moments hesitation I nodded my head in the affirmative. As long as I could get on flying status, I figured my chances were better to move up to a crew chiefs slot later on my own helicopter. I was starting to feel better about things. Garcia had shown me around his flight platoon area, the flight line and maintenance area and then left me to rummage about by myself.

As I sat in my new hooch writing letters home, the guys from C section maintenance began trickling in. Introductions were exchanged, and always, where we were from in the States and how long each of them had been in country. As it always is in the Army, it was all walks of life in my little tent community. “Tyson” was a “cracker” from Southern Georgia, slow talking and sociable. “Wolfe” was from Las Vegas, a big tall sandy haired guy, also soft-spoken but more intelligent and at twenty-four, an old man by the average age in our tent. “Beauprie” was from Beaumont, Texas. He was stand off-ish and said hello but obviously was more of a loner than the rest of the guys. “Albert” and “Morricini” were both from the Los Angeles area. Albert was also the oldest of the crew at twenty-seven and a businessman prior to being drafted. “Cryder” or “the Critter” as he was called by the guys was an old man in a young mans’ body. His MOS was 67A10, an aircraft mechanics helper. Critter was a sweet, innocent kid who spoke with a lisp and was a little slow on the uptake to most conversations. "Davis" was also from Georgia, an elementary school teacher. He was a draftee, quiet and amiable, and a man who loved his wife more than any person I had ever met before. He lived only to be able to return to her. He was a fortunate man, when he arrived in Viet Nam he only had a nine month tour of duty to DEROS. The last of our tent-mates was Castolini who hailed from Philadelphia. Castolini was skinny with acne covering his face and a large mouth out of proportion to his head. He had a hoarse, boisterous way of speaking in a clipped, quick East coast accent.

As we all sat and talked about what was currently happening, and getting caught up on what was going on back in the world, I explained my plight of wanting to get into a flight platoon. Wolfe said in that soft-spoken voice, "Ya know, the life expectancy of those Huey crews is something like thirty-five minutes." I thought if that were true, I'd be in a flight platoon next week! I said to Wolfe, "If that's true, you guys should be patching up helicopters on a daily basis." "We are" Wolfe said as he gave me a hard, serious look. As all the guys more or less affirmed his statement by their silence they started bailing out for evening chow. Maybe I wouldn't have to wait so long after all.

Chapter Five

Three weeks in C section and I'm going nuts. Our usual maintenance routine is to perform fifty and one hundred-hour inspections on the helicopters. This is the same tedious work I had been doing in the states. The only difference now was that I was twelve thousand miles away.

I've started receiving mail from home on a regular basis and it sure makes a day more livable. Most times it is the daily events and happening in the family, or something about my dogs that my mom will write about. My girlfriend in Milwaukee writes to me almost daily and tells about work and the goofy things she and her roommate are up to. I've been in country a little more than a month and the "world" seems so far away.

The company helicopters launch between seven and eight o'clock in the morning. During the day, depending on the type of missions, helicopters would come back and occasionally we are called upon to trouble shoot mechanical or specific aircraft problems. I notice the metal patches along the fuselage and tail section of the helicopters, bullet holes that have been repaired. How I hunger for some of the action.

Garcia hasn't been able to help me out at all, even though I bug him constantly. I have noticed that the guys in the two flight platoons have their own clique, and they stay more to themselves in their respective flight platoons. I have tried to get to know the flying guys, but it's like a wall—that although not unfriendly, is not open to uninvited guests. When I visit Garcia, the looks I get from the guys in his hooch are almost dark and foreboding, somewhat like an interloper at a private party.

I have become fast friends with the men in my hooch tent. The stories and bullshit fly fast and furious. And I have come to know whom I can trust. Albert is a good friend with a guy in California named "Hooker," who also happens to make "headers" for cars. Too cool. Morricini insists on showing us all kinds of pictures of his girlfriend back in California. She is exceptionally hot, and it makes me wonder what she's doing with a goof like him. Beauprie has opened up a little, went to high school with Janis Joplin, and he tells all kinds of great stories. Life in our hooch is pretty good. Each man respects the privacy of the other, and we share our mail and our care packages from home.

I have managed to scrounge a pillow and I'm sleeping quite comfortably, thank you, in spite of some young Warrant Officer pilot's misfortune to not keep a better eye on his bedding. I'm sleeping well at least the two nights out of three that we don't have bunker guard duty on the perimeter. Being in the maintenance section, we pull more guard duty than the flight platoons do, due to the hours that flight crews fly.

We get up at five a.m. and are at chow by six a.m. By seven a.m. we are in the maintenance area and work until five or six o'clock. One thing I begin to notice is that I am perpetually tired. It seems we never have enough rest, and the brain doesn't function in a decisive and critical manner. My entire year, even allowing for R & R —rest and recreation, will continue to be one of sleep deprivation that gets worse as my flying hours increase through my tour.

Early one morning after guard duty, I am walking

backwards against a driving rain up the terraced flight line towards our company area. My rain poncho covering the helmet on my head sounds like I'm on the inside of a snare drum. With the M-60 thrown over my shoulder, the wind is howling mercilessly. As I trudge along, I am weary of the sleepless night I have just spent in the leaky bunker fending off the rats that call the bunkers home, and the mosquitoes that want to suck the life out of me, one milliliter at a time. I am moving in a world of noise. The rain, the wind, my personal snare drum, and for some unknown reason I stop dead in my tracks. I have just reached the top of the last terrace on the flight line. As I turn my face into the driving rain, not eighteen inches in front of me is the spinning tail rotor of a Huey. I can't believe I have just about walked into this high-speed buzz saw. Not allowing myself time to think or ponder, I react by running to my left away from the spinning blades. Just as I reach a safe distance, the tail drops down as the Huey shifts slightly backwards, the torque twisting the tail left and right as the pilot pulls pitch lifting off the pad. As the chopper starts to lift off the pad, out pops the head of the crew chief. Huddled back in his seat from the driving rain, the chief is slow on clearing his tail to the rear; otherwise he would have seen me standing there. As I watch them depart, my knees are so weak, I can barely stand. In AIT (advanced individual training) while learning to become a helicopter mechanic, the instructors talk about Murphy and Murphy's Law. "If it can go wrong, it will go wrong." Or if someone is stupid enough to do something wrong, they will. I was almost a Murphy. Why did I stop when I did? Why did I run to my left immediately? Why did I not stop to ponder for a second all these questions when I was standing looking at the tail rotor? These were all of the questions I asked myself in a nanosecond. If I had paused to ponder even the raindrop on my nose, I would have become a statistic. Life experiences mold a person. That one, like no other, shaped me for life. And that's what operating on the edge of sleep deprivation is like in war. Careless to the point of caring less.

Chapter Six

There are four men assigned to a bunker on the perimeter each night. Although we have to be at the bunker by six in the evening, we draw straws to see who pulls each two-hour shift from ten o'clock until six in the morning. After determining who will pull each shift, there is always some bargaining and haggling. I always prefer the ten 'til twelve shift because most times the guys will stay up and talk until past eleven o'clock. Then I can get a full night's uninterrupted sleep. The bitch shift is the two a.m. 'til four a.m. shift. Getting to know the guys you work with is important. Some on the bitch shift will fall asleep, and they don't care. Even though the sergeant of the guard requires hourly check-in throughout the night, men still fall asleep. We have heard the horror stories of gooks getting through the "wire" at night and killing all the men in a bunker, and it has already happened at Eagle.

Bunker guard has become routine. Every few nights we get to ruin our sleep with this miserable duty. I have drawn the twelve a.m. 'til two a.m. shift and am desperately trying to stay awake. I'm on top of the bunker with my M-16 cradled over my legs as I sit Indian style. I have five fragmentation grenades arrayed in front of me along with three star clusters for illumination. Every night that I have guard duty, I lay out the same pattern of grenades and illumination shells. I can reach for them blindfolded and know exactly where they are.

My field phone rings softly at about one-thirty. It is the sergeant of the guard. "Who is this?" Sergeant Carver asks. "Lahti sarge, what's up?" He responds "you've got dinks in the wire at about your ten to eleven o'clock position." It is as black as that old coal mine again, and I can see nothing beyond a foot in front of my face, the sarge must be using the starlight scope I muse. As if in confirmation of my thought Sergeant Carver continues, "I've got them in my starlight scope" he says. If I can't see them, they sure as hell can't see me I think. "Where are they in the wire sarge?" I ask. "They appear to have made it almost all the way through" he says in a voice that sounds nervous and shaky. Realizing we are remf's, and not front line grunts gives me reason to pause and rethink what we are about to do. This is not a normal everyday event for us. Turning wrenches is what we do best. As we have been talking, I have slid into a prone position, "unsafed" my M-16, slid it to my side and cradle my M-60 machine gun ready to fire. My heart is pounding so hard it feels like someone is beating me on the chest with their fist. My mouth feels like it is stuffed with cotton, and my throat is so dry I desperately need a gulp of water. Bringing my hand to the feed cover on the left side of the gun, I run the top of my knuckles along and under the belt of ammunition out to arms length touching the ammo can. I want to be sure that I have a good feed into the gun on my initial burst and that the belt is not twisted. "I see four gooks" sergeant Carver says, "We're going to put up illumination. When we light up the area, I want you to blow all your claymores." "Do you want me to wake the other guys?" I ask. "Only if they're on top of the bunker with you, there's no time," he says hastily. It had looked like rain that night, and the other three guys had opted to sleep inside. Just my luck, I thought. I grabbed for the clacker that would detonate the claymores as I heard the not to distant wump of artillery and prayed it was my illumination. I didn't have long to wait as the rounds swooshed over my head, the familiar "pop" and the eerie, hollow "whoop, whoop, whoop" as the canister containing the flare fell from the sky. If the gooks didn't know their shit was up with the noise from the illumination canister, it was too late to pray to their God.

In an instant the area in front of the bunker was lit up like the hometown football field at a Friday night game. As the flare swung underneath the parachute, the long swaying shadows created by the brilliant light of the flare danced across the barbed wire in front of me. Off to my left I saw two, then three figures pushing themselves off the ground. It all seemed so surreal as they rose to their knees, slowly standing, looking up at the flare, then at the bunkers, their satchel charges hanging from the sides of their bodies. In that moment of indecision on their part, I mashed down on the clacker three times in quick succession, nervous that one push of the clacker would not be enough. The booming blast was deafening as the four claymore mines detonating simultaneously ripped open the still night air, spewing the steel ball bearings out across the wire. When I lifted my head, the disfigured, dismembered bodies lay strewn across the wire, body parts twisted at strangely different angles. Immediately in front of me another dink was running back to the wire towards safety. My hand rested on a hand grenade in front of me. I grasped and instinctively pulled it to my chest as I reached with my other hand to pull the pin. I lobbed the grenade at the figure trying to escape back through the wire, and watched with satisfaction as it found its mark. As I watched the grenade explode just behind him at his feet, he turned around to look back at our bunker. The gook had been engulfed in the explosion, and I couldn't believe my eyes as he turned back towards the darkness and attempted to run. I thought this guy must have nine lives like a cat. Within seconds as he became entangled in the first strands of concertina wire, three bunkers on either side of me opened up with their M-60's cutting into him, spinning him around and shaking him like a rag doll until he crumpled to his knees, his body still bucking and contorting as the rounds tore into him. As I stared at the now lifeless body, I thought morosely, at least he had three lives to give, which was two more than most of us would ever have.

It grew quiet, as I realized how close that gook had made it to our bunker. A pall of smoke hung low to the ground, it was like a soft billowing blanket covering what was left of the faces and bodies of the dead. The acrid smell of gunpowder overwhelmed my nostrils as more artillery flares continued to light the area. As the smoke slowly drifted over the wire, two Huey Cobras swept in down low over the perimeter searching for any other activity that might require their attention. But the fun was over for now, my throat was parched and I desperately needed a drink of water.

I put my head down, unable to hold it up under the weight of the helmet on my head. As I lay there, Albert, his flak jacket unzipped and flapping open came jumping out of the bunker to join me. As he crouched over next to me, his head darted left and right as he surveyed the scene in front of him. "Are you alright?" he asked. Without waiting for a response, all he could say was "Wow." I started shaking uncontrollably and violently. Just like "buck fever" I thought later. It had all happened so fast, I had only time to react and not think. We were put on full alert the rest of the night, but it remained quiet, and the guys let me sleep. But sleep would not come. I was so charged up with the adrenaline rush, I just told the guys what happened over and over again, talking a mile a minute.

Chapter Seven

At night if it doesn't rain, we watch a movie under the stars. The movies are generally none that I have ever heard about. Some of the movies are so bad, with lousy plots and sad endings that it is depressing to watch. As a rule, as time goes on, I make it a point to not attend them because of the blue funk it puts me in.

We are getting hit with 122-millimeter rockets every three or four days. The gooks are firing from what is called "rocket ridge." This is the first ridge of mountains to our west about fifteen miles away. Five, maybe ten rockets generally come in between eleven and one o'clock in the morning. It is more of a harassment and interdiction fire "H & I" than disabling to us. Because no indigenous "indig" personnel (Vietnamese civilians) are allowed on Eagle, the rockets are not impacting with much success. Although a 122 can penetrate our bunker, I am not too worried about the odds of a direct hit. When the siren sounds however, or we hear the unmistakable, distinctive crack or "shakim" of the first impacting rocket, it's quite literally asses and elbows heading for the bunker. On one occasion, from a dead sleep, I hear the impact of a rocket somewhere in the base camp. The blasts of rockets come quickly, and are landing closer to our company area. There is a blast wall of sandbags about seven feet high in front of our bunker entrance. Rolling out of my cot and running for the bunker the guys are backed up on either side of the blast wall entrance. Instead of waiting to go through the entrance like the other guys, I leapt over the top and don't remember even touching the sandbags as I high vault the blast wall with surprising ease. This is one of my first clear memories about how the body reacts on an adrenaline rush of fear.

The war for me is far away. We are seeing helicopters coming in with battle damage. Two helicopters have been shot down, one was unrecoverable due to the battle, and the other was "hooked" out by Chinook back to our company for repair. As often as I can get into a flight platoon, I listen to the day's events and stories told by the crews. It is almost surreal as I listen to them laugh and tell of deeds done during battle that should scare a normal person shitless. But the laughter overcomes the day's events, and more than just a little beer and "Mary Jane," "grass," or "dew" help ease the stress of the day.

The "Jesus Nut" is a huge four inch lock nut that kept the main rotor blade assembly secured to the splined shaft of the transmission of the helicopter. It came to be called that because folklore had it that the last thing a pilot would say prior to losing that nut and attached rotor blade in flight was "Oh Jesus!" As I sit straddling the rotor head of a Huey working on the "Jesus nut," a charge of quarters "CQ" runner comes in looking for me. "Lahti" he calls, "Yah, what's up?" I respond. "Top wants to see you ASAP" he says. "What's up?" I ask again. "I don't know man, he just told me to come and get you." I tried to think of what trouble I was in, because that would be the only time Top would want to see anyone.

As I knock on the tent pole of the orderly room tent, specialist Derrick responds with "enter." What a dick he is, I think to myself. The guy thinks he's big hot shit because he sits at the right hand of Top. Trying to stay cool and friendly even though I can't stand the guy, I say "Yo, what's up man." All Derrick says is "Top wants to see you." Like, no shit, I already knew that, tell me something new. Standing and waiting in the sweltering heat of the tent, I'm already anxious about what's going on, or about to happen. Derrick in his T- shirt with a fan blowing in his face totally ignores me. I can feel little rivers of sweat running down my back, my shirt starting to show the affects of my profuse sweating.

Top comes into the tent from the backside and calls me into his office area. I try to read his face for the impending doom I just know is coming, but he's stone faced. "Lahti" he says, "I didn't realize you had so much time in service and grade" referring to how long I had been in the Army, and my latest date of rank to specialist four or "spec four." I had joined the Army while still in my senior year of high school. That time prior to entering the active Army had counted towards time in service and for pay grade purposes. As a result, I was promoted earlier than my counterparts because of an extra six months time in service.

I wondered where he was going with all of this when he said "I have a gunners slot open on the maintenance 'bird' if you want it." I couldn't believe my ears. I was ready to jump up and kiss his ugly mug of a face. "What" I said in a shocked voice. "After going over your '201' file," my personnel file, I'm moving you up the list for flight status, and you can gun on the maintenance bird if you still want to" he said. "You bet, Top" I said, "I'm ready right now." "Okay, report to specialist Flores, and he'll hook you up with the details of your job" he said.

I left the tent in a daze. Even the smirk on Derricks' face didn't get to me. I found Flores down on the third terrace of flight line applying polish to the tail rotor drive shaft "dog house" of the Huey. I knew Flores better than other flight platoon crews because he was really more attached to the maintenance section. "Hey Santi" this was Flores' nickname, "how'd ya like a new door gunner?" Flores looked shocked at first as he raised his eyebrows and his mouth formed an "Oh" look, and then his mouth drooped half opened. He regained his composure quickly and said "Did Top send you down?" Not knowing why, I tried to be a little diplomatic and said "Yah, I guess he juggled the list and my name came up." "Oh, okay, well, let me tell you what we do, and what I expect from you," he said.

As Flores talked to me he finished polishing the tail rotor "dog house" on the Huey and then sat on the inside deck of the helicopter as he detailed what he expected of me. He was acting nervous and fidgety like, and I couldn't figure why the hell he was so jumpy. Flores was absolutely "anal" about keeping his bird clean. Most of his dissertation on my job description was in polishing the helicopter, keeping the interior deck and "chin bubbles" clean and free of sand and trash, and the windshields clean. I wondered where in this process the guns were to be cleaned. Then I realized if you don't shoot them, it doesn't take much to keep them clean. The maintenance bird was more than less the "peacock" of our company. It did not do combat assaults "CA's" or logistical missions "log missions" or more colloquial speaking "hauling ass and trash." What we really did was provide VIP services for the battalion, hauling around anybody that was anybody, an occasional maintenance recovery team for a downed helicopter, flight time for "higher-higher," (so they could get their flight pay for the month) and an occasional "General's chow run" down to Danang for food and a day of fun. God forbid the General would have to eat the same food as the troops!!

Finally as Flores was winding down on my job responsibilities he popped the question that had him as nervous as a whore in church, and why he was so damn fidgety. "How long you been a 'spec four'?" he asked. "A little over seven months" I said, "Why?" "Oh, I was just curious why Top would put a spec four in a gunners slot on my ship" he said. All the bells and whistles went off then, Flores had just been promoted to "spec four" from PFC a month earlier. So I said "well it is an E-4 slot, and I just want to fly, you don't care if I just gun for you do you?" I asked rhetorically. He seemed to relax a little when I didn't obviously care about the "chief's" slot on his aircraft. Christ, I thought, all I want to do is get into the action, and I've got to worry about some piss-ant politics on a helicopter that will never get dirty.

Well at least now I had a flight slot and I could get into the air. The longer I stayed in the company, the more I realized that once the dues are paid, doors open up!

Chapter Eight

I get to stay in the same hooch in C section, first platoon, the maintenance section, with my buddies. The helicopter I am flying is technically assigned to the maintenance section anyway. I'm happy with that plan. We had all become fast friends, and we got along well. Moving into the flight platoons area was insignificant as we had very little daily interaction with the flight platoons anyway.

My first flight. Our Huey, a "D" model may be a princess in the company, but it is a most elegant and beautiful ship. Santi keeps the bird highly polished and it's rubbing off on me. Each company has distinctive markings on their helicopters for quick identification. Our company has a white triangle, while the maintenance bird has two white squares and two red squares in a diamond shape painted on the middle of the tail boom. The tail cone and "toes" of the skids are painted a banana yellow. As we fly along, we are able to spot company birds by any of these quickly identifiable ways and communicate via our company "discrete radio" frequency. Without realizing it, I find myself looking for our Company birds whenever we fly, and find myself adept at picking them out almost at will from other companies.

Eight a.m. and we are "pulling pitch" out of the company area and repositioning to Phu Bai airport. "Clear left" Santi says as he checks back behind to clear the tail rotor and anything unseen to the pilot. "Clear right" I say as I dip and bend my head to look back along the right side of the helicopter. The "wop" of the rotor blades increases in intensity as the pitch of the main rotor blade bites into the warm, moist morning air. As we lift off, Captain Wheeler our maintenance officer and aircraft commander brings it smoothly to a ten foot hover as he "walks the pedals" counteracting the torque of the big main rotor. As he lowers the nose of the helicopter, it shudders as if throwing off the grip of gravity, seeking the freedom of flight. We pass through translational lift and quickly accelerate over the company area as Captain Wheeler banks to the right heading for Phu Bai.

All throughout the departure I'm taking it all in. What a different perspective. Watching the ground fall away from me, my head is on a virtual swivel. I look to the maintenance tents to see if anyone I know is watching. But to those on the ground it's just another Huey, another day, no big deal. The euphoria I feel, the freedom, the rush of fresh cool air buffeting my body is an elixir for all that ails!

We are waiting for the "donut dollies." These are American Red Cross girls, "round eyes" that visit firebases and base camps as recreation girls, boosting the spirits of the GI's. I'm kind of excited myself to see an American girl. I've been in country only a month and a half, but it sure seems like a lot longer. As the jeep pulls up to the helicopter with two of the donut dollies, Santi rushes to the braking jeep. I step back as Captain Wheeler makes his presence known and ushers the girls into our bird. Maybe I haven't been away from home long enough, but the dollies are not remarkable in any way. They are definitely nice and pleasant, but not my cup of tea. The girls make small talk with the whole crew on the way out to the firebase, and it makes for a pleasant and quick trip. They definitely perk me up, and make me feel special!

My first ride into the mountains and I continue to absorb the scenery and atmosphere. I occasionally see a Huey in the distance, much lower than we are flying. The mountains extend west in a continuous chain of succession. Cleared off mountaintops look like brown smudges on a green tapestry. These are our F.O.B.'s our "forward operating bases" short for firebase and/or base camp. After twenty-five minutes of flying we approach our destination. "Whip" is a fire base ten kilometers or "kliks" southeast of the A Shau Valley. As we make our approach, yellow smoke rises from the cleared off mountaintop. It gives Captain Wheeler the wind direction and speed as we watch the smoke drift over the encampment. I pull the M-60 out of its stowed position as our Huey comes in range of small arms fire and continuously sweep the gun left to right. As we come over the top of the perimeter the helicopter is descending rapidly and only at the last minute does Captain Wheeler pull up on the "collective" to arrest the rate of descent. Pitching the nose down simultaneously and allowing the Huey to settle down and through translational lift, Captain Wheeler deftly moves the cyclic stick so the skids of our bird touch down with a slight bump on the uneven ground.

A large group of enlisted guys stand by the main bunker on the firebase simply staring at "our" dollies. As the dust is still settling from our arrival, the dollies are met by a small group of officers and NCO's and escorted to the main bunker where cat calls, whistles and whoops of excitement elicit from the gun crews.

A battery of six 105-millimeter howitzers surrounds the camp. A ring of sand bags stacked in a circle waist high protected each gun. 105 shells are stacked by each gun, ready for action. Behind the howitzers, piles of empty brass from previous fire missions sit heaped up like beer cans from a high school beer bash. While we waited, I made small talk with a gun crew. As I stared out over the valleys and mountain ridges, I was very happy to be flying over these jungles rather than "humping" them with a sixty or seventy pound "ruck" sack.

Chapter Nine

The monsoon season is ripping at us with full force, and the flying was becoming more irregular as we waited for breaks in the weather. I am in my hooch talking with Albert when "Smokin Joe" Belinski comes in looking for me. Smokin' Joe has gotten his nickname from the helicopter he crews. "Smokey" is the battalion smoke making helicopter. On combat assaults where obscuring the "LZ," (the landing zone) is possible; Smokey is the first bird in to lay down a smoke screen. "Hey Lahti, are ya flying tomorrow?" he asks. "Not that I know" I responded. "Well Lolkus (Joe's door gunner) is going on R&R, and we got a 'CA' tomorrow down in Vayco valley" he said. "You wanna gun for me tomorrow" he asks. I'm flipping out. "Ya, sure, is it okay for me to do that?" "Why not, everybody swaps around now and then" he says. "Alright" I say again.

After telling Flores what I would like to do the next morning, he gives me an okay with a look like I'm overdue for the funny farm. We are scheduled for take off or pulling pitch at 0700. I meet Joe at breakfast and we go over what he expects from me on the assault. "We'll be laying smoke this morning" he says, "so we'll be the first bird over the 'Z'. It could be a 'hot LZ' (meaning we could be taking fire) so just follow my lead" Joe says. “When I fire, you fire. We will suppress in the Z regardless” Joe continues, “I’m not gettin’ my shit blown away for nothing. On the first run through the LZ we won’t be carrying troops because of the ‘jinking’ and wild maneuvering we’ll be doing. So anything is fair game, it’s a free fire zone.” A good briefing from an experienced crew chief about upcoming action, cool…I can’t wait.

It’s a smoky, hazy, and for the time of year, warm morning. As we crank up and pull pitch out of the company area, we are the last bird to leave. The other nine helicopters have repositioned on the other side of Eagle to pick up the grunts. As we circle over the top of Camp Eagle, I see our flight platoon leaving the pickup zone the “PZ” of the 501st Infantry. We move out ahead of the flight heading for Vayco valley. Smokey is definitely a working, slick helicopter. The cargo deck is dirty, blood stains the deck, rice and dirt clumps fill the cargo tie down rings. The exterior glistens with the slick oil from the smoke ring surrounding the jet exhaust. The tail of the Huey is covered in black soot, baked into the olive drab paint.

Joe’s aircraft commander is smooth and knowledgeable in his flying skills and I relax with the confidence that I’m with a good team. I feel competent yet anxious that I will do a good job for them. As we approach the LZ, we start into a shallow descent as we initially pick up speed going in. I look back to the tail of the helicopter and the smoke is already trailing behind us. A ring extending around the jet exhaust of our helicopter is injecting oil into the exhaust creating a heavy white smoke. As we “get down on the deck” I can smell the fresh earth only feet below the skids of the Huey. The pilot slows his approach allowing the dense smoke to lie down on the ground like a heavy fog concealing and protecting the incoming assault force. Smokin’ Joe begins shooting or “suppressing” the area for enemy fire. All we want to do is keep the bad guys heads down right now. The tree line is about fifty yards to my front as I also begin to shoot. Watching the tracers from my machine gun entering the tree line, I adjust my aim to work over the edge and up to a height of three feet. I see with satisfaction the rounds reaching into the tree line and adjust my fire as we begin a hard left turn out of the Z. Joe stops firing and I follow his lead. As I look back to see the affect of the smoke on the LZ, I notice a glint of sunlight on the palm fronds that surround the landing area. It looks as if the sun is reflecting white light off small pools of water. The pilot makes a hard left pedal turn at the top of our climbing, looping arc and we make a steep descent back to the Z. As soon as we make the turn, Joe begins to fire and once again I follow his lead. This time I am looking to the east at small rice paddies and dikes. I take aim for the dikes and adjust my fire once again to "work" over some areas that have small palms, banana trees and scrub. Once again Joe quits firing and I follow his lead. As we begin the climbing, looping arc and pedal turn I see the assault helicopters setting up to land just behind us. Forgetting to wait for Joe's lead, in my excitement I begin to shoot before I hear Joe starting to shoot. Our next approach over the LZ is slower and lower and the smoke is doing its job. The smoke obscures the tree line as the first of three helicopters touch down and the grunts begin to fan out and away from their helicopters.

As we head back to the PZ Joe comes over to my side of the helicopter. He's wearing his helmet, clear visor down and he's still hooked up with his microphone cord dangling behind him. "So how'd ya like that" Joe says. I gave him a thumbs up and a big smile and said "that was really outta sight man. I love those hard steep turns too, I just laid into them." "So what d'ya think about getting shot at" Joe said. "You mean doing the shootin" I said. "Na, ya know, taking fire, those gooks trying to waste ya" as he talked, Joe looked at me with a smile in his eyes. "I didn't see anybody" I said as I wondered if Joe was pulling this cherry boy's leg. "Hell man, they were light'n up the whole Z. We brought some 'pee' on them for sure" Joe said in an exuberant voice.

As I finally understood what Joe was talking about, I realized I was no longer a cherry boy. The chatter on the radio between the infantry now on the ground and our company helicopters confirmed that the LZ was indeed hot. They were now only taking sporadic fire from the tree line as the grunts moved deeper into the LZ securing the area for the rest of their company.

Trying to sound hip to the action, I said, "Yeah, I saw muzzle flashes around the palmetto scrub just as we broke off the first run" I said. "Ya, that's were I saw 'em too, I 'hosed' it real good" Joe said. Joe flipped around into the crew chief's seat well on his side of the helicopter as he continued to talk, "that clump of trees just north of the palmetto looked like it had a bunker too" Joe said. "Ya" was all I could think to say. I was so disappointed in not knowing or realizing what had just happened. All I could think about was that damn sun glinting off the palmetto bush, and what must have been enemy fire. As I continued to think of the several runs through the LZ, I realized that it had all happened so fast, that the experience had left me befuddled. There was no sense of exhilaration, no doom and gloom, nothing. It left me with a hollow feeling. I could just as easily have been wounded or shot dead in those first few moments. The din of the wind and rotor, my thumping machine gun and turbine engine, had been the only obvious noises I had heard. Those were the sounds of my war. It sure wasn't like the movies. It wasn't the experience I had expected or anticipated.

As we landed at the pick up zone, the grunts jumped on like obedient robots. They've done this a thousand times already I thought. As I looked over my shoulder watching them, Joe comes walking up from the tail of the chopper and stands in front of me. He still has his helmet on, and with a sideways nod of his head he motions for me to follow. As I twist out of my seat around my stowed gun Joe stops and points to the aft compartment we used for storage. Where the tail boomed blends into the fuselage of the helicopter, there in a neat stitch are three bullet holes! Joe just smiles, flips the bird at the bullet holes, gives me a wave and walks back along the tail, past the spinning tail rotor and jumps back in.

"Clear left" Joe said, I followed immediately with "clear right" as I looked aft of the ship. I felt the helicopter getting "light" on the skids, the rotors creating the ever familiar cloud of dust and flying dirt. Joe gave our aircraft commander the damage report on the bullet strikes. As the aircraft commander acknowledged Joe's briefing, he looked over his shoulder at me, gave me a slight nod and said “good work, gun.” I just smiled. Hell of a way to go to war I thought, as I shook my head not really believing how the day had unfolded.

Chapter Ten

The monsoon rains are increasing in intensity. It is raining almost twenty-four hours a day. The temperature is in the low fifties and a low cloud of fog in a drizzly, gray mist persists even when the rain has stopped. We move around the company area in a sea of mud. Being wet becomes a natural part of the daily routine. With very little flying to do because of the weather, we spend a lot of time in our hooch tent. The cold and wet weather numbs me to the bone. To get warm, the guys in my hooch have been burning love letters in a gray metal wastebasket that I have scrounged. We sit around the fire in our tent like we are boy scouts at camp. The tent is filled with smoke from the burning letters, but we ignore it in favor of the limited warmth from our trash can fire.

We play cards, and talk about everything under the sun. With all of us being from different parts of the country, there is a wide range of subject matter and opinions on any particular topic that comes up. We talk about Viet Nam, and get into a game of "what if." What if a rocket hit the tent? What if the gooks penetrated the perimeter? What if we could have a date with a Playboy Bunny? What if a helicopter is on fire? Six guys have six different opinions. We all pretty much had the same opinion on the first two topics. The Playboy Bunny is a different subject all together. Depending on the length of time in country, it can definitely sharpen the imaginations palate of "creative dates" for all of us... As to what I would do if my bird was on fire? I don't really know what I would do if my bird was hit and caught fire. Bob Layman, a new addition to our hooch from California says that he would jump out as the bird got close to the ground. I wouldn't realize until many months later how ominous that simple game of "what if" conversation would be, nor how it would come back to haunt all of us. Most of us agreed that we would ride it in with variations on when they would get out. But all in all, it was always good and spirited conversation among friends.

At around one a.m. there is a loud explosion very close to our tent. I roll out of my cot, tangled up in my mosquito netting half awake and waiting for more explosions. As I lay on the floor kicking and pulling at my self made trap of mosquito netting, people are shouting and hollering but I hear no more explosions. It's not raining, so after disentangling myself, I step out of the tent to see what the hell is going on. Over on the other side of our chow hall is the 501st Signal Battalion. They operate the Military Affiliated Radio Systems or "MARS" station and communications for Camp Eagle. The MARS people handle the long distance calls for G.I.'s to the states. There is a lot of commotion and people milling about, but I see nothing to indicate a need to go nosing around over in another company area especially when I could be warm and snug in my cot. There's been no alert for incoming rockets or mortars, and not really caring about the loud explosion I head back to sleep. I figure I'll hear about it in the morning. Most of the guys in my hooch are sitting on the edge of their cots smoking cigarettes and discussing what may have just happened. Some, not caring, have slept through the blast and are still fast asleep. As I make my way through the tent flap, the guys look to me for some news. I just shrug my shoulders, "don't know man" as I tell them the little of what I did see. As I am curling up trying hard to get back to dreamland, Beauprie comes in with the news of the blast. It seems the first sergeant of the MARS company was a real asshole, and became the victim of a "fragging." Somebody put a claymore mine under his cot, and when he went to bed, they just blew him away. Hell of a way to go I thought as I flashed back to my experience with the sappers on the perimeter. They would be picking up pieces of that guy for a month.

Viet Nam was a nasty place for anybody to be hanging out. The last thing any of us needed was a stateside type of bullshit military harassment. Just let us do our jobs, and press on. A month earlier, Klaguss, a guy in our company had unjustly tried to do a number on our commanding officer over a petty personal problem. It seems that Klaguss' girlfriend sent him a "Dear John" letter, and was breaking up with him. He wanted "compassionate leave" to go back to the world and make nice with her. Our C.O. was a pretty good guy, and treated everyone fairly, but he would not let him go back to the states. Hell, we were all getting "Dear John's." Anyway, Klaguss is going to frag our C.O. and throws a hand grenade on the outside of his tent one night. As Klaguss waited to watch the results of his handiwork, the hand grenade rolled down off the tent and landed on the ground. Just as he hears the hand grenade hit the ground, he begins running for his life as it explodes behind him. Well sure enough, Klaguss gets his ass laced with shrapnel from the grenade, but isn't too much the worse for wear. The following morning we fly Klaguss to Phu Bai with a patched butt to catch the C-130 to LBJ. He got back stateside all right; right to Fort Leavenworth, for twenty to thirty years busting rocks. What a shit bird. As I said, you meet all kinds; thank God most had their head screwed on the right way!

Chapter Eleven

My hooch mate Davis received a "Dear John" letter from his "loving wife" today. She hopes that he will "understand" why she is leaving him for a shoe salesman. Davis came in country with only a nine month tour of duty, and is leaving for home in less than three months. To say this guy is devastated would be an understatement to the meaning of devastation. So many of our guys are getting the "Dear Johns," that it's almost an epidemic. My sweetheart is hanging in there, however, and it sure is nice to hear from her and news from home. There is a lot of antiwar sentiment coming from the colleges, universities and hippies. "Make love not war" is the mantra of the day. I wonder how much of that affects the relationships of the G.I.'s and our civilian sweeties back home. They have to deal with the "cool" or "uncool" aspect of having a husband, boyfriend or lover over in Viet Nam "killing babies." That seems to be the favorite buzzword in the states. You show me any guy over here that would deliberately kill a child, sometimes to the point of giving their own life, rather than taking a child's life, and I'll show you a coward.

Moricini has been showing us pictures of his girlfriend. This guy is the biggest liar I have met in my nineteen years on this earth. If you've done something, he's done it twice as long, and twice as good. He showed the guys in our tent a picture of his girlfriend skiing up in Mammoth ski resort in California. As I've said before, she sure is one hot babe. But one of the pictures she sent to Moricini is torn in half. It shows his girl in the traditional skiers pose standing, holding her skis. The only odd thing is another pair of hands (a man's hands) are also holding the skis on the other side of the picture, the side that is torn off. We have gone beyond good-natured ribbing about this, and he just doesn't seem to get the picture, no pun intended.

I found out on December fifteenth that I unceremoniously made E-5, Specialist five rank on December seventh. I guess it's my own early Christmas present. Two weeks later, I receive news that I am being transferred to a new battalion further north, at Camp Evans.

Christmas is just around the corner, and we have been doing "real" flying out into the mountains, weather permitting. One day we are called upon to retrieve a United States Service Organization "USO" rock band from a firebase that have been stranded out in the mountains due to the fog and rain clouds. They have been out their three days, and I guess it's getting a little hairy for the longhaired dudes and especially the dudettes!

As we pull pitch out of the company area, the view of the mountains to the west is less than welcoming. Large areas of the mountains are fog shrouded, and the blue veils of rain hang in all quadrants of the sky. As we fly along, Captain Wheeler keeps telling us to keep our eyes open for other aircraft. We are flying in and out of the clouds, and rain is coming into the cargo area where we are perched behind our guns. It is so wet, that it's impossible to keep a cigarette dry long enough to smoke, and even though I am wearing rain gear, I am soaked to the bone.

As we weave our way down the valleys, and slowly climb the mountains I wonder how important this rock band extraction really is. Captain Wheeler is in radio contact with the firebase and I detect the strain in his voice as he talks with the radio operator. "We can hear you coming" the radio operator from the firebase says. The only thing I can see to the side or front is a wall of cloud, fog and mist. “We have a strobe light flashing for guidance,” the radio operator says again. We are almost at a hover in mid-air, inching forward, all eyes from the crew straining to see through the whiteness that surrounds us. Captain Wheeler again in that strained voice advises us to keep a sharp eye out. A minute later I scream “STOP” as a wall of green appears out of the fog in front of me. We are so close to the jungle canopy on the side of the mountain I can see the moisture clinging on individual leaves of the trees. Captain Wheeler slows the progress of forward movement of the Huey. As if realizing we need more assistance, the radio operator on the fire base begins relaying our position from thc mountain top LZ. After ten minutes of left and right corrections we pick up the blinking strobe light. As the skids of the Huey settle on the LZ, I say a little prayer of thanks. The rock band is loaded and anxiously ready to go before we have a chance to catch our breath. The smiles of heart-felt relief and elation on their faces could have filled a book of stories on its own. As we lifted off, I said to myself that I was ready to move on to my new unit, I'd had enough of this bullshit flying. If I was going to die, I wanted to go down in action, not making a foolish attempt saving a rock and roll band.

Moricini is still bragging how his girlfriend is going to be in the centerfold of the December Playboy magazine. We have all been anxiously awaiting the arrival of the magazine, just to call his bluff, and to see what kind of a lie he will come up with to explain away why she really didn't make it this month. The Playboy magazine has arrived, and to our amazement it really appears to be his girlfriend! We demand to see candid photo snapshots of her that she has sent to Moricini through the previous months. Sure enough, it's his girlfriend “in the flesh.” I am dumbstruck, confounded and a believer in the new world order. To top it all off, Moricini's dad sent him a Bowie knife for Christmas that is easily twenty-four inches long. This guy never leaves the safety of the company area. He wears it strapped to his hip like John Wayne wearing a six-shooter. It takes all kinds to make the “green machine” run, and Moricini sure fills the bill for the abnormal.

I have received a fifth of “Ron Rico” white rum carefully packed in a styrofoam box from my uncle back in Michigan. My uncle John is a mailman, and as he explains in the note attached to the bottle that it is illegal to mail booze, but he’s sure Uncle Sam will allow him this one indiscretion for a “boy at the front” so to speak. The bottle of clear liquid shimmers in the package of white foam, and I feel a loneliness for family and home that suddenly overwhelms me. I break from my Christmas blues as the guys in the hooch are encouraging me to start celebrating the season immediately. As I carefully lift the rum from its packaging and cradle it in my hands, I hear a “crack” like a rock snicking off a single pane window and the bottom of my bottle of rum falls out and onto the floor drenching my mud caked boots in liquor. I am unable to salvage more than a few drops that have splashed on my fingers, which I immediately lick clean, dirty hands and all. The guys all groan in disbelief at my, or our, misfortune.

Three days before Christmas, the first flight platoon has gone a huntin’. One of our ships is sling loading a young, and now deceased water buffalo in from the rice paddies. With a great deal of excitement, we all watch as the “buff” is deposited on the flight line, its feet sticking up in the air like it just came off a game pole instead of a helicopter. Word spreads quickly through the company that we will have a steak barbecue that night, and each night thereafter until our buff is consumed. The rumor holds true, and sure enough the cooks are grilling on a fifty-five gallon drum cut lengthwise that night. All the officers and enlisted guys are hanging together, knocking back beers like we’re at a luau, giggling about our good fortune and a joke or two about “living off the fat of the land.” I am a little pensive at first about eating something the gooks had been working the paddies with the day before. But as the thick slab of steak hits my plate, all thoughts of disease and dire consequences evaporate as I push a big chunk of juicy medium rare buffalo into my mouth. It’s so good, I just can’t believe its Army chow. We finished the buffalo at another cookout the next night, washing it down with more beer. All in all it was a pretty satisfying departure from the routine of food we had been getting at the mess hall, and it brought the company together in a shared, memorable experience.

Christmas day, all the troops will have a hot meal; at least that's what the generals are saying. Since nine o'clock in the morning, we've been shuttling mermite cans from the firebases loaded with turkey, mashed potatoes, gravy, green beans, yams, cherry and apple pie to the grunts in the field. We also have plastic crates loaded with milk, more mermite cans with kool-aid, sundry packs and the odd mailbag for some of the lifts. The mail going out to the boonies is received with almost a hungry zeal from the troops. Like nothing else, mail from home, good or bad, is the beacon of light, the reality of something better; that sustains us through our tour. I have a good and positive feeling about the deliveries we are making to the guys. You can tell the way the grunts rush to our arriving helicopter that the spirit of Christmas and the food and mail are very much appreciated. We are on a twenty-four hour cease-fire with the dinks, and so far the truce has been holding.

We fly until six o'clock that evening. A steady right from the showerhead kind of all night rain had begun about five o'clock. We slog up to the chow hall, heads bent down against the rain-washing over our faces, and catch what is left of the Christmas meal. The cooks are very good at "keeping the light on in the window" for the late arriving flight crews. The "head shed," either top or our C.O. is good about letting the cooks know when there will be late arriving flights. If they have run out of the evening scheduled meal, they cook for us a la carte. The cooks, most of them "heads" - dope smokers are real good guys. We never lack for the best they can muster up for us. On occasion because of the close ties we share with the cooks, they will gun for a day on our ships for "the fun of it."

I haven't had much time during the day to reflect on Christmas. It has just been another day to scratch off the calendar. Next year I'll be at home with my girl and family, and that makes it easier to deal with the present situation.

The dink that provided our great steak dinner by allowing us to consume his water buffalo has found our lair. In retribution, it will cost two thousand dollars to pay for the loss of his animal.

The C.O. asks for donations to the cause, and I kick in five dollars. In short order the “meal” is paid for by generous contributions from the company, with an admonishment from higher-higher that a culling of the herd will not happen again.

The last seven weeks with A Company, 101st Assault is mostly spent playing cards. We play pinochle, poker, and sit around our love letter fires talking about the World, cars, Harleys, and of course, women.

It is raining non-stop. In all my life I have never seen so much rain. It is a time that I get to know my tent mates on a deep and personal level. Inner most thoughts are shared and confided in the same breath; it’s as if we are all dying a slow death. The pervasiveness of gloomy days and endless rain makes it seem as if we don’t voluntarily speak of our hopes and dreams to our friends, to another human, then our being, even our soul, could die without ever having had any substance. It’s a strange time in an even stranger place. The weather and inactivity works on the mind in strange and mysterious ways.

This is also a time when I start to have waking hallucinations for lack of a better word, that “the World” or home is a great lie. The “green machine” has created and perpetrated the best lie anyone could think of. My hallucination is that we have been “created” magically out of a test tube, groomed and reared, to exist only to fight. We have really been in Viet Nam forever. After only three months, it seems like forever. The thoughts of “the World,” and home, girlfriends, cars and California girls have been maliciously implanted in our brains by the military. It is all a big lie. “The World” doesn’t exist. It is the greatest illusion of all time.

Yet wanting to believe that there really is something to go back to, something to live for, keeps me looking for my mail. I share my hallucination with no one. I believe, only because not to believe, would be the ultimate insanity. And, they can’t create and really medically do this to the brain anyway, can they?

Time goes by slowly as we fly in and out of the monsoon weather. There is very little combat type of activity. On two occasions we have been in the mountains with maintenance crews to rescue our company birds. One bird was disabled by trash flying into the tail rotor and another had the control tube to the main rotor hit by ground fire.

Bob Layman, one of our hooch mates, has transferred from maintenance to the first flight platoon. I am both envious and happy for him. He comes back to visit almost daily after evening chow. His stories are funny and scary all at the same time. I look forward to my new unit and the hope of possibly experiencing some of the same story telling. I have three weeks before reassignment and the time really drags. Between the cold, rain, mud, and limited flying, my hallucination about the "World" not being real intensifies. Two hundred five days and a wake up to go.

Chapter Twelve

It's time for me to move on, my duffle bag is packed, and my pillow is stuffed in my footlocker. It's hard to leave my family of friends, but I am anxious to get onto something new. My tent mates look at me as a "real" combat vet. I've been in the "boonies." So far, I have viewed it as being in the wrong place at the right time. Is this what war is all about? I am more the victim of circumstances, and most certainly, circumstances not under my control. I have mixed emotions about leaving my friends. But there is little I can do, nor would I want to, even if I could. I view this as just another opportunity for adventure in a strange land.

Climbing onto the deuce and a half for my trip to Camp Evans, I hear the same cautionary statements from my friends I had heard when I arrived on the freedom bird. "Keep your head down," "good luck," "drive on" and "take it easy" followed with half-hearted smiles, hand shakes as good friends depart each other not knowing if we will ever meet again.

It was a new day as we rolled out of Camp Eagle in the deuce and a half; it was like I was seeing new surroundings for the first time. I had not physically driven off base since arriving five plus months earlier. My eyes, more seasoned now, took in my surroundings. I felt relaxed and confident as I watched the blacktop road of Highway One "the street of no joy" flow smoothly beneath the big truck. I watched the local populous from the back of the truck, surveying them with a new found awareness of what I was really looking at. They were people just like me who wanted nothing more out of life than enough food for their families and shelter from the elements. They wanted a better life for their children, free of the Americans, Viet Cong, and North Vietnamese occupying their villages day and night fighting for *their* freedom. I felt no more threatened on that drive North to Camp Evans, than if I had been going to the grocery store back home for a loaf of bread. It wasn't really that secure, but I felt that secure in my own mind, that I now had more control of my own destiny. I had fought in a limited way, both in the air and on the ground. As a replacement for a new command, I didn't think I was a seasoned combat flight crew member. But I would put forth all the effort I could muster as a replacement candidate for the job to come.

As we passed through the city of Hue, across the Perfume River and the Citadel, I thought of the Marines, who fourteen short months ago had fought so valiantly here during the Tet offensive. I had watched it all on television with Walter Cronkite. Hue had been a beautiful Asian city with many buildings showing the French influence on the region, but now were bullet pocked, bombed out ruins. A great cathedral with a tall spire still stood, but it too showed the ravages of a great battle fought in and around it. As we passed the Citadel one of the guys on our truck remarked that there were still NVA and VC within the thick compound walls.

Leaving the city of Hue behind us, we continued our drive north, occasionally crossing small rivers and streams now swollen from the monsoon rains as the city and its roadside stands gave way to open country. Palm trees dotted the countryside, and the mountains to the west were lush with green vegetation of the monsoon season just ending. As we came over a small rise in the road, Camp Evans came into view. It was not as large as Camp Eagle, but nonetheless was imposing with a platoon of tanks and armored personnel carriers "APC's" fronting Highway One. Like

Eagle, Camp Evans was a sprawling base located on rolling terrain. Evans was located about half way between the mountains and the South China Sea. Interspersed inside the perimeter were abandoned rice paddies and dikes along with an assortment of burial sites and graves of the Vietnamese.

We rock back and forth in the deuce on the uneven terrain of the road as we pull into the company area of "the Haunted House," A Company, 158th Aviation Battalion call sign, "Ghost Riders." This will be my or our new home with the Ghost Riders. It's the same "cluster fuck" that it always would be. People are scurrying everywhere like mindless drones. Ten old timer enlisted guys showing the cherries how it's done. Oh yeah, we were the ones they looked at now with respect in their eyes. It was strange to be treated like an old timer. The 158th had been in country over a month already. They were in the process of "gearing up," qualifying the pilots as aircraft commanders in there "AO," their area of operations. Most of the battalion had made the voyage over by ship, and had a full "T.O. & E.," a full table of organization and equipment. They had spent the last three weeks unpacking the steel conex containers making preparations to contribute to the effort.

As our new Top came out into the company area to greet us, it was "with hat in hand." Top was a second tour Viet Nam vet. He'd been there, and done that once already back in '65. But nonetheless he treated us newcomers as seasoned veterans in our own right. I felt uncomfortable with the attention he bestowed upon us. But I accepted it as if I deserved it. If the truth were known of my adolescent, "princess" flying in my previous unit, I was afraid I would be immediately thrown back to the horrors of grounded, non-flying helicopter maintenance duty.

After collecting copies of our orders assigning us to Company A, Top started right off with "who's got orders for flying status?" I didn't need a poke in the butt to speak up when I heard that! "Yo, sarge" I said, trying to sound like an old timer, a seasoned killer. Three others in my group also sounded off in the affirmative as Top continued "Hmmmm, we only have three crew chief flight slots right now." My heart began to sink just knowing I would be going back to maintenance. It would be found out that I was an impostor; I had gunned on a sissy princess ship. I'd never been a "real" crew chief. You could see the wheels of Top's brain turning as he chewed on the problem at hand, one too many "chiefs." He continued "Well I guess they screwed up that one! I lost three crew chiefs, but I'll damn sure gladly take four in return" as he smiled to himself at his good fortune.

Top dismissed the remaining mechanics and motor pool guys who had made the trip from Eagle with us to the headquarters tent. They would be receiving further assignment from the headquarters orderly. I breathed a huge sigh of relief, I was going to be in a bona fide flight platoon!

"I'm assigning two of you each to first and second flight platoon" Top said. "Lahti, you and Ridge to first platoon and Gabet and Moorlin to second platoon. The flight platoon hooch's are behind you on the other side of the mess hall. I'll have Briskey, my orderly show you where to stow your gear, and then I want you up on the flight line ASAP," he said. As Top continued with a sense of urgency in his voice "The Company has been given our first orders for combat operations in country and with all the reorganization of personnel, we're in a cluster fuck to get crewed." When Top said "cluster fuck" I thought we were at least on the same page when it came to definitions of importance. I really hoped that this was just the initial jitter of getting a new battalion in country started up. Because when people didn't have there shit together over here, people died. As Top continued, he repeated himself, another sign of nervousness. "We have our first real flight tonight, a combat assault with the First ARVN Division out on the beach. I need you guys to get a helicopter assignment at least for tonight, and then draw your flight gear issue from supply." As Top finished he nodded his head and PFC Briskey appeared out of nowhere. "I'll show you guys where to stash your gear" Briskey said.

As we picked up our gear and walked along, Briskey gave us the cook's tour of the company area. In the middle of the company area was a parade ground with steel conex's on the west perimeter, the long mess hall formed the north perimeter, the headquarters buildings formed the south perimeter and the company's sleeping area, and the hooch's were to the east. On the opposite side of the steel conex was our bath and latrine area, and from there the ground pitched down to an abandoned rice paddy still wet from the monsoon rains. There were several makeshift bridges of boards and logs across the paddy up to our flight line. The flight line consisted of a blacktop type of material called "pena prime" with revetments for each helicopter. Near the top of the gently sloping hill of our flight line were two huge brand new metal hangars that could each fit two helicopters. Just to the south of the hangars was the 18th Surgical Battalion "MASH" unit and hospital.

After dropping off my duffle and footlocker at my new hooch, I went over to the supply area to draw my flight gear. The supply clerk scanned his list for the standard issue of flying gear. As he began throwing my new equipment on the counter, the first item landed with a heavy thump. It was the heavy ceramic body armor or "chicken plate" that protected the chest area from small arms fire. Next came my "K" bar survival knife, a Smith and Wesson .38 Special revolver, flight helmet, nomex shirt, pants and flying gloves and a pair of brand new sunglasses. I overreacted when the supply sergeant asked if I had previously been issued my Rayban sunglasses. "Hell no, are you shittin' me" I said as I stifled a laugh. He was surprised that I was surprised to receive them as standard issue. "Man, if you want sun glasses over here, you go to the PX" I said in way of explanation. I was thinking to myself that I was going to like it here just fine.

I had traded up in life style from Camp Eagle one hundred percent. Navy Seabees had built our new hooch's at Camp Evans. They were brand new "stick" buildings with half plywood walls and screens, a plywood floor, and corrugated steel roof. I was receiving the best flight gear, all new. We had worn our jungle boots and fatigues as flight uniforms down at Eagle. Here the nomex flight suits and gloves were the latest fire retardant gear available, PLUS sunglasses. Life was good. Best of all, I was in a real flight platoon with my own helicopter. It couldn't get much better than this I thought.

Chapter Thirteen

I walked up to the flight line and met a gaggle of guys milling around the hangars waiting for something to happen. Introductions went around, and I discovered that I was one of a very few old timers in the flight platoon created by the cross infusion between the flight battalions. The respect and attention paid to me left me embarrassed and at a loss for words among all these cherries. I had very little to say because I had very little to contribute to their conversation on helicopter action in Viet Nam. The cherries or “FNG’s” (fucking new guys), mistook my silence for a hardened vet not wanting to relive all the horror and gore. If they only knew!

As I was being deluged with questions of every form and nature, our flight platoon sergeant, Staff Sergeant Gilmoyer appeared from the direction of the company area. His feet were wet from crossing the “swamp” as the old rice paddy came to be known. I presumed he must have slipped off one of the boards, because his boots were caked in dark mud up to his bloused trousers. He was a tall and lanky guy, with a kind of hayseed attitude and smile. He didn’t seem to have both oars in the water, or he was one short of a six pack when he talked. But I decided to give him the benefit of the doubt. The original guys in the flight platoon treated him with respect, so for the moment, that was good enough for me.

Sergeant Gilmoyer briefed us on the mission for that night. We were to pick up a load of First Battalion, 1st ARVN (Army Republic of Viet Nam) Division grunts and combat assault them down into the coastal area beach east of Highway 1. A company of the Second Battalion, 506th Airborne Infantry was on a reconnaissance in force mission on a suspect VC village and bunker complex, and the ARVN would be utilized as a blocking force as the 506th made their push. The LZ landing zone was supposed to be "cold," meaning that we could anticipate no hostile fire as we made our approach into the LZ.

The crews were all pumped up for their first real mission, and I was right there with them. Sergeant Gilmoyer walked up and introduced himself to me as he apologized for the manner in which I was being introduced to the Ghost Riders, the call sign for "A" Company. "You'll be crewing '644'" he said. As we walked down the flight line toward a revetment where I presumed 644 was, he continued to update me on the move of the 158th Aviation Battalion from Fort Carson Colorado. "We've been practicing months for this day" he said. I just smiled and thought, yeah, so have I!

"Well here she is, in all her splendor and glory" Gilmoyer said. He was half kidding, smiling, just another helicopter…I was on cloud nine…As I walked into the revetment I was immediately taken with the freshly painted gray deck, the shining Plexiglas, the clean unmarred olive drab paint and the straight unpatched rivet lines. "I've got to get ready myself" Gilmoyer said, "so I'll just see you later when we can talk more. I want to hear all about this place so I can get a better idea about what we're up against." I gave him a silent wave of my hand and continued to stare at my helicopter. She was beautiful. As I walked slowly around her, taking it all in, I arrived at the co-pilots door. I opened the door, stepped up to the toe skid and swung my left foot into the door opening. Putting my foot into the covered step built into the fuselage, I climbed to the top of the helicopter to begin a thorough preflight of the engine air intake and rotor head assembly. There was a broad white stripe painted across the roof of the helicopter just behind the "greenhouse eyebrow" windows. I would learn later, that this white stripe was uniquely individual to our Company helicopters. No other companies had a distinctive marking such as this. As I checked the rotor head and scissors, the gimble ring and pulled the screens on the engine barrier filters, I felt for the very first time since arriving in Viet Nam that I was doing what I was trained to do. It felt so natural to be in that environment.

I continued my preflight inspection walking along the tail boom to the tail rotor. A big red circle or ball was painted on each side of the tail boom area. Beside the white stripe across the roof of my Huey, the red ball was not the only distinguishing mark on my bird. The top of the horizontal stabilizer was painted orange, and the vertical stabilizer has the "Screaming Eagle" symbol on it. Not knowing what the other two "slick" company's markings were at the moment, I made a mental note to keep an eye out for them. As I had already learned from my time flying with the "Commancheros" of Company A, 101st Assault Helicopter; getting to know your companies identifying markings was part of knowing your "family" of brothers.

I was a little disconcerted at first when I saw the red ball painted on the tail of my bird. It reminded me of the red "meat ball" painted on Japanese aircraft during World War II. I would strive to make that red circle a symbol of all things good and righteous. What had been truly "evil" with the Japanese meatball was not going to be applicable here. It was a silly thing to focus on, but I truly felt I was one of the good guys, and that red ball was something I would have to deal with, and prove it, we were good.

I completed my preflight and found the status book on the console between the pilot's seats. My Huey was a year old "H" model with relatively low flying time. Its flight log showed she had just been through a fifty hour inspection and was "good to go" for tonight's show. As I continued to acquaint myself with "my" bird, my door gunner "Jesse" ambled up the flight line carrying an M-60 in each hand. Shortly after Jesse arrived, my aircraft commander "Snoopy" and his co-pilot came walking up with their flight gear and helmets. After a quick exchange of introductions, Snoopy, a first lieutenant, was quick to let it be known that an old timer was crewing for them. He said, "Even though we're FNG's, we'll have to show him that the Ghost Riders can do the job. I kind of smiled as I looked at the "LT," when would this entire "old timer" shit end? Nobody had to prove anything to me.

Jesse had mounted the M-60's on their gun mounts, and seemed to be in pretty good spirits. He was a heavy set, average height guy about twenty-one years old. He had been drafted seven months earlier, and was school trained in the Army as a clerk typist. Jesse had volunteered to fly in a gunner's position on a Saturday as a thrill while still in the states. After that, he more or less fell into the gunner's job by accident as the Company TOE needed gunners slotted for duty while still at Ft. Carson. "Have you had any aerial gunnery training?" I asked. "Not really anything to speak of" he said. "Well if we have to suppress the LZ tonight, just be careful to shift your fire rearward as we land. I don't know what 'Marvin the Arvin' (our nickname for the ARVN's) has on his mind, and I sure would hate to 'zap' the little guys with friendly fire. Even though this is supposed to be a cold LZ, if you see any indication that your taking fire, you call it out, and fire em' up" I said. I thought back to my time with Smokin Joe, and my immaturity in not recognizing the incoming fire as such. So I wanted to make it clear to Jesse that he was to assume the worst in all circumstances. "The gooks generally shoot green tracers, but if you see red tracers coming our way, or muzzle flashes you suppress them. Okay?" I said, as a point of emphasis, as I looked him in the eyes. "Yeah, sure, okay" Jesse said, as he looked at me, trying to comprehend whether I was treating him like an FNG, or because I was "Mother Hen" nervousness because I was an old timer, or maybe both. "Don't worry man," Jesse said reassuringly, "I may be an FNG, but I'm ready to smoke them." Jesse sounded confident, but ignorance could be bliss. I felt he may have a better attitude about the upcoming assault, than when I was first baptized by fire. I sure hoped so.

Chapter Fourteen

The twilight sky was a kaleidoscope of colors ranging from pale orange to pink as the last rays of sun disappeared behind the mountains. As we pulled pitch out of our company area for our first combat assault or "CA", we are repositioning to an ARVN compound near Dong Ha where a Company of the First ARVN Division is located. Using the road that runs by the compound as our PZ, ten of our helicopters comprising the first flight platoon settle in just as darkness quickly envelops the countryside.

Many of the ARVN "little people" traveled with their camp following families in tow. As the soldiers moved, so did their family. Their wives, Mama-sans, along with children standing protectively close, or perched on the hips, stood loosely behind their man, along with pots and pans, goats, chickens and camp rolls. This was their family, their personal support system. It was a very different mind set to observe, so different from an American soldier ready to do battle. But it worked for them. I could never understand how the family repositioned themselves, while the ARVN soldier could move by helicopter sometimes ten or twenty miles away.

This was my first exposure working with ARVN troops. They were small, little, and juvenile looking people. It was difficult to discern the age of any individual soldier. They appeared to be fifteen or sixteen in contemporary Caucasian age, but were in reality probably closer to twenty-five years old. The American surplus "GI" type helmets on their heads appeared way out of proportion to the small frame of their bodies. The load bearing equipment "LBE" they had strapped to their backs with rucksacks, canteens, and ammo pouches reminded me of the literary character Ichabod Crane in the "The Headless Horsemen." As they ran back and forth, their hands flew about the body trying to hold this, then that, as the equipment on their backs and sides slapped at them. Much the same as Ichabod fled for his life from the headless horsemen, his coat flying out behind him in turmoil as his horse galloped at full speed; Ichabod hanging on for dear life. They had cigarettes hanging out of their mouths, absurdly long cigarettes in relation to their small faces. They smoked as if it was their first or last, eyes darting about, the hand moving with quick animated motion, bringing the cigarette in and out of their mouth. Good friends held each other's hands, like little American schoolgirls. I thought they were queer at the time, but I learned over time, of their customs and our cultural differences.

The grizzled old ARVN noncommissioned officers "NCOs," who did look their age, carried big hardwood sticks. They were not abashed at beating on an ARVN trooper with it to affect a desired response. They herded the ARVN grunts into lines on either side of the Huey as we prepared to load for the upcoming assault.

Snoopy had gotten his nickname by the big wide glasses that were constantly perched on his head. Walking around the flight line, he looked exactly like that famous cartoon character Snoopy and the goggles he wore. As Snoopy started the turbine engine on our Huey, the big rotor blades turning slowly at first, became a blur as they came up to operational speed. As the whine of the engine and drumming of the rotor blades made speech impossible, the lines of ARVN troops had a more disciplined look. "Let's get em' loaded up chief" my aircraft commander said. I motioned to the old battle hardened ARVN sergeant as he immediately started shouting and prodding the grunts toward the door of our bird. Four troops broke rank from my side, and four approached from my door gunner Jesses' side. We normally could carry five fully loaded American GI's on the Huey, but we could easily fit eight Marvin the Arvin on board. We had nylon canvas web seating for five strapped and stowed to the aft bulkhead of the cargo area on our Huey. With a fully loaded soldier, the seats were useless and a hindrance for ingress and egress. So it was customary to sit on the flat floor for the normally short ride the grunts would take with us.

The old sergeant screamed endlessly, prodding with his stick, as his charges fidgeted and shifted on the floor decking of our Huey. I had no idea what the old sergeant was saying, but it was having an obvious desired affect on the grunts. They held their M-16's between their legs, the barrel pointed down without the ammo magazine inserted in the weapon. I felt more at ease knowing that an accidental discharge of a weapon would not bring us down in the dark and unfamiliar terrain.

As we pulled pitch once again out of the ARVN compound, my aircraft commander keyed his microphone and announced "Snoopy" coming up. This was the flight platoons notice we were on the way. As I stepped on my microphone button, installed conveniently on the floor deck of my Huey, I stuck my head out to clear the tail rotor and automatically said "clear left." My chest rested on the dual pistol grips of my M-60 as I leaned forward checking the clearance of my tail rotor and the surrounding area, glancing up at the main rotor assuring we would have no clearance problems with wires and antennas in our departure path. I had the clear visor of my helmet lowered to protect my eyes from the inevitable storm of sand and dirt that we kicked up from the rotor wash of our helicopter. The soldiers left behind for the second lift, seated on the ground, automatically lower their helmeted heads as they were consumed in the rolling cloud of dust.

I watched as the main rotor blades cleaved to the load it was attempting to lift into the dark sky. The helicopter "danced" on its skids as the load was transferred through the pilots collective to the main rotor blades, the helicopter torque wanting to twist the body of the aircraft like a child's toy top. The lieutenant deftly "walked" his anti-torque pedals connected to the tail rotor to keep our bird straight as we became unstuck from the pull of gravity. As the pilot brought the helicopter to a five-foot hover, he gently nudged his cyclic stick forward lowering the nose of our bird, continuing to walk the pedals, pulling up on the collective as he gently caressed the cyclic stick in a circular motion fighting the laws of gravity and inertia. As we slowly gained altitude and forward motion, our bird gave a massive shudder as we passed through translational lift and launched into the darkness.

Sitting behind the ARVN grunts watching the engine gauges and rotor rpm, everything appears normal in the subdued red glow cast off by the indirect lighting in the cockpit. I look at the helmeted heads of my "AC", the aircraft commander and the "peter pilot" his co-pilot. Their heads bounce and jiggle on their shoulders like bobble head dolls.

There have been so many firsts for me in the span of this one day. This is my first assignment as a crew chief. This is my first flight with this crew. This is their first flight ever in a combat environment. We are flying people who do not for the most part understand the English language. We are going into a hostile area, at night. What's wrong with this picture? I hoped the firsts wouldn't keep coming this rapidly and overflow my cup of fun. I sit back, cup my hands around my Zippo, light up a cigarette, and stare out at the moving darkness. A little bit afraid...yes, very excited...Hell yes, let the fun begin. That's what a nineteen-year-old American soldier is all about. No fear, just the excitement of the unknown. Nothing can happen to me!

Our flight takes us across sandy scrub and rolling hills at two thousand feet. High enough to stay away from small arms fire, but low enough to obscure the direction we are coming from. We are traveling at one hundred and five knots, about one hundred twenty miles an hour. Generally by the time you can hear and see us, we have already passed the "kill zone" at that altitude.

We are somewhere between Highway One and the beach as we pass over a cavalry "Cav" unit of armored personnel carriers or "APC's" on a night laager. I see the murky outline of tracked vehicles in the dark. As I continue to stare at them, I count approximately eight APC's circled up just like the old wagon train days. They are in the middle of a ferocious firefight with the bad guys. Heavy red tracers from the APC fifty calibers streak out in all directions as the smaller green tracers from the gooks find the armor shell of the APC's. I pull the pistol grips of the M-60 toward me in a small gesture of comfort, instinctively swinging the barrel toward the muzzle flashes beyond the circled "Cav" unit. Not a word is spoken by anyone in the flight crew as we pass over and to the side of the firefight.

Ten minutes later our "AC" the aircraft commander announces "were coming up on the Z chief." "Roger sir" I respond. I look at the old ARVN sergeant and as our eyes meet, I give him the "V" sign followed quickly with a thumb's up. Instantly he begins shouting orders to his men. They move from their slouched resting positions and begin to sit up straight. The sergeant barks an order at his men again as they load their magazines into their M-16's. "Get your gun out Jesse," I said as I swing the muzzle of my M-60 forward. "I've had it out ever since we passed over that firefight," Jesse says. Jesse's going to do just fine I thought to myself.

As we start our descent toward the Z the lieutenant turns on the navigation lights of our bird. About two hundred feet off the ground the lieutenant instructs the co-pilot to turn on our belly landing lights. I sure as hell hope that's standard operating procedure I think to myself. Nothing like giving the dinks a better target than those flashing red and green navigation lights. As the lights extend down and forward, they illuminate the beach sand and scrub in front of us as I pull the trigger and begin firing my M-60 at any obvious and not so obvious places of concealment. I am delighted to hear Jesse open up with his gun at the same time.

There is no incoming or return fire as we enter a flare to land on the sandy scrub brush. As we touch down I cease firing and aim my gun towards the rear of the helicopter. The LZ is totally obscured by the flying beach sand and the yellow smoke of a smoke grenade as five helicopters simultaneously touch down. I now can see a flashing strobe light being held up by a pathfinder for the next flight of five birds. As I looked over my shoulder, the old sergeant is shepherding his men away from the bird, fanning out like this was a routine job. As I visually check the cargo deck area and confirm we have no one left aboard, I immediately say, "We're clear, clear left," "clear right" Jesse responds. We immediately pull pitch and leap out of the LZ.

The second lift proceeds without further consequence and our first action as the Ghost Riders in Viet Nam is now history. With a sigh of released tension our AC says, "Well that didn't go too bad at all, let's head for the Haunted House, it's Miller time."

Chapter Fifteen

The following morning, as I go through another post flight inspection of my new bird, Jesse approaches with the guns. The gun bluing on the barrels are shiny from the wash job and fresh coat of oil Jesse has generously applied. "Can I help you out at all here?" Jesse asks. "Yeah sure" I respond as I throw him a brush. "Would you be so kind as to sweep out the sand from the chin bubbles," I say in exaggerated politeness, as I give him a friendly smile. Jesse smiles back as he opens the pilot's door, stands on the toe of the skid, and bends down contorting himself between the armored seat and torque pedals. "That was pretty cool last night," Jesse says, as he grunts and shifts his weight attacking the fine grains of beach sand in the chin bubble. He continues, "That sure was some fire fight those APC's were in." "Did you see the green tracers?" I asked Jesse. "Ya that was a first for me. What's it like out in the mountains when they're firing you up?" Jesse asks, meaning when we're taking incoming fire. "Most of the time you'll never see it" I respond. "Just keep your eyes open for muzzle flashes, small wispy areas of smoke that look like ground fog, gook bunkers, a difference in the color of foliage or vegetation, even the dinks themselves moving around." Jesse keeps brushing the sand through a drain hole in the bottom of the chin bubble. His voice is muffled as he wedges himself deeper into his cleaning task, "What's it like to get shot at?" I relate my story of taking fire from the palm fronds back with Smokin' Joe and Jesse laughs. "Man I sure hope we don't do these beach assaults too often, this sand is a bitch to get out of here." As Jesse continues to help clean our bird, we continue to get acquainted with each other and my new company.

"BJ couldn't make it last night, ya know" Jesse says. "Who's BJ?" I ask. "He's our AC, our assigned aircraft commander, a 'W-2'" Jesse says. A W-2 was short for a Chief Warrant Officer Second Class. "I didn't know." I was surprised by that news; I had been under the impression that Snoopy would be our aircraft commander. "BJ Baylor, he likes to be called BJ, is a good guy" Jesse says. "He's always in hot water over something with the brass. The guys gave him a nickname; they call him "The Bridge." "Why's that?" I ask curiously. "Well just before we left 'Carson,' referring to Fort Carson Colorado, BJ flew under the Royal Gorge Bridge up at Pike's Peak." "No shit?" I said incredulously. "Ya" Jesse said, "whatathey gonna do, send ya to Viet Nam." We both cracked up over that, and I thought, I couldn't wait to meet this guy.

Later in the morning, as I am putting the finishing notations in the flight log on the outstanding minor mechanical discrepancies on my bird, a shadow suddenly looms over me. As I turn looking into the sun, I shield my eyes to seek recognition of who this new arrival is. This guy is huge! Broad shouldered, a semi-oval face with a square jaw and a big crooked smile, he must stand at least six feet three inches tall. A big bear paw of a hand is outstretched, "Howdy, I'm BJ." He's a fair haired, good-looking guy who you want to like immediately for that disarming smile, and the twinkle in his eyes. As I'm shaking BJ's hand I slide off the deck of my Huey. "How ya doin' Mr. Baylor," I used the formal address of his rank. "Ahh, call me BJ, or 'the Bridge', everyone else does" as he continues to give me the once over. "Okay, BJ." "So I heard it went well last night," BJ continued. "Yes sir" I said, not feeling comfortable enough to call him any nicknames yet, even if I had his expressed permission to do so. "The LT's assigned bird was down for the CA last night, and I was detained on other matters," he said with a sly grin. But unless something should change, we'll be the crew for 644 together." "Okay, I'm looking forward to flying with you." "Likewise" BJ responded.

As the day stretched on, the other crew chiefs and gunners from the flight platoons stopped by to say hello and chat. Ridge, was crew chief on "197," the sister ship to mine. His revetment is just over and down from my bird. Ridge is also a hooch mate of mine. Like me, he had been infused from another battalion, and was an old timer with five months in country. Ridge hails from Chicago, plays the guitar and is a friendly guy. I took to him immediately, as we exchanged and shared similar thoughts and ideas relating to our new company.

As we talk, Castillo, Ridge's door gunner, ambles up. Castillo's a plump, fleshy, Mexican from Phoenix, who obviously loves to eat. His thin, good-looking face, and even white teeth, defies the rest of Castillo's appearance. He is a disheveled, portly character that civilian clothes, or a military uniform, will do little to help in improving his stature with the ladies, or, our first sergeant. As I meet him for the first time, his olive drab tee shirt is half in and half out of his pants, stained with big blotches of gun cleaning solvent, and smelling of the same. His Army issue baseball cap looks as if it has just come out of the box, cocked on his head, the bill of the cap slightly askew, he looks as if he could be mildly retarded. As he pulls one of his big puffy hands from his baggy pants outstretched to shake, Castillo has a contagious smile. As Ridge introduces us, Castillo's disarming smile makes me chuckle for no reason, and I know I'm going to like this guy right away too. "How ya doin' Lot," Castillo says, as he immediately contracts my name, to allow for a more even flow of nonsense conversation that spews from his mouth. Not waiting for a response from me, he continues on rambling about the weather, the Army, Viet Nam, and how there must be a common thread to why all sergeants are basically lifers, dicks, and idiots.

Two revetments over from me and next to Ridge is Jerry Hollandale's bird. He crews for our first platoon leader Captain

Jack Armatidge, call sign "Cracker Jack." Jerry has come over with A Company from Fort Carson. He's about twenty-three, tall with light brown hair, and a take command kind of guy. His face is heavily scarred from acne in his teen years, but his bright sky blue eyes and easy demeanor overshadow the pockmarks on his face.

Hollandale exudes an untested confidence, and I'm unable to determine whether I like it or not. (Later I come to understand that being the Captain's crew chief carries the perceived distinction that being the first flight platoon lead also includes the attached crew members). Well only time would tell...

My hallucination of the "World" the United States being a "real place," a "real entity" continues to play in my mind. I can't shake the feeling that I've been in Viet Nam forever. The hallucination doesn't seem to be getting worse; it's just that it will not go away. I look forward to reading my mail from home. I still have a sense that it really isn't real, but I accept it for what it is. If I don't believe in the States, I have nothing at all to believe in.... What would I do then?

Chapter Sixteen

We are starting to reopen abandoned fire bases that lead into the A Shau Valley area. Sitting idle because of the weather at our PZ, firebase Birmingham; Birmingham has two companies of the 1st of the 502nd Airborne Infantry that we are lifting today. This is the second attempt at going into a firebase closed last year prior to the start of the heavy rainy season. The weather is miserable. The assault was scrubbed yesterday due to the inhospitable weather deeper in the mountains. The monsoon season is releasing its grip on Viet Nam begrudgingly. Today, a single small white cloud surrounded by other separate but uniquely individual clouds bump together and lay low on the horizon to the west, trying to escape the huge rolling white blanket of enveloping weather. The veil of gray clouds intermingled with lavender, purple and deep blues gently obscure the base of the mountains in a veil of fog, rain and mist. All the while the mountain tops try to push their broad shoulders of rock through the overwhelming mass of churning weather.

I don't see us flying today either, and settle in for some zzz's. Field jackets, sweaters and long underwear do little to relieve the cold dampness that permeates the air and body. As I snuggle and tuck my head turtle style deep into the collar of my field jacket, I curl up into a fetal position for warmth.

Today seems exactly like yesterday. So I am surprised to hear BJ's voice creep into my consciousness telling us to mount up. I lay groggy and dazed on the cargo deck trying to clear my head. Sitting up and looking around me, crews are already in an advanced stage of preparedness hopping in their birds, gearing up. Fighting through the fog of sleep that has left me in a stupor, I slide the bullet shield of BJ's seat forward and close his door even as he pulls the trigger initiating the start sequence of the T53 Lycoming turbine engine in 644. The rotor blades initially resist the 1400 shaft horsepower coming up to speed in the bowels of our bird, but finally the blades begin to turn, picking up speed as the whine of the engine and the slap of the blades against the air melds into the familiar sound of a dozen other Hueys churning the air around the firebase.

Half the squad of one of the infantry platoons, their packs bulging with all the necessities of combat, survival and the meager comforts of jungle existence, amble over to the cargo deck I had so recently been sleeping on. Turning, facing out, the guys joke and poke at each other as they sit on the deck, there feet resting on the Huey's skids. It will be a short ride to Veghel.

Far out on the approach to the LZ, I watch through the veil of misty rain the impacting artillery rounds. It's some small comfort knowing that with each yellow orange flash of a round's impact, a bad guy can no longer potentially strike at us. The ensuing pall of black smoke from the massive artillery barrage covers the LZ like a blanket. Finally the signal we've all been waiting for, white smoke from the "Willy Pete" the white phosphorus rounds hitting the LZ is our clue the artillery barrage has ended. Now it's the Aerial Rocket Artillery or "ARA" the "Snakes" our Cobra gun ship's turn to finish the preparation on the Z prior to our landing.

My flight platoon is on the third lift in to Veghel. The tension decreases as the first two lifts on the assault have resulted in no enemy contact. Our machine guns are deployed, but we're not firing. Cracker Jack, our platoon leader is just in the flare to land as the radio buzzes with his terse voice "Cracker Jack taking fire." I immediately begin shooting, suppressing fire on the cleared area surrounding the fire base and the jungle growth. It's then I sense, more than feel, that we are also taking fire and hits on 644.

"Taking fire on the right" Jesse says; followed by…"Holy shit." "Whatdaya got Jess?" I query. "Fuck, they're running around all over the place." The jack hammer noise of his machine gun is amplified in his microphone as Jesse speaks, "I don't know what they're shooting at us, but it's scaring the hell outta me." I instinctively look over my right shoulder knowing I won't see anything anyway. But I do notice our peter pilot staring out the side window, his head darting to the left and right as he scans the LZ for the action.

Ten seconds to landing, no more poking and joking from the grunts now. Their butts are as close to the edge of the cargo deck as they dare. They're leaning back on their packs so they won't fall out, M-16's held across their chests, locked and loaded, ready. I'm firing constantly wishing my M-60 could shoot five times as fast. I sweep the area to the rear and down with gunfire as we enter short final for landing.

As BJ enters the landing flare, the purple smoke from a grenade gripped by the downdraft of the helicopter rotor wash, twists and intertwines itself tightly into the grass, leaves, dust and sand. The purple haze rises vertically, wrapping itself into a horizontal tornado as it disappears in an outward swirl away from the helicopter. As we hit the uneven terrain of Veghel, the grunts lean forward and are away even as the helicopter skids settle to the ground. The infantry already on the ground are moving and shooting, throwing grenades inside bunkers and routing the NVA from their underground hiding spots. I continue shooting throughout the landing and departure from the hot LZ.

Shifting my machine gun fire to the surrounding jungle, the grunts we have just deposited on the LZ are running and weaving.

The smoke and explosions of grenades and rocket propelled grenades, "RPG's" crisscrossed with tracer fire, turn the LZ into an inferno of fire and confusion, making me think of that phrase, "the fog and haze of battle." Surely this must be what it's all about.

Scanning the engine gauges to make sure 644 hasn't been hurt or hit strategically, thirty seconds out of the LZ, I lean out the door of my Huey. Turning my head back into the slipstream looking back at Veghel, I'm astounded by the utter calm that comes over me. Even as the smoke drifts lazily across the LZ, I see movement on Veghel, but cannot distinguish friend or foe. "How ya doing Jesse?" "I'm okay Lot. Damn, it was really hot!... I think I got a gook Lot." "Really." "Ya, I'm not real sure, but he either got hit or took a dive for cover." "Well good shootin." "Way ta' go" BJ pipes in. "Ya, thanks." "We got two more lifts" BJ reminds us. "Whatcha see on the approach BJ?" I ask. "Well there was a lotta shit going on, and I was concentrating on the LZ, but I think they were firing somethin' I ain't ever seen before." "Like what?" I ask again. "I don't know, but I'm surprised we didn't get hit with something." I'm amazed myself that we hadn't taken any hits on our machine, and made a mental note to take a quick look when we landed.

On the way back from Veghel for our second lift, there is communication that one of the first assault ships from our sister company the Lancers has had a crew chief killed and the gunner wounded. Better him than me is all I can think of. I have a vision of the dead crew chief only hours before having chow and doing the same things we all do in preparation for the days launch. It makes me realize how really cheap and easily extinguishable life is. Landing back at the PZ, as we prepare to pick up the next load of grunts, I jump out to take a quick walk around 644 looking for any signs of hits or damage. Sure enough as I move to Jesses' side of the ship I notice three hits on the skid, a couple through the aft engine compartment and one smack dab through the tail boom and out through the dog house cover on the tail rotor drive shaft. The grunts have already loaded on as I give BJ the news. "Whatdaya wanna do Chief?" BJ asks. "Shut her down, and I'll take a look at the tail rotor drive shaft and the engine compartment real quick." As I undo the dzus fasteners on the "dog house" of the drive shaft Jesse opens the engine compartment cowling. BJ has joined me as I open the cover of the drive shaft. We have taken a round through a segment of the middle of the tail rotor drive shaft. The engine compartment hits are clean, no damage other than a little sheet metal work for the boys when we get back to Evans. "I'm good to go on this if you are BJ." I wanted to get back into the action! "Let me talk to maintenance about the tail rotor drive shaft." BJ says.

The flight platoon has continued the assault without us, as we sit at Birmingham awaiting word from our company maintenance. A staff sergeant from one of the lifts waiting to go ambles over inspecting the damage on our bird. "Pretty hot?" he questions as I sit on the cargo deck waiting for news from our company. "Yeah I guess." I try to sound tough, unaffected, half smiling. Jesse jumps into the conversation blabbering like a school kid blowing my whole "everything's cool" philosophy. "They were running all over." "Who?" The sergeant asks as he turns his shoulders and head toward us now that we had his attention. "Well it sure looked like NVA to me." "Jesse got one" I said with affirmation. No maybes, he got the son-of-a-bitch! That got the sergeants full attention. When I said that, Jesse turned to look at me, smiling. In my mind, it was a confirmed kill, period! No more bullshit maybes about that. The sergeant nodded his head, a new respect for us, as he looked at the damaged skid and the engine compartment and said simply "Looks like a claymore hit ya." "Whatdaya mean?" Jesse and I say almost simultaneously. "On our old firebases like Veghel, the gooks will point claymores up into the air. They know we're coming back eventually, so they booby-trap the place with claymores and other fun shit." he says matter of fact, displaying simply a veteran's seasoned knowledge. So that explained why the bullet or should I say pellet holes were so vertical to our line of flight.

The fire fight on Veghel had ceased as we were given the okay from our maintenance officer to continue the assault as is. We made one more lift into Veghel uneventfully, and headed home for repairs. Later I explained to BJ what the infantry sergeant had told us about the claymores and he nodded his head saying "I knew there was something different about that ground fire. It makes sense now. Thanks, I'll put it in the after action report."

At about midnight I am awakened by someone hollering outside. There is a small commotion as I put my pants on and walk over to the parade ground of the company area. Cracker Jack with several other pilots are standing in the middle of the parade ground hollering and screaming up into the air, obviously very intoxicated. It's then I notice the sound of "round engines," radial engines in the night sky. Cracker Jack points toward the mountains, a bottle in his extended hand just as a sheet of flame shaped like a collection of lighting bolts erupts out of the blackness and reaches to the ground. The reddish yellow flame becomes a roman candle as the tracers from the miniguns of a "Spooky" ricochet off the ground in the distance. Again and again Spooky circles as the red tracers of minigun fire seek unseen targets down in the darkness beyond the camp. Cracker Jack stands, screaming obscenities, whooping it up, as he enjoys the show at the expense of the bad guys catching literal hell from the gunship.

The following morning on our way out from Evans on a log mission BJ takes us out to the area that the Spooky had been working over. About a mile from the base of the mountains lying in the beaten down grass, were the bodies of fifteen Viet Cong. As BJ hovered over them for a minute, we got a good look at what a killing machine Spooky was. I was left feeling a little numb at the closeness of death beneath me. I was glad they had been taken out of action. Against an Army such as ours, with the infinite ways we had of killing them, I wondered how any magnitude of killing such as this could continue with these people.

Chapter Seventeen

Days are consumed by flying. I am up, and on the flight line, by 7:00 am every morning, seven days a week. It has become routine. I pull a twenty-five hour inspection every four to five days. This entails pulling fuel and oil filters to inspect and replace, plus grease and visual inspections of flight components. My days usually end between seven and nine pm.

One morning soon after BJ, Jesse, and I have been put together as a team on 644, BJ had "squawked" the fuel pressure gauge as inoperative. I had been unable to locate a fuel pressure gauge, but noticed in my scrounging around for parts that a jeep water pressure gauge was the same size as the hole in the instrument panel. It also appeared the connection would be the same as the fuel pressure gauge. So "liberating" the water pressure gauge and installing it on the Huey, was what I guess you could call "field expedient." The Army loved to talk about "field expedient," whatever it took to get the job done. BJ got the biggest kick out of showing his new co-pilots our water pressure-fuel gauge. It worked, that's all that counted, and I think I got an "atta-boy" from BJ.

My hooch has become a place of refuge. I have built a large box approximately thirty inches wide by three feet long and twenty inches deep that is adorned with every gorgeous girl I can find from Playboy, Penthouse, and other fine girly magazines. I have hung this from the wall, with a pad lock, with the affect of having a storage locker. The area that I consider my private space, including my cot, occupies a space five feet by seven feet. From the top of the ceiling draped down to the floor, I have installed several white nylon chutes I have pulled from expended parachute flares. The chute for these magnesium aerial flares is easily ten to twelve feet in diameter, and when dropped to floor level quickly provides privacy normally unheard of in a barracks environment. Besides my footlocker made by the local dinks out of artillery shell boxes, I have a plastic strap beach chair. I have "acquired" no less than three fans. One is an exhaust fan you would find normally used in a kitchen to exhaust smoke and odors from the kitchen stove. I have nailed this one down on a two by four brace on my wall, canted at an angle, and aimed at my head. This fan moves a tremendous amount of air. I also have acquired a "squirrel cage" type of fan that I placed on the same two by four but mounted at my feet and aimed up my body while I lay on my cot. Finally, I have purchased a twenty-inch box fan from the PX. When needed under extreme heat conditions, I set the box fan on my footlocker and aim it at my midsection. All in all, it is a more than satisfactory cooling system, and I never worry about being too hot. It has taken quite some time to scrounge my little amenities and I am the envy of the boys in my hooch. The only drawback to my cooling system is that with all the noise created by the fans, I cannot generally hear the warning sirens that precede incoming rocket or mortar attacks. On at least one occasion, I slept through an attack, totally unaware.

The guys in my hooch are respectful of each other's privacy. Considering we fly and work together all day, it is a good bunch to be with. Ridge plays the guitar very well, and we get into some sing-alongs, singing Peter, Paul, and Mary tunes, and Simon and Garfunkel. Greg Distoné is our resident joke teller. There are very few times during a day that we don't smile because of the things Greg says, or pranks he pulls. Greg is a

CH-47 Chinook crew chief by training. But for some strange reason he wound up in our Huey Company, and now is a door gunner with Granger.

As we fly back and forth between the Valley and the fire support bases, we catch a glimpse of birds from our company, most notable by that white stripe I've mentioned earlier on the top of the Huey. BJ will call out "Hey Ghost Rider, who goes there?" followed by the Ghost Rider responding back to us with their call sign. It's like family saying "hey" to each other as we go through our daily work routines. Other times it could be the Lancers or Phoenix birds from Bravo or Charlie companies. One day as we fly up high with a logistical load headed for an infantry company in the field, two Cobras from "D" Company fly by us. They are "low leveling" along the mountain passes headed somewhere. BJ keys his microphone and simply says "Snake" followed immediately by the response of "Slither, slither" from the Cobra guns. The feeling of belonging is intimate and immediate, as we gently cajole other birds of a feather, and they respond equally well in kind as brothers. It is that feeling of mutual support that exists between the flight platoons that sustains us in a potentially hostile environment. I better understand the closeness of the flight platoons at moments like this, and why we may unintentionally alienate ourselves from the maintenance crews back in the Company.

I now understand the strange feeling I had when entering the flight platoons of the Commancheros' back in my old company. That feeling of being an outsider, an interloper of sorts, belonging but not belonging. That clique even now exists in our flight platoons. We distinguished ourselves not by the heroics of flight or battle, but by the grind of daily assaults with those young men of the infantry bringing war to the bad guys. Our infantry, who we deposit on mountainous jungle battlefields far from any form of recognizable civilization, are fighting NVA, of equal courage, under the most intolerable conditions. Our helicopters, the tools used to initiate these contacts, return during and after the heat of battle to replenish, to retrieve the wounded, and also the body bags. To know and feel destruction and death, and simply return home disaffected to the quiet of a flight line at the end of the day could not be shared with anyone but those who had experienced that same magnitude of life and death on a daily basis. A knowing look from crew member to crew member said more than words could ever say. Yes, now I knew the difference between our flight crews and the maintenance guys that stayed at home, back on the firebase.

Our platoon sergeant, Sergeant Gilmoyer leaves us alone. If we need to be corrected on something, he will take us aside in a fatherly fashion and "remind" us of the way things should be. He is still a bit of a klutz, and somewhat simple minded, but a genuinely nice guy. Gilmoyer and I have talked a few times, and by sheer coincidence he married a girl from my hometown. It is indeed a small world, so we have more to talk about than helicopters.

Sergeant Kaiser, the assistant flight platoon sergeant on the other hand is a major flaming asshole. The guy is a short, skinny, hillbilly, lifer, with ten years in the Army and four years time in grade. He definitely has a Napoleon complex, and shits on anybody, for any reason. Our interaction with Kaiser is limited, but for some reason he has his sights on Greg Distoné, and has been riding him incessantly.

"Dink," one of the guys infused into our Company along about the same time as myself, has been in country for almost two and a half years. He is an infantry grunt, having extended his tour in Viet Nam to receive his choice of duty postings. He wanted to be a door gunner and so here he is. Not only is he an exceptional gunner, he is seriously crazy. At night, after flying all day, he will clean his M-60's and sit under the water tower and drink himself stupid. Every six months, after the first one-year tour, any G.I. is eligible to extend their tour in Viet Nam. With a six month extension, you can travel anywhere in the world free of charge with Uncle Sam on a complimentary thirty day leave. Dink has not left Viet Nam since first arriving in mid-'66. Without exception, Dink has used his three thirty-day leaves and two weeks of R&R in Saigon.

Once, early in my limited conversations with Dink, I had mentioned that I had trouble precisely placing rounds on a target with any consistency. In a matter of minutes, Dink explained how to shoot and get “on target” with an M-60 in three easy lessons. “This is the way it’s accomplished” he said, as his eyes, glassy from booze, gleamed with excitement in the telling. String thirty rounds of tracer ammunition onto the belt of machine gun ammo going into the gun. The solid red line of tracer coming from the machine gun has a “water hose” affect for adjusting aim as you shoot. After shooting belted ammo like that on several assaults, he told me to break the belt of M-60 ammo so that I shot ten tracers spaced with four “ball” or non-visible rounds, then ten more tracers. This would give the appearance as if I was watching the dashed white markings of the center line on a highway as you drive a car. After firing in that manner several times under different conditions, such as landing or taking off, I put just ten tracers to start the machine gun belt. By this time, after watching the initial flight of the tracers, I could sense the speed and motion of the helicopter, and synchronize my gun and adjust accordingly. After several weeks, I was hitting my target by the second tracer or ten rounds out of the gun. Depending on the speed of the Huey, and where we were at on an approach, I never failed to hit my target with increasing accuracy the rest of my tour in Viet Nam.

Chapter Eighteen

Dink received his nickname by obviously having spent so much time in country. Almost becoming a native by longevity, he was simply a "Dink" as we called the Vietnamese in American slang. Although he was every inch a Caucasian, the nickname stuck. The use of names, in place of call signs like "6" for commander, or "5" for the executive officer, or "one-six" for first platoon commander was uniquely individual to the Ghost Riders. When it came to call signs for pilots, crew chiefs, and gunners, some nicknames described a physical feature or name contraction, while others were earned as a result of an outrageous event.

The Ghost Riders have their own calling card. In the shape of a business card, a stallion rears up defiantly on a storm cloud with lighting bolts exploding from it. Atop the stallion sits the "Grim Reaper" with his scythe in hand. "Ghost Riders" is emblazoned underneath the Reaper. The back of the card has the following slogan:

> " …From Danang to the DMZ…From the Anglo Bridge to the Ashau Valley…

The Ghost Riders are on call to perform Combat Assaults, FOB's, CCN's, emergency resupply, NVA and VC extermination, and Death Defying Aerobatics."

Along with the normal "ass and trash" resupply of firebases and units in the field, we are flying combat assaults, re-opening old firebases and opening new firebases along the way to the A Shau Valley. We perform emergency resupply to field units of ammunition, and emergency medivac. We also fly as flare ships for night illumination "Firefly's," and "RRF" or Ready Reactionary Force, or "Rat Fuck" for short.

Our job when flying as a Firefly flare ship is to sit RRF either at Camp Evans, or set up on a night laager on one of the firebases out in the mountains. Flying as a flare ship entails putting aluminum bins in the cargo door area of the Huey. The bin will hold about twenty magnesium aerial flares. If illumination is needed for whatever reason, we launch. Flying at ten thousand feet over the target area, I would throw the flare out of the helicopter. A wire lanyard attached to the flare would pull the safety pin out of the flare, deploying the parachute and igniting the magnesium. It was simple but dangerous work. The magnesium burned with the light of a million candle power, with a white hot core that could burn ten minutes under any weather conditions.

We also were tasked with flying "Psyops," or psychological operations. We would attach loud speakers to the sides of the helicopter and a Vietnamese operator spoke either directly into a microphone or played a tape recorded message as we flew along low level in the mountains over suspected NVA or VC positions. The object of the message was to "Chu Hoi" to surrender to the good guys, and be rewarded.

People sniffers were also used in the mountains. To find suspect enemy positions we would install this analyzer box in the cargo area of our bird. We would then run a hose much like a vacuum cleaner hose into clean out holes in the chin bubbles underneath the pilots and co-pilots feet. The sniffer would analyze the air we flew over, sampling the air for quite simply the sweat of a human. If we hit a "hot" spot, the operator running the sniffer would mark it on a map for further investigation by the grunts.

CCN's short for Command and Control North were operations involving the Green Berets, our Special Forces, from "FOB's" or Forward Operating Bases. These operations were strictly voluntary for aircrews, and without fail, exciting. All of my CCN operations involved flying into Laos. I referred to it as leaving "candy land" for where the real war was. The instant we would cross the border, shit happened. And it was always a sigh of relief when returning, to cross the border of South Viet Nam and know we had cheated death again.

On occasion we will also provide lift support to the 3rd Marine Reconnaissance Company of the 2nd Marine Amphibious Force (MAF). Like CCN operations with the Special Forces, time spent with the 3rd Marine Recon units usually doesn't lack for some exciting moments either.

Chapter Nineteen

Flying ass and trash and combat assaults with no action, has not allowed us to fire our machine guns. Just coming out of monsoon season with intermittent rainsqualls, fog, mist and high humidity has resulted in rusty ammunition. BJ has taken us out over the ocean to shoot at sharks and get a little target practice. But the whole company has the same problem, rusty ammo. Rumor has it that our commanding officer Major Dockert will give out Article 15's to anybody caught with rusty ammo. An "Article 15" is a non-judicial form of punishment available to a Company commander to reprimand a soldier either by reduction in rank/pay grade; monetary fines, extra duty or whatever punishment they deem fits the misdeeds. Talk about chicken shit!

As I lay in my cot, Greg Distoné comes charging into the hooch and drops his two hundred twenty pound frame into my PX lawn chair. "Man, I'm going to kill Kaiser." "What's up Greg?" as I roll on my side, propping my head up with the palm of my hand. "That little fuckin' Napoleon asshole put me on K.P. because I have rusty machine gun ammo in my can." "We all have rusty ammo" I say in Greg's defense. "What the hell is new about that?" "I know" Greg says. "That lifer dick, is gonna get a frag shoved up his ass." When the ranting and raving was over, Greg told us, as he had attracted quite a crowd by that time, the story of Sergeant Kaiser harassing him up at his bird while cleaning his guns.

"So, Kaiser comes up to me while I'm cleaning the guns in that military walk he's so famous for. Ya know how I mean?" as Greg bounces out of my lawn chair and imitates in exaggerated form Kaiser walking. We all chuckle as Greg continues, "Nosing around, he's just lookin' for some excuse to rag on me. Then he sees my ammo can, rubs his fingers over the belt, and says my ammo's rusty! Like no shit! So I say to him, 'We haven't had any opportunity to shoot it, whatdaya want me to do about it?' So he says clean it in the solvent tub where I clean the guns, or I'll get an Article 15. 'You gotta be kidding me.' I said. All that ammo, that's sumpin' like twenty-five hundred rounds?" We're all shaking our heads in disbelief. I can't believe the balls this guy has. "Then Kaiser says he'll be back after chow to inspect it! Well guys, I broke the belt down, and I musta cleaned and scrubbed five hundred rounds easy" I interrupted Greg "You mean you cleaned that shit? I woulda told him to inspect this" as I grabbed my crotch and made an obscene gesture. Greg sat down on my footlocker, his head hanging down, shaking it from side to side. "I don't know what I'm gonna do." "So what happened when he came back up?" Ridge asked. "Oh the usual. He said that's not good enough, but instead of an Article 15, I can go on K.P. tomorrow and really learn how to clean something." I just couldn't understand where Kaiser was going with all this, but I was determined to find out.

I grabbed Greg under the arm and lifted him up. "Come on, we're going to find out what's going on here," I said to Greg, as I let go of his arm and motioned for him to follow me. As we left the hooch, Chip Granger, Greg's crew chief followed along with us, as we went over to see our platoon leader Cracker Jack, Captain Armatidge. As I knocked on Captain Armatidge's door, I was seeing red. A lieutenant came to the door as I asked to speak with Cracker Jack. Giving me a questioning look, he stepped aside as Greg, Chip and I entered the hooch. As I gave the lieutenant a don't fuck with me look, he ushered us further into the hooch as Captain Armatidge pushed his chair back from a card table full of paperwork. "Hey boys, what's going on?" Not bothering to salute, I have been going over in my head what I want to say and how I want to begin. Unfortunately, it comes out in a rush of words "Sir we have a problem with Sergeant Kaiser and it's not fair to Distoné" as I continue to gush without making much sense to the whole issue. "Whoa there, wait a minute, slow down" Cracker Jack says, slightly bemused by my blabbering. "Distoné you say? Well specialist Distoné', what's going on here and what about Sergeant Kaiser?" Greg gives a watered down version of what has happened. I keep looking at him to get his attention. He's got to spice this story up, because it really sounds like cry baby shit right now. But he ignores me and shoulders slumped forward babbles on. After a few clarifying questions, "Well let me look into it" Captain Armatidge says. "What about K.P. tomorrow Sir?" I ask. It's obvious Greg won't speak for himself anymore. "Are you supposed to fly tomorrow?" the Captain asks. "Yes sir" Greg says. "Well, you do your job, and I'll take care of the K.P." Captain Armatidge says. "Thank you Sir" as I now give Cracker Jack a deserved salute. Greg and Chip clumsily follow suit, giving half salutes and thanking the Captain as we bump into each other exiting Cracker Jack's hooch.

"I don't know what I did to him, but I can't take this shit forever" Greg says as we walk back in the dark between the officer's hooches. "Just don't think about it Greg, we'll think of something," as I turn and look back at Granger for affirmation that something had to be done. I know Kaiser has to either go or be taken care of, but I'm at a loss as to how to accomplish the impossible, short of fragging the son-of-a-bitch.

Chapter Twenty

Every day is something new, even if it's just ass and trash; there is always a twist to it. Today we are flying up to Dong Ha to recon potential LZ's for elements of the 3rd Marine Recon Company. We don't very often fly with the Marines, and it is always a kick to see how the other half lives.

It's still early spring, and rain threatens, with low lying cumulus clouds and fog. This morning we have a young first lieutenant and a well conditioned and muscled gunnery sergeant as our passengers. Flying towards the now abandoned Marine fire support base at Khe San, the sky is dark. The heavy, rain laden, dark blue and gray clouds spit fine mist and drizzle.

The helicopter bumps and bounces along in the unsettled morning air, as we sit in the door with machine guns at the ready. The gunny and lieutenant sit on opposite sides of the cargo door looking at their maps and coordinating potential landing and extraction sites for future operations. Occasionally the lieutenant will jump up, and leaning over the back of the pilots' seat, confer with BJ as to direction and sites, pointing with his arm, and then quickly move back to the door, glancing from his map, to the terrain outside.

We are flying two thousand feet above the ground. High enough to avoid the small arms fire, and low enough to still make out good terrain features. It is mid-morning. I am buffeted by the cold air and drizzle. As we fly along I tuck my neck deep into my field jacket huddled against the foul weather. We are deep in bad guy country. Just west of Khe San is Laos, and just to the north lays the DMZ and North Viet Nam. There are no firebases to be seen, no brown scars on the earth from abandoned firebases, just jungle, hills, mountains and vast fields of elephant grass. The rain swollen streams, with the pounding, cascading white water, create waterfalls over huge rocks and boulders as it rushes toward the ocean. The only thing that keeps me from looking upon this panorama of rugged countryside as virgin are the bomb craters filled with water that belie other nastier things have happened here.

As I sit there, trying to stay alert, I place the M-60 between my legs. I keep my cigarettes in a small pouch on the front of my body armor, my chicken plate. As I pull a cigarette out, lighting it with my Zippo, I cup my hands protecting the cigarette lighter's flame from the wind and rain. Trying to get my attention, as I hunch over attempting to light my cigarette, the lieutenant is pushing and pulling at my right shoulder. As I look at him, confused by this un-officer like abuse, he's not looking at me, but looking straight out the door of the Huey. The lieutenant's right arm is outstretched, his index finger pointing, with a look of object horror on his face. As I look in the direction of his outstretched arm, an F-4 Phantom appears out of the rain and mist, as if a great explosion has just blown it out of the clouds. The Phantom is no less than a hundred yards abeam our position, and coming straight at us! The lieutenant looks at me in dread, then back to the F-4, his jaws moving, mouth wide open, uttering unintelligible words, still pointing.

My knees relax the grip on my M-60. As the gun drops down, the bag attached to my gun, used to catch my expended ammo brass catches in the slipstream of the Huey. Ignoring the gun as it swings rearward away from my hands, certain the F-4 is going to collide with us, I scramble to reach for my mike button.

As I fumble for the mike button, the F-4, not a hundred feet away now, “wags” his wings up and down, appearing as if the pilot in his dismay is unsure he wants to turn left or right. Small, tight conical vapor trails magically appear on the wing tips of the huge Phantom as the wings dip. As I look into the cockpit of the F-4, the pilot in his white helmet looks at me, a huge grin of white teeth on his face. At the very last moment he dips the nose of the big fighter, and head tilted back, looking up, still smiling, disappears underneath our helicopter. The roar of the Phantoms engines passing underneath our Huey is analogous to the laughter I am sure is coming from the cockpit of the F-4 as the “fly guys” have a little fun at our expense!

BJ’s head immediately turns, looking quickly left and right, and then left again, “What the hell was that Lot?” Finally gaining some composure, and pressing my foot down on the mike button located on the floor I respond “Uh, well Boss,…we just had an F-4 go under us from left to right.” “What!!” He exclaims, “Dammit Lot, you gotta keep your eyes open!” As BJ kept shaking his head, I said, “Shit Boss, he literally came outta nowhere.” There was nothing else I could say in my defense, so I said nothing.

Chapter Twenty One

Early April, and we still are fighting the lingering affects of the monsoon season. We have repositioned our flight platoon to Phu Bai. The last time I was here, I had been flying the Red Cross donut dollies. It seemed like a long time ago.

The olive drab Army busses arrive with a strange cargo. Out pours a bedraggled mixed crew of men and equipment I have heard about, but have never seen. Mercenaries. Americans, British, Irish, German, French, South African, Dutch, about a hundred in all. White, black, Asian, their "uniforms," as well as their weapons, are as varied as their nationalities. Vietnamese tiger stripe fatigues, as well as every variation of camouflage battle uniform can be seen. As individual as every nation can be in uniform, some are obviously individual in their own unique style of dress. One guy has a red handkerchief tied around his neck. Others wear berets, different styles of helmets, boots, knives, and load bearing equipment. Others are clean cut. Shaved heads, crew cuts, flat tops, and yes even that long unmilitary-like hippy hair. One man carries a BAR. A Browning automatic rifle, of World War Two vintage. A Dutchman, judging from his speech, has a new Swedish K nine millimeter. Several carry sniper rifles, an M-14 and a German Mauser.

Sitting in my crew chief's seat, a blond haired, blue-eyed "merc" catches my eye as he ambles over to chat. He appears to be an American, about thirty-five, well conditioned, but attired in the combat gear and uniform of a foreign country. "How are ya mate?" he says in a voice that sounds European, which confirms he is definitely not American. "Great, how ya doin'?" "I'm okay. Say I notice you have some of those new 'LRRP' rations under your seat there." In slang, he is referring to the new Long Range Patrol rations "lirps" that I keep under my seat for those days when we miss lunch. The LRRP rations are freeze-dried bags of food, light in weight, and nutritious. The LRRP's will go out on seven-day patrols, and to sustain them for that length of time, the sheer weight of C rations would be prohibitive for the type of movement and activity involved. So the lightweight food designed especially for them is a highly sought after product. On those days when I feel like snacking on them, I just pop the dry food into my mouth and suck on it to give it moisture. It will expand as it sucks up the moisture and is really tasty considering it's Army chow. "Yeah, they're pretty good" I respond. "Would ya be interested in trading some?" he asks. Curious where this merc is from, I dodge the question and counter with "Where you from?" "Besides my majstro aplikajoj, my matré, my moeder, my mother, you mean" he says trying to make it a joke. "I'm Afrikkan, Sow' Africa," he says in a slur. "Well, whatdaya got to trade?" I ask my South African friend. "I got a Thompson sub-machine gun here." As he reaches behind his back, he pulls the machine gun, barrel first, around in front of him as I just stare. Holy shit, how cool is this? So much for Moricinni and his Bowie knife I think. "Deal" I say. "Wait a minute" he says, "I only have two ammo clips for it." "That's okay, I'll make do." I just can't believe I just traded a box of rations for a Thompson sub-machine gun like my television hero "Sergeant Saunders" carried on the TV show "Combat"!

Finishing our barter, the Huey's started "cranking up" and the merc's started to pile on board. We flew them into a small valley south of the A Shau Valley near the Laotian border. As we dropped them off, there was no visible signs of additional support for them as they unloaded and quietly melted into the nearby jungle. Although over the span of the next month we hauled two additional loads of mercs into the mountains, I never saw my South African friend again.

Chapter Twenty Two

A few weeks ago, we were instructed by our higher command to begin wearing seat belts or Monkey straps while sitting in the gunner positions. The belt was about five feet long and attached to our waist and then to a cargo tie down ring on the aft bulkhead. The monkey strap term came from the "tail" we had whenever we unhooked to exit the helicopter. Everybody hated the restriction to freedom of movement, but it seems that several gunner crew members had "fallen" quite inadvertently from helicopters while in flight.

Returning after a day of ass and trash, I was completing a post flight inspection of my bird when Ridge's door gunner Castillo comes running up to my ship hollering "The seat belt saved me, the seat belt saved me" in an excited almost hysterical voice. "What?" Knowing how everyone felt about these monkey seat belts, I didn't comprehend what Castillo was saying. "Yeah, we were on a CA about lunch time, and Preacher starts doing some jinking from some 'shit' (alluding to ground fire) we're getting on short final to the Z. Well at about the same time, I was twisting in my seat to get a better angle to shoot and was ya know, kinda' in and outta' my seat like this" as Castillo duplicates this absurd, contorted position simulating his gunners position. Unable to contain a stifled laugh, I shake my head and bend over laughing just imagining the bobbing, bouncing and twisting of the helicopter as Castillo tries to move his chubby frame around in the confined area of the bird. Ridge walks up with a scowl on his face. "You stupid Mexican" he says. "What?" Castillo says in feigned bewilderment. Ridge ignores Castillo and turning to me, begins to give me his version of what happened. "Well the Preacher starts jinking, and this fool" as Ridge lifts his arm with finger pointed at Castillo "thinks it's a good time to go for a stroll. All I heard was some high pitched scream and then this terrible wind noise." Castillo indignantly interjects "That's when I went out the door." "The air noise just about ruined our hearing for life!" Ridge interjects. I look at Castillo as he tells of being ejected from the helicopter. His face shows wounded pride, but his lips are defiantly pursed together in a manner that says it wasn't his fault. "So I think the Mexican's been shot," as Ridge continues, "and the grunts are all leaning out the door looking at him dangling by his Monkey strap! By the time I crawled over to his side of the ship, two of the line doggies had hauled this tub o' lard back up to the skid, and we finally hauled him back in. Man, you gotta lose weight," as Ridge turned to look at Castillo for the first time, "cuz I ain't pullin' your fat ass out of the fire the rest of the war! Preacher was pissed too! In fact he said, and I quote, 'If he falls out again, let's just cut our losses and cut him loose!'" "No way!" Castillo says in feigned defiance, but still that silly smile on his face. "You fall out again, and you can get yourself back in. And I don't care if we're taking fire or not!" With that, Ridge waves a hand of disgust at Castillo and walks away. "Well anyway, it did save my life." Castillo says boldly to Ridges' retreating backside.

Replacement Warrant Officer pilots continue to trickle in to our Company. BJ is one of the training officers responsible for getting them up to speed on the Huey. Most are coming straight out of flight school. One of them, a dough boy named Hackett shows up one morning, green as the new flight nomex on his back. Hackett can't be much older than my twenty years, if that. He has a baby face complexion with freckles. Without even opening his mouth, he looks goofy. He even reminds me somewhat of Castillo. Hackett is overweight, his flight uniform looks disheveled, and he simply looks very "un-officer-ish." All the baubles and bangles he has dangling from him, like the big aviator's watch with nine different time zones and buttons, sunglasses and associated sun glass carrying case, plastic ear plug case, and survival knife, remind me of the time we wore everything we were issued (like gas masks) that would never be used. He seems unsure of himself. The new bars of a W-1 Warrant Officer sewn on his shoulders that should command, without question, our respect, gets just the opposite response. He talks to me and Jesse like we're boys from his neighborhood. He finishes with a hollow attempt of expressing a "father like" in-the-know maturity of what's really happening in Vietnam and what we are going to collectively do to fix it.

I walk with Hackett trying to show him the respect deserved of an Officer and pointed out the preflight process we go through on a daily basis. I explain how we check the status of the log book, and how maintenance is performed and maintenance items of question cleared for flying status. He listens intently, almost studiously and I feel better that he really does want to learn and be familiar with what it is we do to support my bird.

Just as we finish a walk-around, BJ ambles up, his big Texas frame relaxed and congenial as usual. We were going to take Hackett out for autorotation practice and basically re-familiarize him with the Huey. As BJ gave me a friendly good morning nod and smile, we exchange knowing looks that we have another lamb ready for the slaughter. He nimbly hops in the left seat and reaches around for his shoulder harness as I slide the bullet shield forward and close his door. Hackett follows BJ's lead as he clumsily gets into the right seat as he knowingly slides his .38 revolver into his crotch and begins looking around at the cockpit. The .38 in his crotch was to protect his "family jewels" from harm. Somebody obviously had already given him a heads up on that small survival technique as I smiled to myself. BJ begins running through the check list explaining the training event as he performs the duties of co-pilot for Hackett. "Well let's get it started" BJ says to Hackett. As BJ reads the start check list, he points to switches helping Hackett through the almost mechanical process we all could do in our sleep. "Okay, start her up" BJ says. I'm watching Hackett from my seat, waiting for him to pull the start trigger; half turned watching the engine gauges. There's silence for a moment as Hackett sits immobile. BJ looking at the engine gauges half turns his head looking at our new co-pilot in training. "Well?" BJ says. "I...I...uh...can't remember how to start it." Hackett says in a low mumbling voice. His head hung down, not looking at BJ, I was at first surprised, and amazed that he couldn't remember how to start a Huey. Then as he explained the memory lapse I began to feel sorry for him. Hackett had just finished flight school; he had gone home on a thirty day leave and then spent two weeks traveling and in-processing in country. It had been over two months since he had last sat in a Huey. "Well don't worry about it Kid" BJ said as he picked up his instructor's voice and casually pointed out where the start trigger was and walked him through the start sequence.

His soothing voice rambled on as we lifted out of the revetment, BJ's hands now firmly on the controls. It was another beautiful, cloudless warm summer day as we headed south and east toward the flat land and rice paddies. It was always a kick to do autorotations; we had done this many times already with BJ training the new pilots. The bottom would fall out, leaving our stomachs in our mouth as BJ would simulate the loss of engine power. Then the glide, searching for a suitable emergency landing spot, checking the wind direction and clearing for potential obstacles in the landing zone. We would do this over and over, and I never tired of the carnival like ride. But once again, our higher command had nixed the crew chief and gunner from going along on these training flights when autorotations would be practiced. Real crashes had occurred during training, injuring non-flying crew members. So now we searched for a suitable place for Jesse and me to wait while the training flight proceeded without us.

Landing on the dike of a rice paddy situated in the middle of a large area of rice paddies; we hurriedly unloaded our machine guns and a case of C-rations as the training commenced with "Kid" as BJ had taken to calling Hackett. "See you in a bit Boss." I said to BJ as I took my flight helmet off and secured it to my seat belt. He waived and with a final check to make sure we were clear of the Huey, pulled pitch off the dike as I once more waved a final goodbye.

I had selected this particular area because of the one and only shade tree available in miles of surrounding rice paddies. Not bothering to set up our guns, we could see for miles if anybody tried to sneak up on us.

As Jesse and I lounged under the shade tree, we talked easily about life and the war. As we talked, we noticed four or five figures making their way towards us across the dikes of the rice paddies. Intentional or not, we began casually setting up our machine guns and confirmed our weapons were close at hand. As we watched the group slowly approach, it turned out to be five little Vietnamese boys carrying watermelons. Smiling, I waved to them and they waved back as they approached us in a friendly, easy way.

Sign language as usual was the easiest way to communicate with the boys who seemed to be about eight to twelve years old. There was the usual "G.I. number one" and "V.C. dinky dau number ten" which meant Viet Cong crazy, cuckoo bad guys. This wasn't the only verbal communication that was understood by all of us. The boys spoke other fractured English sentences. "G.I. want number one boom-boom," or, "G.I. like fucky-sucky?" We all understood that. After the boys had tried to barter with us on everything from marijuana to their sisters, Jesse and I settled on the watermelons which were large and looked great. We had not had fresh fruit like this in our chow hall ever. My first obviously absurd inclination was that the boys were going to just give us a watermelon. However, as I took the watermelon, the oldest boy pointed to our case of C's. It was a brand new box, and had twelve individual boxes of meals. I thought fair is fair as I opened the C ration box and pointed to it allowing the boys to each take a box. The oldest boy shook his head "no" as he pointed to us and then once again extended his hand toward the C rations. So I pulled out a box of rations and handed it to him. He again shook his head "no" as he leaned over and randomly pulled a box out and gave it to Jesse. Smiling, satisfied a deal had been struck, the boy picked up the case of remaining C's and heads for the rice paddy dike. Suddenly realizing he wants the whole case, I tell Jesse to grab whatever he likes out of the case because "it looks like that's the trading price." "Wait" I say as I motion with my hand for the Vietnamese boy to stop. I motion to the leader of this gang of fruit traders that I want another watermelon. The little guy's eyes widen in surprise as I take another watermelon from the boys hands shaking my head in an affirmative no-bullshit manner that, that IS the deal. Once again that innocent smile crosses his face as he turns, the bartering done, and moves back down the dike. I hoped the meals would be put to good use for the kids' families, but in reality, I probably had just fed the enemy.

BJ and the Kid were all smiles and happy on their return as I rewarded them with a portion of the fruits of my labor, the ill-begotten fruit of bartering.

Returning to the company area after our training exercise, the Kid's new moniker was official, as it was explained in detail how the name had come to be, accurate, but ridiculous as it was. That evening in the hooch Greg tells me of another attempt by sergeant Kaiser to harass him. It's all bullshit, and collectively the guys in our hooch don't know what to do. Today it was unshined boots and the length of his hair, which looked fine to me. Greg wore his hair short, like a football jock. He even tried to put him on KP, but the roster was already set for tomorrow, so it didn't work.

Chapter Twenty Three

We are flying endless days of ass and trash, interspersed with moving troops in company and platoon strength to different parts of the AO, or area of operation. Each day for "log" logistical missions, we are assigned to a particular battalion, and then support the companies of that battalion. For instance, we will go over to the log pad of the First Battalion, 506th Infantry. We provide the "lift" support flying mail, C rations, ammunition, uniforms, replacements, troops coming in to go on R & R, or to go home, anything that needs to go back and forth from the battalion, to the boonies.

One day, as we land on the battalion logistical pad, the grunts throw us the mail bag, and then start piling jungle fatigues, boots, several sundries packs and a few crates of ammunition and hand grenades on board. I have never flown fatigue uniforms before, but don't give it a second thought as the grunts finish loading and we depart for the mountains.

As we reach our destination, an LZ located on a small mountain top near the A Shau, the ground commander pops smoke. The area around the LZ is cold, no contact, and none anticipated. It's a straightforward kind of day as BJ easily settles the Huey down in the hastily prepared, makeshift LZ. Several grunts, hunched over to keep clear of the main rotor blades, come running to Jesse's side of the ship as I get up to throw out the cargo of uniforms and ammo. As they eagerly reach for the cargo, I realize why the uniforms are being sent out to these guys. The faces and necks of the grunts are caked in grime and dirt. The creases in their necks as they lift there head to pick up a load of ammunition from the deck of the Huey, or a quick smile is the only revealing evidence of the fair skin underneath. The uniforms the men are wearing are absolutely black. The blackness of the uniform, on closer inspection, is from the sweat and body oils of these men, combined with the dirt and grime of a hard month in the field. After over a month of continuous use, not having a chance to bathe or wash adequately, the uniforms are nothing more than oily rags draped over their bodies.

The guys are happy to see us. We have mail and the sundries packs. The sundries packs are filled with the little essentials of life we all take for granted. The sundries packs contained four cartons of cigarettes, Camels, Winston's, Marlboro, and Kool's. They also had tablets of writing paper, pen, pencils, toilet paper, chewing gum, lifesavers, salt and pepper and other niceties to make life tolerable if not somewhat bearable. I always managed to "scarf" or "barter" an occasional sundries pack from the log pad grunts on missions like these.

The grunts we were resupplying that day also had a back-haul for us. As we finished unloading their cargo, two men carrying a body bag came out from behind some bushes on the side of the LZ. As they silently slipped the body onto the cargo deck, I exchanged looks with the buck sergeant carrying the bag. His eyes looked sad, but otherwise emotionless, and I wanted to know...but, this was Viet Nam, and I already knew.

Along with the body came the KIA's weapon, a new M-203. The M-203 was a combination M-16 with a grenade launcher underneath the barrel. The grenade launcher opened up with a slide action where the round was inserted much like a shotgun. I had seen a few of these new weapons in the previous weeks, and they looked pretty cool. On the way back to the log pad, I decided to keep the new M-203. They sure wouldn't miss it, and it would always be useful if I ever got shot down. As we landed back at the battalion log pad, I tucked the weapon on my left side, under my arm up against the bulkhead, like it was a part of me. The grunts were so focused on getting the body bag off and freight loaded, that they never even inquired as to a missing weapon. Cool....

When we landed back at our Company area that night, we learned of a second flight platoon gunner who had been killed in action that day while flying a small combat assault. This was our first KIA in the company. It came as a shock. We had been doing an extensive amount of flying, and our Company aircraft were taking some hits, but nothing of a nature where we felt truly endangered. The reality of war has struck home, and yet the nature of his death has left me disaffected. It was somebody else, not me, not Jesse or BJ, better him than me, and we carry on.

I've been in country over seven months. I'm ready for a break. My mind wanders, and I think of home. Does it really exist, or was it all manufactured by the government just for my mind? Are we merely pawns in some bizarre world that plays with human kind? I can't tell anyone what I'm thinking, they'd put me in a straight jacket...

Chapter Twenty Four

The air assault, airmobile concept is spreading its wings far and wide across Viet Nam. With great flying weather, the monsoon season is now only a chilly and wet memory. We support the troops in every aspect of the fight. One afternoon we are tasked to move a company from one location to another.

En route to the LZ we are informed that contact has been made, and we should expect light ground fire on the way in. A combat assault "on the fly" is much more intense than one that has been thoroughly planned in advance. We are not yet accustomed to hot LZ's as a normal course of business yet, so the heartbeat quickens and the adrenaline flows freely with the excitement of the impending approach. As we flare on the LZ it is clearly obvious that the LZ is hot. We have caught the NVA in the open, or they have caught us. I'm not quite sure who has the advantage of surprise. The grunts, spread out over the entire area of the LZ are returning fire into the surrounding jungle. They fire a searching, covering, protective fire for us as they lay in prone, exposed positions. I will momentarily catch a glimpse of an American GI in his jungle fatigues firing full automatic as a string of expended shell casings eject from his M-16.

Moving my machine gun about on its gun mount to provide supportive fire, I can see an occasional muzzle flash in the surrounding tangle of splintered palm trees and grass. I quickly send three or four tracers, about fifteen or twenty hard rounds into that spot and the surrounding area just in case the gook may have moved. Jesse is firing long bursts of machine gun fire on his side of the ship also. The assault is getting intense.

Through the green haze of the smoke grenade marking the LZ, our guys hop nimbly across fallen trees, or clumps of torn up earth, dodging, weaving, left and right, as they play the game of life and death. To a casual bystander, a seemingly careless frolic in the LZ, the big rucksacks, filled with the meager possessions of a combat soldier sway on their shoulders and backs, as they jump across the uneven terrain. They move much like a child playing hop-scotch on a sunny day, or simply jumping from rock to rock across a small stream. The only consequence to be paid, losing a turn or getting your feet wet. But here today, the outcome could be death or mutilation. Some have already paid the price for the gambol in this LZ. Here lays an unmoving body, or over there a medic lying next to a GI ministering a wound, the price being paid, a toll exacted by the enemy for this grassy space in the middle of nowhere.

As the Huey hits the ground hard, telegraphing to me how uptight BJ is flying this assault, I see in my peripheral vision the movement of the troops unloading the helicopter, joining in the dance of war in the LZ. "Crack, crack, crack"... one crack following the other in quick succession. What the hell was that? I turn to my right insuring the helicopter deck is clear, and also try to ascertain what noise I had heard, or thought I had heard. I continue to shoot, stopping for a moment to scan the engine gauges. "We're clear, clear left." I say automatically, as Jesse follows moments later with "Clear right." The Huey still rocking from BJ's hard arrival leaps off the ground. All is well as the power of the engine and massive rotor blades pull us back into the warm tropical air. The turmoil in the LZ quickly slips away beneath the deck and skids of the helicopter. Shifting my fire forward, I shoot continuosly until we are well clear of the LZ, accelerating and gaining altitude.

The entire assault sequence from the landing flare to lift off has not lasted more than fifteen seconds. My mind is dull or overloaded, I don't know which. Something happened; I try to concentrate on what should concern me. "Lot, you didn't clear the area pulling pitch out of the Z," BJ says in an almost abstract fashion. Now I am even more confused as I concentrate on what has just happened, and my mind spins. I could have sworn that I had cleared my deck and tail rotor of grunts and elicited a response confirming that.

Not looking to the cockpit, staring out the door, I am captivated by the emotions that are overwhelming me. With my gun still extended, cooling in the slipstream of the helicopter, my foot pushes down on the microphone button located on the floor deck of the Huey. "I think I did clear coming off the LZ, BJ." Shit, I knew full well that I had cleared lifting out; I just tried to be a little diplomatic until I could sort things out. But my mind was in a whirl, even my voice didn't sound convincing. Still baffled with a conscious thought that something crucial has happened, I sit in a trance trying to concentrate on what it is.

"Lot" BJ says, once again breaking my concentration. I key my mike again, I'm trying to think and now he's really irritating me "Yeah, BJ." This time I don't hide the frustration I am feeling; a moment of silence, then with a hint of annoyance in his voice, "Lot" BJ says again. I look over my shoulder and see Flashy, our co-pilot looking at first concerned and then quizzically back at me like "What's up?" I step on my floor mike button again, and looking at Flashy I say "Can you hear me?" Flashy shakes his head in the negative and responds, "No, can you hear me?" I pick up the microphone switch that hangs at my side and holding it so Flashy can see me pushing down on the talk switch; I respond "I can hear you" as I move my head up and down in the affirmative. Flashy shakes his head in the negative again as I check the connection between my microphone cord and my flight helmet. I can hear them, but they can't hear me. What in the hell is going on? I have a good connection to my flight helmet as I run my hand up the communication cord that runs up into the sound proofing and ceiling of the helicopter. Where the wire runs just past the top of my helmet, I feel a small fray and a pick on my gloved hand as I turn and look closely at the communication cord. A small cut, jagged and frayed has cut across my microphone cord. Pushing on the torn cord with my thumb, trying to make a connection, I ask Flashy if he can hear me... A smile on his face, problem solved, Flashy says, "It's distorted and unreadable, but I think you found your problem."

As we fly back to Birmingham for another lift, I search further as to the cause of my broken mic cord. My M-16 is always tucked behind my left shoulder, readily available in case my machine gun should jam. As I grasp the combination handle gun sight of the M-16, it disintegrates in my hand. Upon closer examination, the whole receiver of the weapon has been smashed by a bullet. The realization then comes to me that the "crack, crack, crack" I heard were bullets flying past my head and body. As I continue to survey the cubicle that I sit in, my head now on a swivel, a smoke grenade hanging behind my head on the sound proofing has also taken a round through the body of the grenade.

I'm no longer confused or in a daze wondering what I missed in the LZ. It was more like what had missed me. It was good that I was still sitting, as I shivered and my legs quivered and knocked uncontrollably together with the realization that I had once again been spared.

Later that week while returning from the mountains mid-afternoon, after a relatively uneventful day, we are all in a good mood as we talk of the day's events. BJ has "AFVN" Armed Forces Viet Nam radio on as we listen to "The Doors." They are playing a new song "Light My Fire"...It's a great song, and as we listen it stimulates conversation in that relaxed atmosphere. I recall one particular lift out to the Valley. There was a Mule that had been sling loaded underneath the helicopter. The Mule was simply a small flat bed vehicle about four feet wide and six feet long with a driver's seat and steering wheel. Nothing fancy, but it sure could save a guy's back, and hauls a ton. They would use these vehicles to haul materials around the fire base. It would be the very earliest version of today's modern All Terrain Vehicles. As we left the logistics pad of one of the infantry battalions, the Mule began to twist and finally spin underneath our chopper. As I lay on the floor looking out and underneath, I kept BJ apprised of our load. Halfway to Cannon, the firebase destined for this load, and in the middle of nowhere, the Mule began to twist rapidly, threatening the aerodynamics that kept us flying. "I don't think this looks good BJ. It's twisting pretty badly in one direction, and the lines are winding up real tight." You could feel the Huey slewing through the air as the twisting Mule fought the air resistance and its tether. "Aw shit" was all BJ could say as suddenly the Huey jumped in the air like we had flown through a small thermal of rising warm air. Looking down once again, the Mule rapidly fell away toward the jungle far below. Tumbling slowly in the air, rolling, then flattening out, as red dirt and dust streaked from hidden crevices that had not been cleaned by the earlier turbulence of air. "Holy shit Boss, we just lost the mule." "Nah, I punched it loose." BJ said. I laughed as I continued to watch the Mule streak toward the jungle. Occasionally I would lose sight of it as it got closer to the jungle and it blended with the green foliage. The red mist of dust still streaking from it giving its position away until finally it was gone. "Wow, one hell of surprise for Charlie if he's in the neighborhood. What are you going to tell the guys back at the log pad BJ?" "That they did a shitty job of rigging that thing, and they coulda' killed us!" I looked over my shoulder at Jesse as he smiled back at me. Back in A Company 101st Assault, when I was on the maintenance bird, we had an I.G., an Inspector General's inspection coming up. We had one turbine engine too many on our T.O. & E. and that was as bad as not having enough engines. So we had flown out over the South China Sea and punched loose this Huey turbine engine that was "excess." Just so the I.G. wouldn't ding us for having one too many spare engines. What a splash that bugger made! Anyway, the pay was the same whether we were getting shot at, dumping Mules in the middle of the jungle, or jet engines in the sea. The music continued uninterrupted, a sunny day, good company, we were all in a good mood as we flew home, what a waste this war was.

A conversation always developed as we flew over "Rocket Ridge'" the last chain of mountains before the flatlands leading to the ocean. The gooks would set up their 120 millimeter rockets behind that ridge and fire them at Camp Evans. BJ, Jesse and I had spoken on several occasions as we flew over rocket ridge that we should "bomb" them back, just so they would know that we were thinking of them as much as they thought about us. "Hey BJ, let's bomb em' today." BJ half turned his head in his seat, looking over his shoulder at me, smiling, "Ya okay." That's all I needed to hear as Jesse and I collaborated as to how we would drop "the bombs." The bombs for us would be hand grenades. Going on hot mike so BJ and our peter pilot could follow what we were doing; Jesse and I met on the cargo deck, grenades in hand. We each had two grenades. Holding a grenade in each hand, I stuck my index finger out and looped it around the ring of the grenade pulling the pins on Jesses' grenades as he pulled the pins on mine as we approached the ridge. BJ lowered the nose of 644 as he aimed for the top of the ridge. Jesse on the right side of the helicopter, me on the left, braced ourselves as we raced towards the ridge. "Standby" BJ said. Finally as the mountain side rushed up to meet us, BJ says "Bombs away!" as Jesse and I threw the grenades out of the Huey. BJ pulled hard on the cyclic stick as we did an arcing rotor climb up and away from the mountain. As I released the grenades I immediately hoped that four to five seconds of delay would be enough time to get away from the impending blast. All eyes glued to the mountain, our helicopter banked ninety degrees to the side of the mountain, we watched with satisfaction as the grenades explode safely far below on the rocky hillside. "That was a rush" I said, as we all burst out in a roar of laughter; we talked about "the bomb run" all the way back to the POL pad.

Chapter Twenty Five

Today we got a call for an emergency re-supply to a Marine fire base on the north end of the A Shau. The fire base is just west of "Salt and Pepper," twin mountain peaks that have an unusual characteristic. "Salt" is a mountain covered with a preponderance of white rock, whereas "Pepper" has more the characteristics of a mountain with dark, or black rock. Hence the name "Salt and Pepper," and a familiar landmark to aircrews as a point of reference.

The 155 millimeter howitzer battery on the firebase is nothing more than a cleared off mountain approximately sixty yards in diameter. The Laotian border is less than a half mile to the west at this point. We bring several sling loads of artillery shells in to them first thing in the morning. I notice the gun barrels on the howitzers are pointed almost straight up, about a seventy-five degree angle to the ground. The bad guys must be damn close. The firebase is intermittently covered in fog and rain clouds, and we can't make another lift in until late in the afternoon. With the last lift of ammunition, I notice that the barrels of the artillery are pointed straight down the hill, and the Marines are firing point blank downhill even as we make our approach. Don't you believe for a minute that the artillery guys had it easy. I never found out what happened to them, as we never went back to support them. But I know a "bee hive" round from a 155 would be nothing to mess with on an attempted ground assault of any kind.

The following day, May eighth, we are still supporting Marine operations. Flying with an element of the 3rd Marine Recon Company, we have a "gunny" sergeant, and a first lieutenant doing reconnaissance up near the DMZ. The first lieutenant is much older than the norm; he looks to be in his early forties. As we stop to refuel after a morning of flying up on the DMZ I ask the gunny what's up with the lieutenant.

"You are looking at an officer who was a gunny like me once upon a time. He goes back to Korean War days" he says. "What'da ya mean?" I ask, confused. "He's one of those guys who received a battlefield commission." "No shit!" "Yeah, ya see all those scars on his neck and by his jaw?" the gunny says. "Those are old bayonet and knife wounds he got in hand to hand fighting over there." I am truly impressed and honored to have a distinguished guy like this on my ship. It's almost as if I had a real John Wayne riding with me! The gunny continues "You should see him with his shirt off, he's got more bayonet scars and a few bullet holes in him too." Wow, a real damn off the shelf G.I. Joe! It was sooooo cool...

We stop in Dong Ha for lunch with the Marines. Hovering into a parking spot, I look across the ramp to an HH-53 "Jolly Green Giant." It is painted in camouflage shades of green. The Jolly Greens are used as a search and rescue aircraft, picking up our downed airman flying north of the DMZ. This one has been hit by anti-aircraft artillery fire. Aft on the tail boom is a jagged hole over two feet in diameter. When I think of our excursions into Laos, and these guys on the Jolly Greens going up into North Vietnam, I realize how lucky we are to have the "cake" job we do.

The gunny invites me to his hooch for chow. As me and Jesse sit in his tent eating C rations, we swap war stories. The life of Marine Force Recon doesn't often allow the pleasure of sleeping much in tents. The gunny has "upgraded" his tent by using pine cargo pallets for flooring material. The monsoon season turns everything to mud, and one of life's simple pleasures is to get out of the wet and mud if at all possible. The cargo pallets helped the gunny do that. Unfortunately, it also provided shelter for other creatures.

As we sit eating and talking, all of a sudden the gunny jumps up, pulls his .45 automatic from his holster and begins blasting the floor in his tent. Not only is the noise incredible, but his wild shooting scares the shit out of me.

"What the hell are ya doin' gunny?"... "Did ya see that big ass rat running through the pallets?" he asks chuckling. "No" I say in a manner that lets him know that I think he's gone whacky on us. "Well if you see any, don't be afraid to blast um'" he says with a straight face. "I hate them fuckin' things" he says. Back in my home town in Michigan, high school day's weekends were spent with my buddies at the local township dump shooting rats for fun, but this was something that didn't have the same appeal.

Back in the air, our lunch time fun complete, we head back to the DMZ. The countryside is beautiful in its wild serenity. The undulating oceans of elephant grass, wave like huge fields of Nebraska wheat blowing in the wind. Mountains and escarpments breathtakingly beautiful look like sculptures formed by the hands of a master artist; and the wild rivers match the fury and grandeur of any category five rapids found in Colorado and Idaho.

As we swing back to the southeast headed for Dong Ha, the Rockpile rises in the distance. We pass over Khe San, abandoned and leveled by bull dozers. We are flying parallel and down the length of the now abandoned Khe San runway. The floor decking of the helicopter suddenly erupts into shavings of aluminum as the old lieutenant begins shooting at the ground below. "We're taking fire Boss," as I simultaneously pull the trigger on my M-60 and join the lieutenant suppressing the area.

Jesse and the gunny follow our lead.

"We're losing hydraulics Lot" BJ says moments later. My head snaps to the right, forgetting about the ground fire, looking at the instrument panel confirming our loss of hydraulics. "You're losing fuel pressure too, BJ" as I watch the fuel pressure gauge flicker and then go to zero. Not far to the South of Khe San is Highway 9, an east west single lane pot holed black top road running out of Dong Ha towards the Laotian border. BJ is nursing the helicopter in that direction as he suddenly loses directional control and automatically dumps collective and begins an autorotation to the jungle below.

Zeke, our peter pilot, is quickly sifting through radio frequencies talking to both the Marines and Ghost Riders in the area. The Marine lieutenant is also talking on his radio, and I can tell from his soundless but emphatic conversation, his fingers tracing details on his map that they are doing all they can to affect a rescue. We need help, and we need it fast. We're going down in Indian country and we need the cavalry. My mind moving at warp speed anticipates the upcoming landing, and I stretch out of the door looking to our possible landing sight. BJ appears to be aiming for a large open area of elephant grass. Highway 9 is no longer an option.

Having been a crew member with BJ while he performed additional duties, acting as the instructor and company check-out pilot, we had countless practice auto rotations already under our belts. I had no doubt and great faith in his abilities to get us down safely. An autorotation is synonymous with gliding like an airplane; only instead of a wing we have rotor blades. As the chopper falls from the sky, the rotor blades "free wheel" like a child's pin wheel. Timing is crucial with the input of the collective as it changes the pitch of the rotor blades to "flare," much as an aircraft would flare to arrest its descent to make a soft landing.

As the ground rushes up to meet us, I instinctively brace for a crash, and not the usual normal landing. BJ walking the anti-torque pedals of the tail rotor moves the cyclic to the left turning our aircraft to make the most of a headwind that I can see now is bending the tall elephant grass right below us. As he makes his turn BJ begins talking to the co-pilot, "Ya see that Zeke" BJ says as he nods his head forward out the windshield to something that I can't see. "Yeah." "Well now as you get a sense of ground rush" BJ's instructor voice drones…the voice I've heard so many times before, as he instructs Zeke on the fundamentals of an autorotation! Not wanting to break BJ's concentration, I say nothing. I can't believe even now he finds the need to instruct and teach. "Okay now" BJ says as he pulls hard on the collective flaring as we softly touch down in the middle of a small dirt road.

"Let's go Jesse." Not waiting for a response, I unhook my microphone cord. I pop open BJ's door and slide his protective bullet shield back even as the lieutenant jumps to the ground. The lieutenant, M-16 in hand, moves forward to talk to BJ as I remove my ammo brass bag from my gun. Opening the feed tray of my machine gun to release the belted ammunition I simultaneously pull my machine gun from its mount. "Jesse?" "Ya Lot." "Set your gun just off the road behind the tail." "Okay." In one fluid motion I grab my gun and an extra two hundred round can of M-60 ammo. I move to the left side of the road ahead of the nose of 644. As I open the tripod legs on the gun I reconnect the belt of ammo and slam the feed tray closed. Setting my gun just off the road, I half run, half walk back to get my M-203 and my bandolier of ammo for it.

I realize how muffled and quiet everything is, forgetting I still have my flight helmet on. As I remove the helmet, the cool breeze on my forehead suddenly feels like a north wind as the wind evaporates the sweat of my brow, calming in light of the current situation.

I look to the rear, confirming Jesse is set up and ready. I glance to BJ, still talking with the lieutenant. The gunny comes over to me, his head turning on his neck like a swivel, his eyes narrowed to slits as if squinting from the sun. But as he got close to me, I could tell he was in an infantry recon mode of thinking now. As he takes a knee on the sandy red dirt road, I follow his lead. The gunny hawks up a spit and with perceived nonchalance turned his head and let it go. "You got one back there ya know." He reached for his canteen, the water spilling around the corners of his mouth as he alternately filled his mouth with water and swallowed, and filled his mouth again. "I didn't see anything." "Well you walked your rounds right into him. Good shooting." "What else did you see?" I ask, not more curious than if we were talking about a ham sandwich. "Well I saw a couple more.... regulars, NVA. I think I got one too. Emptied almost a whole magazine on him, hard to tell though, they were rolling and scrambling when you guys opened up with the 'sixties. I don't think they expected that number one, they would even hit us as we flew over, or two that we'd shoot back so fast."

"Well what da ya think? Are they going to be comin' for us, or what?" I ask more than just a little nervous. I am totally out of my environment out here in the boonies. Without answering my question the gunny gets up and walks back toward the helicopter where BJ, Zeke, and the lieutenant are just breaking up their conversation. Then as we walk he says "We've been reconning the hell outta this place as ya know for the better part of two months. But it's really hard to say. The 320th NVA Division jumped across the DMZ and mauled two Regiments of the 1st ARVN a week ago. We've got some hardcore battalions out there, and if they saw us go down, they'll be coming." The sarge finishes with another hawk of spit into the road, which turns into a brown ball of dust as it splatters on the road.

The Marine lieutenant turns to us as we approach, and as if already knowing our questions states, "We've got some Army mechanized APC's on the way with one of my Recon platoons for security"...As he stares down the road back towards Khe San, he continues, "should be here in forty-five minutes, assuming no other problems materialize along the way. BJ or should I say Zeke got a relay to the Ghost Riders and we should have support within fifteen mikes." The lieutenant using the abbreviation for minutes looks to Zeke for confirmation on the estimated time of arrival of our company helicopters.

Jesse has joined us by the helicopter and we listen to the conversation nodding our heads understanding we'll be okay, but we've got to take care of business. As we turn to leave, Jesse says "Hey Lieutenant, did ya get hit?" As he speaks, Jesse leans and points at the Lieutenants' cheek of his left thigh. We all gather around as the Lieutenant grabbing his fatigue pants feels the blood now trickling down his leg and pulls at the small tears in the fatigue trousers. "I guess so." He says. BJ says "We better get a look at it." Unbuckling his pants, the LT drops trouser, and sure enough he's been hit by the metal shavings from the floor decking. Nothing serious, the blood is just a trickle, but it's good enough for another purple heart. Rubbing the blood trail from his thigh, the LT pulls his pants back up. Rubbing the blood from his hand onto his pants, he continues "Gunny, I want you at the rear with the co-pilot, dug in, cover and concealment." "Aye, Aye sir." the gunny acknowledges, as the lieutenant gives him a knowing look, that says officer or no officer, meaning Zeke, the gunny's in charge. I wouldn't think Zeke would have any problem at all with that! As the Gunny turns to go with Zeke, I holler to Zeke, "Hey Zeke let me give you my over and under, it'll be more help than that thirty-eight you got." Zeke half smiles and nods his head. "I'll show him how it works." "Thanks gunny." Zeke and I say simultaneously. And that was that!

"BJ, you and the chief with me" as the lieutenant walks away from the helicopter, towards Khe San. BJ had recently purchased a Swedish K nine millimeter submachine gun, new out of the box, and he carried that with him now. How in the hell do you purchase a submachine gun by mail? I hadn't given it much thought, but I put that on my list of what inquiring minds want to know from BJ.

"Listen, I don't know for sure what the hell is gonna happen, but I can tell you with utmost sincerity if they saw us go down, they'll be coming. So you guys cover up and stay off the road. If the gooks come down the road and think we've been extracted already, maybe we can catch them by surprise and hold them off for a bit, or at the least take a few with us. 'Cause we sure as hell will be outnumbered. The gunny and I will be doing a roaming security on the flanks behind you, so just keep your eyes forward. If the shit hits the fan and ya need help, I'll be close by." BJ looked at me and I looked hard right back at him, "Well Boss, I'll go back and get all the smoke and frag grenades I have." BJ just kept looking at me, slowly nodding his head. "Make it quick time chief" the lieutenant said, "we're burning daylight."

Grabbing all the grenades and as much of the remaining ammo I could carry, I ran back looking for Jesse. I couldn't see Zeke or Jesse! Getting nervous, I hollered in a loud whisper "Jesse!" "Ya Lot" "Where the hell are ya?" Jesse sticks his foot out of the elephant grass about ten feet from me. From the other side of the road, about five feet closer to me, Zeke waves a gloved, camouflaged hand. "Shit, I couldn't see you." As I hand some of the grenades and ammo to him, I can tell Jesse is scared too. His big frame shivers and he starts making stupid small talk. "Damn, Jess, I just want to give you some of these grenades, I gotta get back." "Okay Lot, well good luck, and keep your head down." "You do the same" as I pat Jesse on the shoulder once. "See ya." I give a nod in Zeke's direction as I hurry back up the road.

Chapter Twenty Six

A single blade of elephant grass looks much the same as a single blade of Bermuda grass so abundant in Florida. Only, a single blade of elephant grass, as the name implies, can grow sixteen to twenty feet in height and be two inches wide and one eighth of an inch thick. There are miles of elephant grass throughout northern South Viet Nam, especially in the area of the DMZ. Once immersed in this grass, anything can become invisible.

Lying in the elephant grass, I think of home, my girl, and my dog, a black lab Shepherd mix. It is hot, but not unbearable. The elephant grass sways in the wind, shading me somewhat from the afternoon sun. Listening intently for anything out of the ordinary, I realize how peaceful it really is. A gentle breeze fills the air with the freshness of spring greenery and the freshly turned soil I have dug into reminds me of the freshly plowed potato fields back home. Then the realization hits me that I have been shot down! Not quite the experience I had expected, but nonetheless terrifying in its own right. My mind had conjured up more intensity of everything. My vivid imagination has portrayed gunfire, rocket fire, the smoke and din of battle, torn earth and mangled wreckage. Yet 644, my Huey, sits languishing in the middle of a little dirt road, injured, but a far cry from the pile of junk it could be. And here I lay thinking of fresh cut grass, apple blossoms in bloom and potato fields.

The wop of Huey rotor blades in the distance breaks my train of thought and my heart skips a beat. I can't believe they are already inbound. I look at my watch, and I'm surprised to see more than twenty minutes has elapsed since BJ and I have dug in on the road side. BJ slowly steps out to the side of the road and I follow his lead, smoke grenade in hand. As the rotor noise increases in intensity I can detect the sound of multiple ships inbound. I look at BJ and lift the smoke grenade asking without words if he wants me to pop smoke. He shakes his head in the affirmative as I pull the pin and roll the smoke grenade into the middle of the road. The slight flash and pop of the smoke grenade's ignition, followed by the tentative sputtering and finally full blown eruption of yellow smoke fills the road and surrounding jungle grass. I enjoy the smell of the smoke grenade as the smoke rises up and drifts lazily on the air currents not yet disrupted by the violence of the incoming helicopter's rotor wash.

The lieutenant seems to simply materialize from the field of green as he steps out of the jungle grass radio in hand, telephone shoved to the side of his face. Talking intently, he catches our eyes, smiles and raising the radio with his hand gives a thumbs up, radio held high.

As two of our Ghost Riders orbit the crash site, we await the arrival of the 5th Mechanized Infantry armored personnel carrier's. Thirty minutes later, APC's and a platoon of Marines secure our site, as our maintenance bird lands, bringing fresh hydraulic and fuel lines for quick replacement.

Back in the air in less than an hour, we complete the two hour reconnaissance flight none the worse for wear, and maybe a little bit smarter.

The APC's make a quick dash during that time to Khe San. With no further enemy contact, the 5th Mechanized Infantry guys confirm several blood trails and drags from the area we had received the crippling ground fire. I am left again feeling disturbed at how quickly things can and do change. With more than half my tour complete in Vietnam, I still react with a naiveté that has no place out here.

Chapter Twenty Seven

Combat assaults, CA's, are in simple terms a planned movement of troops under combat conditions. The Huey was used to quickly envelop the enemy or a position by "combat assaulting" our grunts to a designated area. These assaults were commonly well devised and planned operations. Others were accomplished out of sheer necessity to get infantry to a grid on a map in response to time critical situations. Generally those were the operations where we hung our collective asses "in the breeze" and just simply hoped for the best.

An assault was developed in our S-2 intelligence section, where experts would piece together bits of information gathered from aerial reconnaissance, infrared detection, our "sniffer" missions, and other intelligence sources. From this information a picture of potential enemy activity was developed to determine the necessity to proceed with action to contact. The enemy situation would become more exact when local intelligence from ground units, pilots, captured or surrendering enemy troops (Hoi Chanhs), and the local populace contributed the links that tied all the information together. Our S-2 would then generally have reliable information as to the enemy Unit designation, its size, their weapons, and the particular habits and activities of the enemy force.

In a general briefing, the aviation unit will discuss the exact timing of the operation, artillery preparation, aerial rocket artillery support, any special requirements, ingress and egress routes for the helicopters into the assault area and chain of command. The chain of command on a combat assault begins with the C&C bird, the command and control helicopter. Onboard the ship is the battalion commander and the LNO, the artillery liaison officer. The C&C ship will have absolute authority during the assault pertaining to the mobility of the troops. Orbit points are also discussed for the command and control ship and any other friendly aircraft that will observe the assault without actually participating.

The assault companies will then plan PZ's, LZ's, routes, altitudes, timing schedules and check points, so that the pilots will know what to look for as they approach the assault landing zone.

A day or so prior to the actual assault, a reconnaissance flight would determine the acceptability of the LZ and its approaches. Detailed map sheets will then allow the pilots to visualize the LZ with the associated timing schedule and check points. The total number of lifts and sorties, along with the units being supported are also detailed at this time. Rules of engagement are described (including whether the LZ will be hot) as well as POL refueling and rearming points. Maintenance recovery and forward aid stations are also established at this time.

The artillery liaison officer works with the infantry commander to develop a fire plan for the LZ. This includes priority and critical targets, likely avenues of approach to the LZ by the enemy, and targets of interest selected by our Intelligence section. The size of the operation, artillery batteries within range of the LZ as well as intensity of fire are also considered.

On the day of the assault, a spare Huey with crew sits on standby, ready at a moments notice, should one of the scheduled aircraft be unable to launch. In the orbit area, a maintenance ship like I flew with the Commancheros of "A" 101st Assault Helicopter would circle the assault area ready to assist as needed in case of mechanical problems. On the maintenance bird were two qualified maintenance officers and mechanics with tool boxes and spare parts.

Artillery "preps" the LZ and intensifies in volume as the assault Huey's approach. A smoke ship will also be used to cover the approach if possible. Aerial rocket artillery will hit the LZ and surrounding designated targets keeping the enemy under constant fire during the approach and landing phase of the assault. As the combat assault develops into a ground operation, the LNO coordinates with the forward observer attached to the unit on the ground to hit preplanned on call targets or targets of opportunity or necessity as the combat action evolves.

With the details and knowledge of the planning and preparation behind us we are going to the "Valley." The early morning air thick with moisture makes the rising sun coming up out of the South China Sea a hazy red ball. We were in the groove. Two and a half months of ass and trash, combat assaults, CCN's and some intermittent work with the 3rd Marine Recon Company had honed our three-man crew (aircraft commander, crew chief, door gunner) into a lethal and volatile weapon of war. We were synchronized and tuned into each other's thoughts like a well-oiled machine, or a fine Swiss watch. We were smoooooth. As the peter pilot's, our co-pilots, rotated in and out of different birds for experience, I came to think of our crew as three "hard-cores" plus a co-pilot. As a crew we had amassed close to three hundred flying hours during that time.

BJ called me "chief," and I had taken to calling him "Boss" in lieu of sir, Mister, or "the Bridge." It was easier to show him my respect in this way, rather than a regulated or "camp" manner. BJ had proved to us his savvy and extraordinary skill as a pilot on many occasions in the previous months. He had been flying since he was sixteen, and had been a civilian flight instructor prior to joining the Army. BJ was four years older than me, and we got along like brothers, always kidding and pulling pranks on each other.

Finishing my morning preflight, Jesse had shown up with the guns. Installing them on our gun mounts, we talked about girls, home, and R& R. I was within two weeks of heading for an R&R to Hong Kong. I had tried to hold out for Hawaii so I could see my girl. But my unit would only give allotments to the married guys for R&R in Hawaii. I had been in country seven and a half months, and I was more than ready to get the hell out of this place for a couple of weeks.

To keep the pressure on the bad guys, we've been re-supplying the infantry at firebases like Anzio, Bastogne, and Veghel with all sorts of equipment and gear. We have been flying an inordinate amount of logistical runs day in and day out, and I was totally bored with no action.

We were going to be doing a full Battalion assault of fifty plus helicopters this morning to various LZ's in the A Shau Valley. We're reopening old firebases and creating new ones. Doing combat assaults like stepping-stones, we are opening these new firebases heading straight for the A Shau and feeder routes of the Ho Chi Minh trail, the "Yellow Brick Road." It was called the Yellow Brick Road because of its appearance from the air as a yellow path or trail. The trail itself was made of a "rip-rap" of bamboo laid criss-cross fashion to support the weight of bikes, animals, and Viet Namese loaded with war material. The NVA are filtering supplies down into southern South Viet Nam along this trail, and our ultimate goal was to interdict and sever the many routes coming out of Laos on the north end of the A Shau.

It was a beautiful day for flying and I was looking forward to the combat assault. I had none of the jitters or sense of foreboding that would be natural for a combat assault going into "the Valley." It's just another day. War is like that. No premonition, no warning, everything's cool, let's go fly. Unknown to us at the time, there are over 50,000 enemy North Vietnamese soldiers in or around the A Shau.

Chapter Twenty Eight

The A Shau Valley is a large, beautiful and well-defined valley lying along the western edge of South Viet Nam bordering Laos. The mountains surrounding the valley run in generally a north and south direction in continuous rugged ranges eastward to the flatlands of the South China Sea. It is a very inhospitable terrain with mountains forty-five hundred to five thousand feet high covered with triple canopy jungle.

We pick up our first load of grunts for our run out to the Valley. They are from Company B, 1st of the 327th Airborne Infantry. As our flight platoon lifts off, we form up in a “staggered trail” formation one behind the other. It is a twenty-minute ride out to the Valley as I sit back, light up a cigarette and stare at our cargo of five grunts. I love to read the writing on the grunt’s camouflage cover that covers their helmets, their “steel pot.” Some of the guys have their hometown, or their state scrawled with an ink pen. Others have short timer calendars, peace symbols and “FTA” - “fuck the Army,” along with some very interesting “art.” I search for names of cities or states close to me, that I might reach out to someone I know, or touch a bit of home through someone else. The camouflaged helmet cover is held in place by a rubber like band. This same rubber band also had tucked into it mosquito dope, C ration cigarettes and toilet paper, matches, playing cards or pictures and an occasional magazine of M-16 ammo. Anything that was deemed important enough to be in easy reach, but most importantly, kept dry while crossing rivers, creeks and rice paddies was kept in that helmet band.

I still am enamored by the gear and stuff all around their rucksacks and butt packs. The "LBE" load bearing equipment suspenders, used to distribute the weight of the rucksack over the back and shoulders, also carry an odd assortment of gear hanging on the front of the suspenders. Squad leaders and higher will generally have a flashlight and maybe a compass that they carry. A bayonet or "K" bar may also be taped to the suspenders, usually upside down for easy access. Then depending on degree of time in country, they carry an odd assortment of smoke, white phosphorous, fragmentation "frag" grenades, and the round "CS" tear gas grenades that look like baseballs. The longer a guy has been in country, the more smoke grenades he carries. I think the belief or philosophy is that if the grunt has to use a frag, the bad guys are too damn close. If he has smoke, help in the form of a Huey is close at hand, or, if the bad guys can't see 'em, they can't shoot em'. There is always at least one compress bandage on the suspenders that is for their own use. If he's wounded, the first to provide aid, or a medic will use the bandage from the wounded soldier because it is carried and readily available for just that purpose. Some of the guys will also have attached to the suspenders a tightly coiled green nylon rope for climbing and pulling themselves and their gear up the never-ending vertical mountain slopes. There is always a fresh cloth bandolier of boxed M-16 ammo that has eight boxes of twenty rounds each draped across their chest, along with a hundred rounds of M-60 ammo carried criss-cross fashion across their chests like Poncho Villa for their squad M-60. Every third or forth man also carries a LAW, a Light Anti-tank Weapon for bunker busting. These are small, sling carried, self contained, and disposable weapons. "E" tools, entrenching tools, small self contained shovels are carried on the hip or back pack as well as an occasional machete for clearing the jungle vegetation. Rarely, unless absolutely necessary will the grunts walk on established trails. Established well used trails are called “high speed” trails. These trails and paths are booby trapped, and protected by rear guard NVA soldiers and VC for ambushes.

The pistol belt that the LBE suspenders are attached to have ammo pouches which will hold two standard twenty round M-16 magazines. I notice that the grunts usually have four ammo pouches, and three or four canteens of water on the web belt. The butt pack is also attached to the pistol belt. The average load carried by the grunts is sixty pounds and generally eighty pounds is more the rule than the exception.

Chapter Twenty Nine

There is a lot of radio chatter. BJ hasn't told us anything about the assault, other than it will be into the A Shau Valley. We are lifting several battalions of infantry today. I can pick up bits of conversation trying to develop a picture in my mind of what's going on. I can hear the call sign "Blackjack," the infantry commander of the battalion we are responsible for lifting, and assume he is in the "C & C" "command and control" bird overseeing the upcoming assault. He sounds pissed at someone for some indistinguishable reason. I hear "Bird Dog," our artillery and forward air controller guy talking, and the general consensus is everything seems to be behind schedule. Oh well, it's a lovely morning for a helicopter ride.

We are number three in formation. As I lean out to look back at the string of Hueys behind, I snap a picture with my Kodak Instamatic camera. It's a great picture. Three Hueys are stepping stone fashion suspended behind and above our bird. Each Huey slightly higher than the one it follows, is silhouetted by a hazy sky, backlit by a lemon yellow morning sun. Listening to the radio, the "arty" or artillery prep on the LZ has been delayed and we go into a circular holding pattern over the Valley. I lean over and tell the grunt seated next to me on the floor that we're in a holding pattern, and to pass along to the other guys they have time for a smoke if they're so inclined. A couple of them light up and seem to relax a little.

BJ talking to our co-pilot Beastie on the intercom mentions that our commanding officer, Major Dockert "the Bull" is flying with our platoon leader Cracker Jack. "Some of the AC's don't think that it was a good idea for two command staff to be flying the lead bird. I kinda agree with them." BJ said looking over at Beastie. The co-pilot nodded his head in agreement. "This CA could get nasty today, and I just can't believe they wanna be together on this assault," BJ said as an afterthought, as he shook his head side to side. As we continued to orbit in a large circular holding pattern over the middle of the A Shau Valley I could see my shipmates on the opposite side of the circle with the easily distinguishable white stripe on the top of the Huey's. "What a cluster fuck and a waste of gas this is," I thought to myself. Over our UHF aircraft radio I heard our "gun company" check in with Blackjack. Finally the "ARA" or aerial rocket artillery had arrived, and would begin to "soften up" the LZ.

This was going to be a single ship assault into an artillery LZ. They had concentrated artillery on one specific grid coordinate and blown down the trees so we would be able to land or hover over the LZ to unload our grunts. The LZ was located on the northeast ridge of the valley about midway between the top of the mountain and valley floor.

With the artillery barrage complete, Black Jack gives the okay to begin the assault. As we remain in our circular holding pattern, the Bull and Cracker Jack begin their approach to the LZ. The radio chatter begins to increases in volume, as the assault gets under way. The Bird Dog guy is talking to Bull and Blackjack. "We've got hostile fire coming from multiple directions on the east ridge and floor of the valley" he says. Major Dockert, Bull, is telling Blackjack the LZ conditions. "There are still some triple canopy trees that are of concern on the approach, and it will affect ingress and egress from the Z, which will affect the timing for all the assault birds going in" Bull says, as the static and hiss on the radio continues for a moment after his radio transmission. There is so much communication over the radio, it is hard to discern who is talking to whom, and what conversation is directed to which command authority. A moment of silence and then a voice presumably Bird Dog says, "Black Jack, the Bull is down, I say again the lead ship has crashed in the LZ." After an elongated silence, to allow this news to sink in, the radio erupts with everybody trying to talk at the same time. "Everybody shut up," Black Jack screams. "I want priority on this radio 'freak." Blackjack is seething, you can feel it in every fiber of your body as his voice, his words measured and emphatic comes through loud and clear. "Bird Dog————, did they get shot down?" "I can't say for sure how they went in" Bird Dog responds; "I was overhead the Z when I saw them lose control and crash." Black Jack is now trying to raise Bull on the radio. "Bull, this is Black Jack, over." There's no response. Again, "Ghost Rider lead, Bull, this is Black Jack, over." Again, there is no response "I want everybody to stay off this freak unless I specifically ask for you" Black Jack says as if to emphasize the silence and his frustration. "Alpha one six, this is Black Jack," as Black Jack tries the formal military call sign procedure with Cracker Jack, our platoon leader, who was on the lead ship with Bull. Again there's no response.

I'm thinking about Jerry Hollandale, the crew chief on Bull's chopper. He's a real good guy. He knows his shit and can take care of himself. Many emotions run through my head, "poor Jerry," "what's he doing right now, IF, he's still alive, what kinda shit is he into?" My mind is numb, "Just another everyday combat assault" I think to myself. Yeah, right!

"Black Jack, this is Bird Dog." "Go ahead Bird Dog." Black Jack responds. "The LZ is still open, Black Jack." "Holy shit'" I think to myself "this thing could still be on." "Okay" Black Jack responds, "I'm going to make a pass over the Z and take a look" he says. Several minutes later, Black Jack says, "it appears the bird has rolled down in the LZ and kept the Z open. I can see some activity around the downed bird." Black Jack calls for "Big Bird" the call sign of our number two helicopter on the assault commanded by CW2 Sparrow. "Big Bird, the Z is still open. I need to get people on that Z, I need to know what's goin' on, I want you to continue with the assault." "Roger, Black Jack" Sparrow responds.

I watch as Big Bird breaks away from our oval formation heading for the LZ. As I strain to see over the pilot's glare shield, the mountains are an artists' palette of greens, from a shamrock green to varying shades of dark, almost black green. The sun and cumulous clouds creating shadow and overwhelming brilliance all at once makes the mountains shiver and come alive. The LZ is not a recognizable spot or point I can see from where I sit in the back of the helicopter. "Good luck Zimmerman," I say to myself, wishing good fortune to Big Birds' crew chief.

Big Bird disappears from view as I cue myself to pay close attention to the radio chatter. As Big Bird approaches the LZ he reports back on observed conditions to Black Jack. "Black Jack, this is Big Bird, we have triple canopy trees as previously reported that are making the approach marginal. We are inside and clear of the canopy now, and continuing the approach." "Roger, keep me advised," Black Jack says. Immediately Big Bird responds with, "We're taking heavy fire from the Z." Static and radio hiss.......a long pause, Big Bird unknowingly still has his microphone key held open... then, "Shit!" Over the radio you can hear the staccato fire of the M-60's and the dull mechanical crack of the grunt's M-16's. I've never heard the grunts shooting out of the chopper on an approach before.

A minute of silence as the assault continues. Then Black Jack, "we have communication from the Z." A slight pause as if to collect his thoughts, "Big Bird has been shot down, but the Z is still open. Who's number three?" Black Jack asks. He sounds like a man who has resigned himself to having a very shitty day. BJ immediately responds, "The Bridge is number three sir." "Okay Bridge, let's go," Black Jack says. As if we've been picking our asses all morning and oblivious to world events and current happenings, Black Jack continues "You've got triple canopy trees on the top of the approach and close margins down under the canopy with heavy ground fire...Over." "Roger that" BJ responds.

As we break off our holding pattern and head for the East ridge of the Valley, my mind is clumsy with all kinds of thoughts. Home is always first and foremost in my mind, then my R&R, the situation in the Z, how my fellow crew members on the ground are doing, can we help them and finally....as I fill with unselfish emotion... let's do this! I lean over to the grunt I had earlier talked to during the holding delay. He looks up at me, his eyes questioning what's going on. This has been no simple assault, and he knows it. It has been over forty-five minutes since the first ship has gone in. There is nothing "standard" or "business as usual" now. Throw the playbook out the window. "The LZ is hot," I say to him. Now I guess I'm talking his language, he nods his helmet at me in the affirmative and leans over to spread the word to the other grunts. The grunts as a group are unaffected visually by his pronouncement. However, they shift their gear and rucks just like they're getting ready to make a parachute drop. The same grim determination is set in all their faces. The grunt looks back to me, his eyes questioning. I flip my switch to "hot mike" so BJ, Beastie and Jesse, can all hear my comments to the grunt. "We have two Hueys shot down in the LZ." The grunt's eyes widen in surprise, but his face remains otherwise emotionless. I continue, "the last bird in was taking heavy fire on the approach. If you guys want to give us fire support on the way in, we'd be more than happy. And remember we have eighteen 'friendly' on the ground." The grunt gives me a thumbs up, and once again leans over to pass along the information. BJ jumps in "I really don't want them to fire until we are closer to the bottom of the Z." "Okay Boss" I respond. "And remind them about our main rotor, I don't want to accidentally get shot down" BJ adds. "Okay Boss" I say again as I pass the information on to the grunt. He gives me another thumbs up. We are nine totally united and goal oriented men on our bird. We all seem to be leaning together, into the trace of the plow, a grim determination to be successful in the outcome of our endeavor.

Chapter Thirty

BJ has the pedal to the metal as we head for the LZ. I still cannot see the LZ from my vantage point. An LZ is normally the pinnacle of a hill or mountain that is devoid of trees and obstacles, or a flat open area allowing for some form of stabilized approach. As we get closer to the mountain ridge, I can detect a spot on the mountain that BJ appears to be aiming for. There is a "hole" in the mountain vegetation that is only discernible because of a fog or mist that rises from the vegetation like a sleeping volcano.

As we approach the "sleeping volcano" it becomes evident that this is our LZ. In my entire time in country, I have never seen a more God forsaken landing zone that we collectively have been asked to fly into. As BJ "stands on the brakes," he smoothly brings the Huey to a hover over the canopy of jungle below us. "Everybody on hot mike?" I ask as BJ slips the helicopter towards the edge of the abyss in the mountain. Voices tight with emotion, all crew check in. BJ deftly slides the Huey into and around the first layer of triple canopy trees drawing a bead on the center of the hole in the jungle. "Jesse I want you to concentrate on keeping the main rotor clear," I say as I twist and turn to look out the right side or Jesse's side of the chopper. Jesse acknowledges with a terse "Roger." The two trees that are the nemesis to the initial approach, one on each side of the LZ, are enormous. Inside, and underneath the first layer of triple canopy trees, the trunks of the trees are over three feet in diameter and growing, and we're only on the inside of the top canopy! "Jesse I don't want any suppressive fire until we get closer to the bottom of the Z. Don't worry about incoming fire; just keep us clear of that damn tree!" I say again. "Okay Lot" Jesse responds.

The main rotor clearance is less than a foot varying on either side of the chopper. "Clear left," "Clear right," as Jesse and I talk in rapid fire speak, keeping the main rotor clear for BJ as we begin our descent into the top of the second layer of jungle canopy. I feel like I'm on the floor of the New York Stock Exchange negotiating with Jesse for every spare inch of rotor clearance on my side of the chopper. "Go left" Jesse says, as we drift closer to the tree on the right side. "You have twelve inches on the left Boss," as I respond to Jesse's correction. BJ slowly shifts the helicopter away from the tree on his right. As we continue the descent, "clear left and clear right" no longer will satisfy the defined margin of clearance needed to keep the pilots apprised of our rotor clearance. The communication becomes a rolling banter of "nine inches on the left," "fifteen inches on the right," as we continue to break it down even further, until our contractions sound like an auctioneer; "six left, twelve right, seven left, nine left, nine right."

Our hot mike picks up the slightest of noises, someone is breathing heavy, they catch themselves, quiet for a moment, and then heavy breathing again. BJ mutters unintelligible comments under his breath. Beastie offers an occasional word of encouragement to BJ, his hands and feet lightly riding the controls, just in case the worst should happen, and BJ cannot continue.

BJ drifts left, "STOP, Boss" I shout, forgetting our protocol of left or right. Thank God the Bridge knows my voice. We have almost whacked the tree on my side. My eyes have been constantly fixated on the end of the main rotor, and we have virtually no clearance. I can't understand why I'm not seeing wood shavings flying, but we couldn't have been any closer without disastrous consequences. "Nine inches on the right" Jesse says. Thank you Lord! BJ, without comment, corrects and we continue the descent.

We have been descending very slowly, clearing our main rotors for about thirty seconds. As the bottom layer of triple canopy opens up, the opening in the LZ is getting larger. The jungle surrounding the hole of the LZ is dark and foreboding. But the LZ is bathed in sunlight, much like the narrow focused beam of a flashlight. We now have at least three feet of rotor clearance on each side of our bird, and the LZ is getting ever larger.

I take time to look down into the LZ. Once again, I cannot believe my eyes. The "bottom" of the Z is choked with huge trees and limbs. Trees blasted into jagged splinters, sit at angles incongruous to the mountain and imagination. It looks as if a tornado had alighted on this one spot, and after exhausting its fury, vomited the spoils of its rage on the mountain. The only thing is, the spoils are tree trunks and limbs three or four feet and larger in diameter. A piled mass of matchsticks, pick-up sticks, tinker toys, Lincoln logs, and then throw in a few telephone poles for variety.

In all this conglomeration of destruction, lay our two Hueys. Bull's helicopter is lowest in the Z. It is at a precarious angle, almost upside down. The underbelly of the helicopter is exposed, its cargo hook peeking out of the "hell hole." Big Bird's helicopter sits upright just below the center of the LZ. The skids are bent and buckled, but otherwise intact.

With no rotor clearance adjustments necessary for BJ to continue his approach, I began to suppress into the darkness of the trees below the LZ. Occasional tracer fire streaks up at us with no apparent affect. I hear Jesse also open up with his "sixty" as our load of grunts join in, firing selectively at potential areas of danger. As I continue to shoot in long sixty round bursts, I continue to survey the fast approaching LZ. Now that our rotor clearance is not an issue, BJ has picked up his rate of descent to minimize our exposure to ground fire. Within seconds, the helicopter is parked over the gore of broken, twisted, shattered jungle, as BJ enters a stabilized hover. Due to the steep pitch of the mountain, we are at least twenty feet off the ground on my side of the ship as I half turn to the grunt who has been sitting next to me. I reach over to tap him on the shoulder, his cue that this ride is over. Before I can touch him, he disappears over the side of the helicopter. As I scan the cargo deck of our bird, we are completely empty, as if our load of grunts has never shared this space with us.

We are hovering on a mountain slope that has at least a thirty-degree pitch. I have just watched men, who I've spent the last hour with, jump into the most horrific shit hole imaginable. These men did this without the least hesitation. "Clear left," "clear right" Jesse says. "Let's get the hell outta here" BJ says.

As we begin our ascent away from the melee below, I quickly scan the area. I can now focus on some of the grunts, moving about the tangle of trees. They look like toy, miniature soldiers in comparison to the trees they are crawling over. As I look at Big Bird's helicopter, I see Jerry Hollandale crouched behind the aft end of the ship by the door gunner's position. We see each other at the same time. Hollandale gives me a sardonic half smile and waves, moving the stiff fingered palm of his hand facing me, side to side, and then finally, a thumbs up. The best sign of all, "thumbs up," everything's cool…I'm relieved to see he's still alive.

Taking a quick cursory scan of the LZ, I see a body on the north edge of the Z near the edge of the jungle. The black boots on the legs are twisted at angles not humanly possible. From the belt line up, the upper torso of the body is completely blood covered with no shirt covering the body. The shoulders and head are missing. My eyes are transfixed on the bloody carcass of human flesh. Staring at the torso for long seconds, I realize that I am looking at the body of one of our flight crew. The pants are Nomex flight pants that a grunt would not be wearing, and the boots are black leather, not jungle boots. Realizing that I am staring, I still have a job to do getting out of there. I begin to suppress the interior of the jungle, watching the tracers from my M-60 disappear into the darkness, as if being devoured by a black hole.

We repeat the routine of clearing our main rotor on the way back out of the Z. As we clear the jungle below into the welcome sunlight and spaciousness of the valley, everybody lets out a collective sigh of relief.

BJ is instantly talking with Black Jack as to the conditions on the approach, and what he observed in the Z. He ends his report with a recommendation that trees are blown prior to any more lifts into the LZ. I brief BJ on the body I've seen in the LZ. At first he is disbelieving, asking if I'm sure of what I saw. "They were Nomex flight pants with black leather boots, I'm positive," I say with sincerity in the best tone of voice I can muster. BJ says nothing further, as we fly in silence. If what I have seen is truly one of our crew members, then this will be the second KIA in our company since coming in country.

Chapter Thirty One

We're getting low on gas as BJ advises our battalion C&C that we are heading for the POL pad. As we depart toward the south end of the valley, we hear Black Jack order the number four bird, commanded by "Lizard" into the Z. I couldn't believe after BJ's report that the assault would continue.

I was relieved. We had made the assault, and come out unscathed! My joy was short lived as "Thor" our battalion commander began to query aircraft as to fuel status. Thor had arrived on site to provide command and control, since our company commander Bull had been shot down. Thor was looking for a volunteer to go into the LZ with a load of explosives, so the grunts could blow the trees down.

BJ responded, "Thor" this is the Bridge. ETA to POL is five minutes. We can pick up the explosives in fifteen mikes." BJ used the phonetic abbreviation for minutes, "mikes," to let Thor know, we could be back en route to the Z in less than a half hour.

"BJ, let somebody else go back into the Z" I said. "Let somebody else put their time in." I KNEW that...we....would.... not....make...it...back in and out of the Z a second time. It was just too hot. That was pushing our luck too far! "We're the best bird suited for this" BJ said. "We'll have the fuel, and we've been into the Z already," he said matter-of-factly. Beastie and Jesse said nothing. His logic made sense, and if I raised too much of a stink, it would be for nothing. BJ had his mind made up.

Shortly after arriving at the Ghost Riders, I had been told that the 158th Aviation Battalion was out to set a mark as the most decorated aviation unit to come out of Viet Nam. I've been in country seven months, I'm ready to go on R&R, and fuck their medals! In the back of my mind I'm thinking to myself, if BJ is doing this for a damn medal, I'm going to kick him hard in the ass after the crash.

While Jesse is "hot" fueling our bird at the POL pad, I make a quick survey of the ship. I am relieved to see we don't have so much as a dent on our bird.

It's a ten-minute flight to Berchtesgaden where a combat engineer outfit has a stockpile of C-4 and blasting caps waiting for us. As we land in the usual cloud of red dust on the mountain top firebase, the engineers on the helipad immediately begin throwing cases of C-4 and sandbags filled with sawdust and blasting caps onto the cargo deck of our ship. In less than a minute we are loaded with fifteen cases of C-4, "det" cord, and four sandbags of blasting caps. "Clear left" I say, as Jesse responds immediately with "clear right." In a cloud of dust and a hearty "Hi-O-Silver" we're off.

As we approach the LZ for the second time, BJ updates Jesse and me on the assault. Lizard, number four on the assault was shot down or had a blade strike on the approach inside the LZ. The number five Ghost Rider, "Preacher" with my buddy Ridge has made it in, and out of the LZ. At that point both Black Jack and Thor had agreed to shut down the operation until the trees could be blown in the LZ. I listen in utter disbelief. Three out of five birds are down. Twenty-five grunts and twelve crew are inside the Z.

I am not concerned for the immediate safety of the people in the LZ. They have between them collectively eight machine guns with tens of thousands of rounds of ammo. After seeing the Z for myself, I didn't believe the NVA could mount an attack of any proportion that would not result in their utter annihilation. The triple canopy would prevent the use of enemy mortars, and once the NVA were inside the Z, such as it was, any tactical movement or control would be impossible.

The approach to the Z is uneventful. As BJ once again begins the slip and side step around the first canopy of jungle, I take up my observation of the main rotor blade. One hundred feet down into the jungle we slowly descend on the approach toward the top of the second layer of jungle canopy.

BJ arrests the descent and stabilizes at a hover as I stick my head over the edge of the cargo deck and look down at the junkyard of Hueys below. Lizard's bird is pointed nose down the mountain resting up against Big Bird. I see tracer fire, red and green criss-crossing the LZ. "Alright, kick it out" BJ says. "Say again," I can't believe my ears. "Kick it out; this is as far as we go" he repeats. I eagerly spin around the seat post separating me from the cargo deck and the explosives. Jesse joins me as we indiscriminately throw the explosives and blasting caps out the door on either side of the ship.

Even before I can sit down, I announce "we're clear, clear left" as Jesse looking around over his shoulder at me, an ear to ear smile on his face and in his voice as he says "clear right."

Although we don't know it at the time, our day is over. The assault grinds to a halt as we wait for the big trees to come down. Two more hours of ass and trash and we're back to the Haunted House.

Chapter Thirty Two

As I head up to the company area, BJ corrals me and throws a heavy arm around my shoulder as he directs me to the headquarters hooch. As I look up at him, no words need to be expressed about how we are feeling. Through the grace of God and good team work, we are home. Nothing needs to be said, our mutual expressions of despair as we look at each other says it all.

In light of spotting the body in the LZ, I have to fill out an AAR, an After Action Report. I press the company clerk in the command tent for any news of the assault, but with a grim look on his face, he is tight lipped. As he moves around in the tent getting the carbon paper and AAR form, his body moves in a stiff jerky manner. He's wound as tight as a spring. I try to relax him, telling him all I had seen in the LZ, keeping it on the light side. I omit telling him about the crew member's body, but tell him how Hollandale had waved and smiled at me from the LZ. I finish my commentary with "he looks like he shit his pants and didn't want to tell anybody even though everyone can smell it." That gets me a weak smile and he seems to loosen up a bit.

After finishing the AAR, I am interviewed by our company

operations officer and some Major from battalion HQ. They review my written statement, confirming the position of downed helicopters and other seemingly inconsequential bull shit.

At chow that night the men in the company are subdued by the day's events. Twelve men are spending the night in the Z, one of ours, Cracker Jack, my platoon leader, is now confirmed dead. The conversation is subdued. The flight crews know we will do it all again tomorrow.

That evening as I lay in my cot, Everly, nickname "Pup" who is the crew chief for Lizard stops in to see me. "How the hell did you get out of the Z, Pup?" I ask shocked and confused to see him standing in front of my cot. "I wasn't flying today, I was on maintenance stand down." Maintenance stand down for flight crews occurred when chiefs or gunners flew more than 125 hours in a month or pilots flew more than 100 hours in a month. It was a two or three day mandatory rest period that was deservedly needed by anyone flying that much in less than a month's time. "Oh... Well who was chief on your bird today then?" "Miller asked to go today" Pup responds with a sad look on his face. "I should be with them now" he says almost to himself. I feel Pup's pain, I think the only reason we made it in and out was BJ's excellent flying skills and crew coordination. "What was it like?" Pup asks in a hushed voice. For the fiftieth time I recount the story of flying into the LZ. Depending on whom I feel should know, and how they will be affected, or can appreciate it, I relay more, or less, on the details of the assault. I know Pup is feeling really bad. I feel he should be told everything from the delay getting the ARA or aerial rocket artillery in 'till we had dumped the C-4 into the LZ. I tell it all.

As I finish the story, Pup looks at me. "You know why I'm here don't you?" Frankly, I was clueless, as I shook my head in the negative. Pup says softly in a very subdued voice, "Can I crew 644 for you tomorrow?" I was surprised, even amazed, that he wants to crew my bird!! Leave my crew with a strange chief? My mind raced, I was leaving on my R&R in three days, it was going to be another nasty day tomorrow, his crew was in the Z, but my crew needs me. “Sorry Pup, I can’t, I just can’t.” I wanted to help, but not at the expense of my crew. “Okay” Pup says softly, “Okay, I just thought, maybe…ya know” he doesn’t finish his sentence. “Luck” he says, as he barely lifts his hand hanging at his side, his head hung low, shoulders drooping, he turns and slowly walks out of the hooch.

Five a.m. comes quickly, I have slept like the dead. The mental exhaustion of the previous day, and the coming attractions of today, leaves little doubt in anyone’s mind that the shit has hit the fan, just knowing there’s a fifty-fifty chance we can be dead by tonight… I feel a very strange sense of excitement knowing that we will definitely be in action today. But this excitement also carries an inexplicable foreboding of danger, that is intrinsically entwined with all that will happen in the coming day. In this troubling time I have renewed my faith and made my peace with God. I make no promises, nor do I ask for any. I simply ask for His guidance to do the right thing and be strong, whatever the outcome.

The familiar sounds of the mess hall, the scraping utensils on the aluminum mess hall trays, the smell of coffee, bacon, eggs, the low buzz and chatter of the flight crews and mechanics, all seems like I’m really only hearing it for the very first time. I mean really hearing it. My senses feel totally alive and aware. Most everyone has a mask of concern on their faces. No laughing or joking today. The news this morning is that Mr. Cauldrea, co-pilot for Big Bird was killed overnight in the LZ. No details other than he was KIA during the night. The news hits home like a punch to the stomach. I hadn’t known Mr. Cauldrea well, but the loss of another crew member brings home the reality of risk we take on so casually everyday.

My preflight of the ship complete, Jesse and I await BJ and our peter pilot. The sun glows under the horizon to the east of us out in the South China Sea. The air is cool and fresh, the sky clear and it promises to be another beautiful late spring day. It is still dark on the flight line as figures of flight crew and mechanics are just discernible grayish shapes, as they move about getting ready for the days launch. An occasional beam of a flashlight pokes out of the dark, dancing with the rhythm of a crewmen walking around his bird on a preflight, or disappearing for a moment and then magically reappearing as the light beam is shoved into an inspection hole in the engine cowling. I lay on the deck of the helicopter as I light up a cigarette, my legs and feet half hanging in and out of the ship. The strain from the position I lay in feels good on my back, which is tight with tension. "Here they come" Jesse says. "Can you see who our peter pilot is today Jess?" I continue lying on the deck, neither bothering to move or get up, blowing the smoke from my cigarette straight up in the still morning air. "It looks like Beastie again." That's good I think to myself. Beastie is going to make a good AC or aircraft commander some day. I had appreciated his poise and skills yesterday under fire, and knew he would be an asset today also. "Good, I like him" I say to Jessie as an afterthought. "Yeah, me too" Jessie responds. "Hey Mr. Baylor, Beastie" Jessie says to the pilots as they approach 644. "Guys" BJ says in way of a hello, an insincere half smile on his face. He is obviously uptight also as he goes through a quick preflight walk around the Huey. "You guys have heard about Mr. Cauldrea?" BJ queries. Jessie and I both silently shake our heads in the affirmative. "Have you heard anything else?" I ask him. "He got hit during the night by an RPG, that's all I know" BJ says after a pause. "Well it's more of the same today." As if anxious to get on with the day, BJ and Beastie open the aircraft doors and jump into the pilots' seats strapping in as Jessie and I slide the protective bullet shields on the sides of the pilots' seat forward.

We reposition all of the company aircraft to firebase Bastogne. Shutting the engines down, we sit and wait for the cogs and gears of the military machine to begin grinding into motion for the assault. The grunts begin to appear in little groups along the sides of the logistical pad. Quickly the number gathering explodes to several hundred, with more coming down the hillside. This is going to be one hell of an assault, I think to myself.

The grunts look capable and seasoned, as I look once

again to their LBE and packs. The jungle fatigues are stained with the red dirt and dust of uniforms that are seldom changed. There are no cherry boys I can detect in this bunch. Short timer calendars on helmets, towels wrapped around necks, bulging cargo pants pockets, M-16's with beat up stocks, well oiled and ready for action, their eyes stare at us with hard, unabashed certainty. Certain that they are going in harms way, but very certain that they will be the ones doing the ass kicking today. I felt good about these guys.

We are not going to be assaulting the same LZ we had assaulted the previous day. I am overjoyed to hear the news. Our entire battalion of sixty "slick" helicopters together with sixty plus helicopters from my old battalion, the 101st Assault Helicopter Battalion would join in the attack today. Infantry battalions would be combat assaulting throughout the entire northern portion of the A Shau, from the "Warehouse area" in the northeast Valley, to fire base Airborne, A Luoi, and the area around Dong Ap Bia to the west. The offensive is aimed at making contact with the NVA while searching for their caches of equipment and supplies. We would be supported by units of the 4th Battalion 77th Airborne Artillery (ARA), and ten Huey Cobras from our own Delta Company Redskins. The ensuing days were to become the beginning of an operation of some epic proportion that stirred the hornets nest in what would come to be known as Hamburger Hill. The battle for Dong Ap Bia.

Chapter Thirty Three

The sky is filled with big, white, puffy fair weather cumulus clouds, and helicopters. Hueys hanging in the air are strung out in long lines, wedges like flocks of geese, and the odd lone straggler off in the distance. Some are coming and others are going; Cobras in ones and twos, Chinooks with sling loads of 105 millimeter Howitzers and boxed crates of ammunition hanging in cargo nets even further below the big gun. Once in a while I catch a glimpse of an Air Force forward air controller "FAC," in the distance. The white and gray painted aircraft has an unusual design with a propeller on the nose and tail, a "push/pull." Down low, the FAC glides over the top of the jungle canopy like a hawk riding the unseen currents of warm air rising up the mountain slopes; they look for NVA and provide target information for the "fast movers," our fighter bombers.

We have five grunts on board. It is a fifteen minute flight from Bastogne to the new LZ we will be assaulting today. There is a lot of chatter on the radios, coordination of operations stuff, and nothing too exciting to write home about. As we lift off Bastogne and follow the river northwest toward the A Shau, the helicopter picks up speed. The cool fresh air buffeting my body feels good after the long, warm morning sitting on the log pad waiting to go. It had started out to be one of those "hurry up and wait" kind of days. It was good to be on the move again. I have the pistol grips of my machine gun wedged between my knees as I sit back and enjoy the soothing view of the dark lush green of the mountains letting my mind wander to other faraway places.

As we leave the mountains behind us, the vast A Shau Valley opens before us. The lead helicopter lazily makes its way out to the middle of the valley, our gaggle of helicopters dutifully strung out following behind. There has been a lot of intermittent ground fire on the east ridge of the Valley, so as a precautionary move we stay a thousand feet above the ridge and well out in the valley.

Paralleling the East side of the valley, I strain over the back of my seat trying to spot the smoking volcano of yesterdays LZ. Just as we start making a slow easterly turn for the new LZ, I spot the hole in the jungle canopy. I think of our crews sitting it out down there, even now as we make an attempt at coming to their rescue.

As we reach the north end of the valley, abeam Salt and Pepper, the lead bird is flown by the "Magician" now more informally known as "Magnet Ass." The Magician has picked up the Magnet Ass moniker more because of his ability to attract like a magnet enemy ground fire resulting in the battle damage of several of our flight platoon aircraft.

The Magician is the new platoon leader for our first platoon. As he makes a sixty-degree turn to the right, setting us up for a long high final approach, I drop the clear visor on my helmet and stick my head out into the slipstream looking forward. We are the number three bird in on the lift. I look forward trying to judge the interval or separation between our bird and the one in front of us.

There is a small, higher ridge of mountain running northeast on the north end of the A Shau Valley that cuts across the grain of the mountains that generally run north and south in the area. At the end of this ridge, there is a precipitous drop into another valley followed by the north-south chain of mountains once again. The ridge appears to be about a quarter of a mile in length. They obviously have had a heavy artillery prep on the Z. The pinnacle is devoid of vegetation. Blasted apart by artillery, rockets and bombs, some shattered tree stumps are all that is left standing in the smoking red earth. This will be our new landing zone for the assault. As LZ's go, it appears to be at least as good, if not better, than most.

As I pull the pistol grips of my M-60 to me, an F-4 Phantom slides by level with the helicopter, slightly nose low. The jet fighter has its landing gear extended, flaps down, speed brakes and spoilers extended. The pilot is doing everything in his power to not go rocketing by us. I wasn't aware of the close air support we would be receiving on this assault. We had never had this type of support before, and this huge machine mesmerized me, as it passed within fifty yards of me. I look at the pilot sitting in the cockpit, hoping to get his attention and maybe wave to him. But he is completely absorbed in the task at hand. Remembering our previous encounter with an F-4 up on the DMZ, I called out to BJ the approach of the fighter. "We have an F-4 going by us on the left side Boss." As BJ looks back over his left shoulder, Jesse calls out an F-4 approaching on his side of the bird also. BJ moves his head to the right nodding acknowledgement that he also can see the Phantom on the right. Damn, this is going to be hot, I think to myself.

Just as the Phantom is abeam my position, the twenty-millimeter Vulcan cannon in its nose roars into action. Shell casings from the Gatling gun spew from the chute below the F-4 in a torrent. I look forward of our bird to see the effect this awesome display of firepower is having on the jungle. The rounds are impacting just to the side of the LZ. The impact of each round is like the explosion of a firecracker exploding in a line that snakes through the jungle mountain. Magnet Ass is just in his landing flare in the LZ as the Phantom continues to lay down a withering, unrelenting fire around the side of the LZ and jungle surrounding it. The F-4 driver "walks his rudders" as the twenty-millimeter rounds twinkle their mini explosions left to right through the jungle foliage. Magnet Ass' Huey disappears in a cloud of red dust from the rotor wash, as the rising dirt and dust envelops the LZ. God how I wish my eyes could be gun cameras at this very moment!

As the Magician lifts off the Z, two more F-4's pass us, their Gatling gun cannons spewing long sheets of flame as they cover not only the departure of Magnet Ass but also the arrival of the second bird in the LZ. "This is Magnet Ass, we were taking small arms fire on the Z," as I see his helicopter jinking over the mountain ridge. To keep Charlie's head down, I am suppressing the jungle with my machine gun in sweeping arcs, slowly elevating and depressing the pistol grips to cover as much ground as seven hundred rounds per minute will allow. My machine gun feels and sounds like a pea shooter in comparison to the six thousand rounds a minute coming from the twenty-millimeter cannon on the F-4's.

As the number two bird lifts off, BJ is entering the flare to land on the LZ. We are in our most vulnerable position, committed to land. Again, the F-4's go gliding by us, as if in slow motion. They fly as slow as possible without stalling, in slow flight, they are traveling at one hundred sixty knots. I have been shooting non-stop. I shift my fire to the jungles' edge, searching for signs of incoming fire, muzzle flashes, tracers, or puffs of dust. As we touch down I turn to the grunt that has been sitting on the floor next to me. As usual, they have jumped even as we touch down. Hunched over, making a low profile target, their big rucksacks hanging on their backs, the troops fan out forward and away from our bird. "Clear left, clear right" come the automatic response from Jesse and me. As the Huey has just started rocking forward on its skids, BJ pulls pitch and we leap off the ground, as if rebounding from a trampoline. Again we have the support of the Phantoms as we pull out of the LZ. As the helicopter accelerates through translational lift, the F-4 giving us support on the way out sucks up the landing gear, brings the boards in, goes into afterburner, long sheets of flame extending from the twin tail pipes as it disappears in a near vertical arcing climb to his left.

I am shooting straight down into the jungle. The twenty-millimeter shells from the F-4 covering our departure impacts the trees to our side and I can see the devastation close at hand. Small trees, three feet in diameter, are blown into splintered stumps by the impacting shells. The splinters from the trees create their own deadly shrapnel. The jungle is sparkling with the twenty-millimeter hits.

Looking back at the LZ, the number four bird has just landed. As we accelerate, BJ is climbing for altitude as rapidly as possible. I place the pistol grips of my gun between my legs to light up a cigarette. I take a deep drag on the cigarette feeling the smoke biting into my lungs. As I take one last look back to the LZ, the number four bird is burning, completely engulfed in flames. The main rotor is still turning, but canted forward at an odd angle. I see three burning bodies, two on the left side of the chopper, and one on the right, the familiar hump of the rucksacks still strapped to the bodies.

A Huey can burn "to the ground," to gray ashes, in less than fifteen minutes. Nothing will remain of the hulk except small pieces of the engine core, and pieces of the main and tail rotor. As I report the burning Huey to BJ, the radio comes alive. I try to look back, but the tail of our Huey blocks my view as BJ begins a right turn away from the LZ.

As we turn to parallel the LZ, I swing around from my seat into the cargo deck area to get a better view of the LZ as we climb away. Even now after only a few minutes, there is very little left of the Huey. Staring at the flames, I look to see if I can see the pilots or gunner. But nothing is left that is recognizable as human in shape or form. I turn away, but I am drawn back to stare again. The men who had been lying outside of the burning wreck have been pulled away from the flames and are being ministered to by the medic on the ground.

"Who was it BJ?" I ask. "Dude and Barfy" BJ responds, his throat tight with emotion. They were the pilots from second flight platoon, which meant PJ Navetta the crew chief, and his gunner Ray, from Alabama, were the other crew members. I didn't know either PJ or Ray well, but they had seemed like okay guys. "Better them than me" I thought to myself. "It don't mean nuthin'. It... don't... mean... nuthin." It was the only way I could deal with the death of people in an immediate way, and still keep functioning. The dead were the "lucky" ones. Their hell on earth was over, they were going home early.

During our assault from start to finish, I have not seen one hostile act. We may have been taking ground fire, but I didn't hear or see a thing. You could be here one minute, and the next minute, simply cease to exist, like you were never born.

The assault continues as we continue to put more infantry onto the mountaintop LZ. There is nothing left in the burned hulk of the helicopter. It provides no obstacle to our approach into the LZ as the business of war goes on as usual. We've lost four helicopters in two days, six crew members killed, and two wounded. It is our first real taste of war. It is a dark place. Yet through it all, looking down the flight line Sergeant Kaiser struts around pissing people off and still continuing to rain on Greg Distoné's parade. I watch as he gets in Greg's face, although I cannot hear what is being said, the hand movements and "jaw jacking" tells it all. This has gotta end too...

The fifth day of "Hamburger Hill" and we are re-supplying the "Hill" all day long. New replacements are coming in to fill the ranks as the hill exacts its toll on the battalion. We fly CBS and NBC news crews in during the afternoon. They ask all kinds of questions of us, what's it like out there, have we been shot at, shot down, wounded, where are we from, everything and anything. Sometimes it's hard to give them answers. Every back haul off the hill we carry body bags and wounded. Killing and death is a very personal and emotional thing that is best left in the hooch before we fly. It's just a job. As we drop the news crews at the bottom of the hill, a camera man spins around to film us leaving the Z. I raise the dark visor on my helmet and wave like hell hoping I'll make the six o'clock evening news. But in reality my spontaneity probably sent me quickly to the "the cutting room floor" as my actions weren't very "heat of battle" or "war" like!

Back on the flight line, our birds come straggling in, flights of one or two depending on how we were dispersed or assigned other missions, after the assault. We compare notes, check for any damage, pull inspections, and fill out the log books. But Ridge and I are preparing for a quick get away for R&R. In less than a week we're outta here.

Chapter Thirty Four

One week of travel, and a week in Hong Kong on R & R has done wonders for my spirits. There indeed is still a "world" out there. Upon arrival in Hong Kong, I talked with my girlfriend in Milwaukee for over an hour. The telephone reception was so good; she could have been, and I wished she was, right next door.

While waiting to go on R& R, I bumped into an avionics specialist, a specialist five or "spec" five from my company. I had never met him before, or even seen him in the chow hall. Making idle conversation, I discovered that he was on his way to Sydney Australia for his R& R. Surprised that he had received a much sought after slot for Australia, I stated my astonishment at his good fortune. "How long have you been in country?" I asked. "Three months" he replied. Not having an opportunity to go to Hawaii to see my girl, I had held out for a long eight months at a chance to go to Australia myself. Seniority supposedly prevailed, and the longer you stayed in country prior to R & R, the more likely you could have first pick on the many places we could go. "Three months" I said, "You mean to tell me that you've been in A Company three months and they let you go to Australia?" "Yeah." He chuckled as if he was privy to some inside joke as he

continued "They want to retain me in the company. My skills are needed everywhere in country and I told them I wanted a transfer if they didn't give me a couple of R& R's and a promotion." This guy had no idea how close I was to trampling his pompous ass into the ground at that very moment! Watching him stand there smiling and oblivious to what was dribbling out of his mouth, I said, "You know what, you smug piece of shit; I've been in this shit hole over eight months waiting to go to Australia. And gee, guess what I'm told, no slots available for Australia. Now how do you suppose that is?" I asked him. Surprised at my sudden outburst, and my transformation from friend to foe; the Spec. 5 immediately started to babble and back up as I got in his face with a snarl, fists clenched, ready to back up my words with action. "If you don't wipe that fucked up grin off your face, you aren't going to be able to slip a beer bottle into that hole you call a mouth when I'm finished with you!" "Hey man, I'm sorry, I'm sorry" he said quickly. His hands up in surrender, his head snapped left and right, his eyes bulging out of his head as he looked for some way to extricate himself from my presence. "You know what asshole, a lot of men better than you and I deserve that slot. So next time you think your so damn invaluable, take a look around at the guys getting there ass shot at, while you sit in some air-conditioned hut somewhere dreaming of what a legend you are in your own mind!" Glaring at him waiting for some form of response, or just a simple reason to knock his perfect teeth down his throat, I snorted with disgust. Shaking my head, I turned and walked away, feeling a little better, but still really pissed a guy like that could manipulate the system. I definitely was going to have a talk with Top when I got back.

Ridge had come with me on R & R. Ridge's Huey had been the only other bird to make it in and out of the smoking volcano that first day. It was nice to have a friend along. I slept late; saw the sights and night clubbed the week away. Time went by fast. But a carefree week couldn't have come at a more opportune time. We both needed some down time after the previous two weeks on Hill 987 assaults, and Hamburger Hill.

We had left for R & R prior to the extraction of our three

crews shot down on May 10 at the smoking volcano. I was anxious to hear how Jerry Hollandale and the rest had fared during and after the action.

Feeling rested and my batteries recharged, I was ready to come back to Viet Nam, or so I thought. As I deplaned once again at Tan Son Nhut airbase, it felt as if suddenly a chicken plate, my chest armor, had been laid over my shoulders. It was such an oppressive, heavy feeling; I was surprised at myself that I would react mentally in that manner. The weighted feeling stayed with me, however, and after awhile I chose to ignore it and get on with getting back "home" to the Ghost Riders and my friends.

We were fortunate to catch a C-130 North to Phu Bai. From there Ridge and I hitch hiked to Camp Eagle for the night. Back in Commanchero country, A Company 101st Assault, my old company; we sacked out with my friends that were still left and caught up on what was going on.

Albert was on the short hairs of DEROS, a ten digit midget, going back home to Ontario, California. It was great seeing him again. When I stepped into the C section tent, followed closely by Ridge, Albert was sitting in his web lawn chair in the same spot I had left him three months earlier. He looked a little shocked and skeptical seeing me standing there. "I heard you got zapped back a month ago." Albert said. "Who said that?" I responded, a chuckle in my voice. "Aw ya know, just rumor. Somebody hears sumthin' and that's how it goes." Laughing, I look at Ridge who shrugs his shoulders and says "Well, we came close a couple weeks ago." Waving my hand at Ridge like he's blowing smoke and still chuckling over my supposed demise I introduce Ridge to Albert.

"So how's it going?" "Aw ya know, the same. Wolfe's gone, so is Davis." "Yeah, I figured. Poor Davis." I said. Albert shook his head in the affirmative, a scowl on his face, knowing what a raw deal Davis had gotten from his wife. "How's Critter?" "He's good, still the same ol' Critter. Oh yeah, Layman was killed last week down in Chu Lai around a place called Tam Ky" Albert

said. "What? How the hell did that happen?" I said suddenly feeling the need to sit down. Al continued "The whole crew got it." "No shit." I said again in astonishment. Ridge leaned up against the tent pole as he first looked from Albert back to me and then back to Albert, as we continued our conversation about my friend Bob Layman. "Well what we heard was, did ya know his gunner Smithe? Oh you wouldn't know him." Albert wanting to get the story out, started speaking in broken sentences, even answering his own questions. "He came in after you left. Anyway, I guess Smithe carried a frag grenade in the front pocket on his chicken plate." I immediately sensed where Albert was going with the story and all I could do was shake my head slowly in disbelief, knowing what was coming, as he continued. "A whole bunch of our birds were shuttling ass and trash back and forth in the mountains. As the story goes, they would reach a mid-point and say 'hey' back and forth like you guys do out there. Ya know what I mean, right?" Albert looked to me and Ridge for confirmation of his statement. Ridge and I absorbed in the telling of the story just stare back at Albert. Without waiting for affirmation he continued, "Well anyway, one of the other Commanchero flights, I don't know who, reaches the mid-way point and no Layman. So as they fly along to the fire base, there's no sign of Layman or the bird ya know? Well when they get to the firebase and find out they had dropped their load and left on schedule, our guys got worried and put out the call for help."

Albert takes a deep breath and continues. "As the story goes, the C.O. got ten of our birds and they all flew on line in formation from the log pad back to the firebase. They missed Layman's bird on the first pass, but found the wreckage heading back to Tam Ky. After securing the area, the Huey had burned bad, and they found the pilots and Smithe still strapped in. Well, what was left of them anyway. The helicopter had burned in place, no evidence of crashing, so they musta' went in under control. Crazy huh?" All I could do was shake my head, still numb, thinking about Layman. Albert continued, "Well Layman wasn't near the crash site." "He jumped," I mumbled. I remembered our game of "what if" so many months earlier. "Exactly!" Albert said, surprised by my comment. Albert looked at me sideways, like I had already heard the story, or I was psychic. "The C.O. was the one who found him... He was lying in the grass about seventy-five yards from the chopper. He was lying on his side with one arm up over his head, like this." With that Albert stopped talking and draped his arm over the side of his head showing us the position of Layman's arm holding his head. Ridge and I both nodded our head, understanding and acknowledging Al's morbid demonstration. "They say when the C.O. rolled him over, he had been decapitated." I just shook my head. Layman had been the nicest of guys; I couldn't believe he was dead. I also couldn't believe that months earlier we had virtually talked of his precise manner of demise. "Do you remember Al, when we played 'what if' with the Playboy Bunnies, and helicopters catching on fire?" Al shook his head, nodding. "I couldn't remember if he had been in that conversation with us though,' Al said, shaking his head, realizing now why I was so affected by the manner of his death. "That's how you knew he jumped." Al said. Bob had been the only one who had been completely convinced that jumping was the only way to possibly survive an in-flight fire. It appeared that the helicopter had fallen faster than Bob, and the rotor blade had got him. He was dead before he ever hit the ground. The arm over his head was probably an instinctive self defense move.

Later I would hear that the accident investigation confirmed that the fragmentation grenade had exploded on Smithe's chicken plate. The explosion had killed Smithe outright and penetrated the fuel cell under his seat. The pilots had indeed landed the helicopter under control, but were unable to get out of the burning ship in time.

Returning to Camp Evans the next day was like getting home after a long vacation. It felt good to lie in my own cot and catch up with the events we had missed while away. Likewise, the guys wanted to hear our "pussy" stories in every minute detail, over and over again. I could now appreciate how in my early days with the Commancheros I had felt like an interloper in the clique-like atmosphere of the flight platoons. Here in my own flight platoon, we were in our inner sanctum. Unless you were a flight crew member, your presence was not welcome; you couldn't understand the closeness we felt toward each other. We were a team.

In my absence, Greg Distoné had a major blow out with Sergeant Kaiser and had been threatened with an Article 15 for once again ignoring Kaisers' bullshit orders. Greg was becoming increasingly more disturbed and despondent about the unfair harassment from Kaiser. Short of killing Kaiser, there wasn't much we could do. But it was fast becoming an option.

Chapter Thirty Five

Getting ready the following morning, I see Jerry Hollandale crossing the rice paddies heading for his bird. As he gets closer, shielding my eyes from the bright early morning sun, I smile and give him a wave. I haven't seen Jerry since he was crouched beside the helicopter in the smoking volcano.

Shifting direction towards the revetment where my helicopter is parked he smiles back. My hands on my hips awaiting his approach, Jerry walks up opening his arms his smile growing bigger, we give each other a bear hug slapping each other on the back. "Damn it's good to see you Lot." "Likewise, Jer." I have a bad habit of contracting people's names. As I continued, "You've been on my mind since... ya know" nodding my head towards the mountains to the West making inference to the shoot down. "Ya I know" as Jerry's smile fades and takes on a more serious look.

Without asking, Jerry begins telling me about the days spent in the smoking volcano LZ. "The Bull was flying. Boy, did that LZ suck or what? Somebody really missed the 'intel' and reconnaissance on that one." As Jerry looks again into my eyes, knowing I had seen everything with my own eyes also. It was a rhetorical question, as he continued, “We were almost at the bottom, ya know where that big mother of a tree branched out and had that screwy looking corkscrew limb?” I knew immediately what and where he was talking about, as I had marveled myself at the sight of the strange looking limb. I nodded my head, waiting for the story to unfold.

“We started taking fire from all over the place. Christ, that was the first time I ever saw them shoot an RPG at a helicopter, I couldn’t believe it! Thank God it missed. I mean I actually saw this gook standing on the edge of the LZ, Lot, aiming that bitch at us. God knows they had enough time waiting for us to get down into that hole they called an LZ. I smoked his ass just after he fired it at us; I never killed anyone before ya know?” Jerry was running his thoughts together, but I was keeping up with him in the telling of his story. “I don’t know what happened after that to cause us to lose control and crash. I still don’t know if it was a blade strike or enemy fire. Bull said he didn’t or couldn’t remember either.” “What happened to Cracker Jack?” I asked Jerry. “Well after we hit the mountain, we rolled and bounced and then slid down to the edge of the LZ.” I remember the picture in my mind of Jerry’s helicopter, almost rolled over on the crew chief’s side, the left side. “There again, I almost got speared twice by tree branches as we slid. I still can’t believe that. But everyone, even the grunts were okay. That was amazing! One guy had a broken arm and leg. Another had a compound fracture of his right leg. That really looked like shit; I almost lost my breakfast seeing that. I think two of the grunts actually jumped as we went down.” Looking at Jerry as he relived the crash, I asked again, “Well what happened to Cracker Jack?” “After we got Bull and Cracker Jack out, Cracker Jack grabs Gary (Jerry’s door gunner) and says follow me, I want to see where the fire is coming from on the LZ.” Jerry makes a small chuckle as he continues, “Gary says, ‘Sir, my job is to stay with this bird, I ain’t no infantry.’ Well Cracker Jack got half pissed and saw the infantry RTO the radio telephone operator crouched next to Gary. So he points his finger at the RTO and says ‘Troop, your with me, let’s go!’ We kinda lost track of them in the confusion after that. But shortly after that an RPG exploded over by where we found his body. I heard you think you saw the body too." I nodded my head again, remembering the nomex pants and bloody torso. Jerry continued "Well the RTO was right behind Cracker Jack. It looks like Cracker Jack was hit in the head or shoulders by the RPG and the remaining blast took out the RTO too." I shook my head, remembering my own visions of the LZ.

Jerry paused, allowing the story to sink in, collecting his thoughts he continued. "Man we had RPG's banging all over in the Z, in the trees, and the tracer fire made it look like the Fourth of July." Listening closely to Jerry's words, I can imagine the conflagration of noise; the din of battle, explosions, gunfire, the human and even the inhuman noise of hell.

"And then, I can't believe it, here comes Big Bird. Well when Big Bird came in the grunts were firing em' up." Jerry uses our slang term "firing em' up" meaning bringing maximum rates of fire on the bad guys. I watched Zimmerman hosing the Z. That was pretty cool! I just tucked my head behind this big ass tree not knowing where the rounds were goin'. It was crazy! Big Bird musta' compressor stalled, cuz all I heard was somethin' like a big long fart and then he was crashing almost on top of us. That scared the shit outta me too! To be honest Lot, I was scared the whole time I was in there. I mean I could tell Big Bird was taking a lot of fire, but we were like helpless to do anything about it. Those blown trees in the Z were major obstacles for everyone." Jerry sounded almost like it was his fault Big Bird was shot down.

"What the hell were they thinking up there Lot?" "I know" I said, a look of disgust pasted on my face. "I couldn't believe they just threw us into the mouth of the lion like that. Then after we got in and out and BJ gave them a situation report, they still let Lizard go in and get shot down." We both shook our heads in utter amazement that we had even been a part of that whole operation.

"Man when you came in and the guns were all blazing between you and the grunts, what a sight." As Jerry continued with a quick series of one line sentences like a machine gun, "I thought for sure you guys were going to buy the farm too! I just imagined having an AK-47 aimed at you. God, I could have hosed you guys real good. I'm surprised the dinks didn't get you too." "Thanks a lot friend" I said half smiling, as I made a fist and feigned a punch at his jaw. "We didn't have so much as a dent on our bird, thanks to the excellent skill of its crew!" "Well ya know they fired at least one RPG at you too, I mean you guys had it all hanging out." As I responded "Well I thought it seemed pretty quiet myself. I mean, I didn't see any tracer fire or that RPG. Hell, I really wasn't much concerned about taking fire. I had those big ass trees on my mind, and getting the grunts out!" "It sure was a few days of nightmares" Jerry said nodding his head.

"The whole deal was bogus man. Those grunts are crazy mother fuckers too." "Why, what happened?" I asked. "Not so much what happened, it was just the way they were. Well ya know through the next couple of days we could hear non-stop explosions, bombs I guess, maybe artillery, sometimes real, real close. But those guys just ate their C rations and played cards like they were on vacation. We had a mad minute a couple times during the night; they would just shoot, hoot and holler. The dinks returned the favor. Like about every twenty minutes we'd have an RPG smack into the Z like clockwork. That's how Mr. Cauldrea got it during the first night. Wrong place at the wrong time." "Really" I said, as I continued "Yuh know his wife just had a kid too." "That whole thing was a real bummer man."

"I gotta get going Lot." "Well thanks for catching up with me Jer." "Hey how was R&R?" I made a face and hand gesture that lacked nothing in interpretation as Jerry laughed while walking away.

Chapter Thirty Six

At night there is a curfew for sampans and watercraft on the rivers. This is to stop the movement of supplies by the bad guys. So for fun, entertainment, and a little work, we are tasked with flying the rivers to ensure the curfew is kept. BJ likes to go out early while the Mama sans are bathing in the river. The sight of some real tits and ass jiggling in the water is a welcome sight for sore eyes, even though the smiling and bashful women are Vietnamese, it's still tits and ass.

One night as we do our low level search on the Perfume River, enjoying the view, we come across four sampans that are not obviously abiding by the curfew. BJ does a quick low warning pass over the boats. As Jesse and I aim our machine guns at the men on the boats, they just wave and smile. "What the hell" Jesse says. BJ stands the Huey on its tail; pedal turns, and comes to a low hover abeam the boats. "Check it out Lot" BJ says in an authoritative voice. As he continues to hover over the boats, I do my best to scan the boats for any sign of contraband or weapons. The boats definitely have cargo covered with canvas tarps. They look like fishermen to me, but I guess that's what they are supposed to look like. "I can't see anything Boss." As BJ hovers lower and closer to the boats, I continue to watch them carefully. "Shit" BJ says. We are in a stand off with the sampans as I ask Jesse to come over with his M-16 on my side. BJ says "motion to them to get off the river." As I start making motions with my hands to get the dinks to move, Jesse comes around with his M-16. "How 'bout I put a burst across the bow so to speak BJ? See if that'll motivate them to move." "Yeah, go ahead." BJ responds.

The dinks are all dressed in either black pajama bottoms or white cotton-like shorts and black silk tops. They all have the typical conical straw hats on. We are not thirty feet away from the boatmen as I move the barrel of my machine gun slightly to the left. The dink in the second boat looks into my eyes with a mixture of hatred and disdain. Immediately I know this is going to go bad in a hurry. "Check out the guy in the second boat BJ" I say as quickly as I think it. But the look on his face is masked again, but I know...

As I squeeze the trigger on my gun, the bullets smack the water between the two sam pans and alongside the second boat. The shooting startles the gooks as I see them flinch perceptibly and duck. I motion for them to move again. Now they seem to have got the message and begin to pole and scull for the side of the river.

Jesse inches closer to the door, bringing his weapon up to cover the dinks. One of the boatmen pulls the tarp back and reaches for some unseen object underneath. As I swing my gun to cover the dink, the boatman in the second boat begins scrambling under the tarps. "Watch it Jesse" I bark an alert not knowing what the hell is going to happen. Both dinks now holding fish in their hands throw the tarps further back to expose baskets full of fish. The other two boats follow suit, and along with some bleached fire wood from the river, the boats appear to be okay.

"Shit" is all I can say. Realizing my muscles are all tense, I relax my grip on my gun and just stare at the boatman. I was ready to waste the little people over some damn fish. At this point I didn't care if they had anything else to hide, I just wanted outta' there. BJ musta been reading my mind because he said, "Let's make sure they get off the river, its beer thirty, and we're burnin' daylight." BJ has coined the phrase taken from our old Marine lieutenant friend and made it his own. As BJ is saying this, we hover over to the opposite river bank offering the dinks the opportunity to beach the sam pans, and end the stand-off. As they pull up to the waters edge, BJ dumps the nose over on our Huey and leaves the little people in a veil of mist and spray from the rotor wash as we pick up speed exiting the river heading back to Camp Evans.

Pulling a fifty hour inspection after chow that night entails, among other things, pulling fuel filters and replacing the filter elements. One of the filters quite literally takes a contortionist or someone with a lot more patience than me to change. Lying on the open engine deck, I pull the filters replacing the elements, new "O" rings and safety wiring back in place. I've done this dozens of times now, and it has become fairly routine. Taking an hour longer than it should have taken me, I finally get a Warrant Officer to come up to my revetment to do an engine run-up and leak check the filters.

With the engine barely at operational speed, I bring my hand in a slicing motion across my neck, the signal to kill the engine. The filter I dread replacing the most is leaking like a sinking submarine. Son-of-a-bitch, I am dog-ass tired and now I've got the fuel filter I detest most leaking fuel like a cow pissing on a flat rock.

"Sir, can you give me a few minutes to check this fuel filter. Its leaking quite a bit and I know it will take only a minute to fix" as I tell a straight faced lie to the Warrant Officer. "Sure go ahead chief" he responds. Doing my magic with the filter, we go through another start up and damn if it still isn't leaking! "Call me when you get it fixed chief" the WO says.

Damn, it's not like this is the first time I've changed this filter. But why does it have to be the worst one to change. Frustrated, I pull the filter cartridge again. Going back to the maintenance hangar for a new O ring and filter, I jump back up on the engine deck and for the third time go through the motions of replacing the filter. Darkness is closing in as I walk up to the company area to get the run-up officer to do another leak check.

Once more we go through the motions, and once again the filter leaks like I've never touched it. "Well chief, if you need any more runs tonight, get the tech sergeant. I'm going to bed." As the Warrant walks away, I reach into my toolbox for a "BFH", a Big Fucking Hammer, and a screw driver. Crawling back up on the engine deck, I wail on the filter in every which way I can possibly attack it.

Satisfied, I get the tech sergeant for the run up. As the engine comes up to rotational speed, I can tell quickly my BFH has done the job. Instead of a shower head spray, I have mere drops of fuel. "Shut her down, we're good to go." I say to the tech inspector.

Buttoning up my bird, I am beyond exhausted. It's not until the following morning, as we head once again for the mountains, that I continuously look to the tail of my bird for telltale signs of smoke and flame. I spend the next two uncomfortable weeks checking that filter again and again. The thoughts of Bob Layman rest just behind my consciousness. The fear of going down in flames is always a heartbeat away.

Several weeks later I will learn from a maintenance team leader responsible for the 100 hour inspection of my bird that although the "O" rings I had been using on that fuel filter had the right part number, they were not the right size. The "O" rings had simply been packaged incorrectly.

My waking hallucinations pertaining to the reality of the "World" have all but disappeared. Talking with my girlfriend and riding the "freedom bird" with round eyes to R&R seemed to be the cure. I can't believe that my mind could have conjured up such a crazy thought, but over the long months in country it had almost become a very irrational but real possibility to me.

Chapter Thirty Seven

Two weeks after my return from R & R, Jesse was killed in action. We both "cleared" coming out of the LZ, and the best anyone can figure is that he was hit sometime after that. There were multiple wounds to his face and neck, but no other damage or hits to the Huey. He bled out, and I can't understand why we didn't hear anything. We had shared a lunch of C rations together at Birmingham, swapping lies, and joking as usual.

His simple and quiet departure from this earth was another unexplainable phenomenon of war. No call for help, no nothing. He was simply here and gone, no last words, no goodbye. If I was going to get wasted, I didn't want to go like that. He was all alone. It had taken me the better part of a day to clean the blood from the gunners' position.

His replacement, Anthony (don't call him Tony) W. Pratcher was the exact opposite of Jesse. A tall skinny kid, extremely quiet, he kept to himself and contributed nothing to a conversation; up until the point of getting himself wounded on a combat assault. Anthony lasted three weeks.

We were lifting into a small valley South and East of the

A Shau. The initial lift had not produced any hostile fire and therefore was reduced to a more or less routine, lower stress situation. As we were in the transition to land on the second lift, Anthony started screaming uncontrollably. It was a continuous scream. However it seemed an intermittent scream as he would step on the floor mic button opening his radio to the flight crew, as his feet thrashed about with the pain of his wound. When the microphone was not open, we could still hear him screaming, but it was more muffled with all the other external noises.

It scared the hell out of the grunts on that lift. Hell, it scared the shit outta me! He was in real pain. I could tell that two of the grunts on the lift were new in country, as their jungle fatigues and boots were still brand new. They looked to me and their buddies for reassurance that this was normal. But ya know...this was Viet Nam, and nothing here was normal. It was their baptism by fire, welcome to Viet Nam. They shrank from his screams, pulling their legs up to their chest, not looking at him, wide eyed, the look of fear on their faces with nowhere else to go until we hit the ground.

Landing in the LZ, the grunts quickly and mercifully unloaded, casting sideward looks back at Anthony. I asked BJ to give me a minute in the LZ to help Anthony, so I could determine the extent of his wound or wounds. "Yeah, okay." He said, "I told the guys behind us to slow it up a bit..., that Anthony's been hit." As I unbuckled and jumped over to Anthony's side, his eyes were closed tightly, his face contorted in a mask of pain. Whimpering now, shock was starting to set in as I unbuckled him and tried to determine where he had been wounded. The gunners' area was splattered with a light spray of blood, reminiscent of when Jesse had been hit. But the blood was not as intense or deep red in color. "Where you hit boy" I ask as I try to get Anthony to talk to me. His lower torso is soaked in blood, and I can't determine precisely where any specific wound is. Still whimpering, and unable to speak, Anthony points to his crotch, any man's worst nightmare. He resists as I attempt to pull his hands away from his pants. But he relaxes as I speak softly to him that I'm there to help. The crotch of his pants is peppered with small jagged black tears. It looks as if he's been hit by shrapnel. "Can you move?" Anthony quickly shakes his head in the negative. "Well let's just try a little, okay? We gotta get you out of here. The other birds are behind us on the way in." Silently, his face still a mask of pain, I can feel the tension in his body relax in a non-verbal sign of acceptance. As I pull and then lift him out of the gunner's seat, he groans. Laying Anthony on my shoulder, my arm wrapped around his butt, the moans are louder as I try to avoid the wounded area of his body. I am aware that the simple weight of his body pressed against my shoulder is causing him some excruciating pain. I lay him on the cargo deck; he appears to have passed out. His body is limp, lifeless, running my fingers to his neck, I check his pulse. He has a strong pulse. I unplug Anthony's mic cord and plug it into my helmet. "BJ, let's get out of here, he's either gut shot, or got one in the groin, I can't tell what the hell hit him." "Coming up," BJ responds immediately, as I clear right and look out the cargo area to my left.

Unbuckling Anthony's pants, I pull them down below his knees. Wiping the blood away from his legs with a compress bandage, the flesh of his thighs is speckled with dark welts of red, purple and black. It almost looks like a fish hook had been pushed into the flesh and then ripped out over and over again. There are a few three to four inch jagged tears in the skin, like he has been hit with bigger pieces of shrapnel, but nothing near his arteries. Fortunately I can discern no bullet holes or traumatic wounds. Pulling his underwear down, I'm glad to see that Anthony is still intact, and will still be able to father many children in the future.

BJ will occasionally glance over his shoulder watching me minister Anthony's wounds, but he says nothing. I catch his eye and give him a thumbs up and smile. "He's going to be fine." I say. "He still has his family jewels." BJ gives me a grim smile, and nods his head.

I cradle Anthony's head and shoulders on my thighs. Not knowing if he can hear me, I shout to him over the noise of the helicopter, “You’re gonna be fine Anthony. We’ll have you back at the hospital in twenty minutes man, you’re gonna be fine and you’re going home for sure.” There is no sign Anthony has heard what I said. But he appears to be okay as we finally land at the Dust Off medical pad at Camp Evans. Anthony is quickly transferred by orderlies into the bowels of the heavily sandbagged fortress of the hospital. Some beautiful “round eye” American nurses and a doctor accompany him.

Much later that day, as I walk back up to the flight line to my Huey, I struggle with the emotional weight of another door gunner gone. I make a half-assed attempt at cleaning the blood from the soundproofing in the gunners area, but I just don’t give a damn anymore. Let the next guy do it. Removing Anthony’s machine gun from its mount, I can see where the support tube for the M-60 is deformed and dented. It appears that a bullet had hit the support tube and disintegrated into Anthony’s groin area. At the level of his seat, just about exactly where Anthony’s knees and crotch were, small fragments of the bullet punctured the sound proofing and littered the floor around his seat. I’m sure it had been painful, but it had been Anthony’s ticket home. Thinking of home, I wonder when it will be my turn to leave. I’m a “double digit” midget, eighty three days and a wake up to go, I’m getting real, real, “short”… It is a surreal feeling.

Craig was Anthony’s replacement. He was a Canadian volunteer from the North shores of Lake Erie in Ontario Province. Craig’s father had been a Sergeant Major in the Canadian Army, and Craig wanted so much to emulate his father. The Sergeant Major had finished his career with eleven medals, and Craig wanted to match or exceed his father’s medal count during his tour in Viet Nam!

Except for his fascination to have more medals than his father, he was so much like me it was scary. We were the same size and stature, had the same personality, the same sense of humor, and the same outlook on life. How could I not like this guy?

Chapter Thirty Eight

Just like the Island Campaign of World War Two in the Pacific, with the ultimate goal of reaching Japan; we are hopping (air assaulting) a string of fire support artillery bases out to our final objective, the A Shau Valley. Following the new road QL 547 out of firebase Birmingham, we opened Bastogne, Blaze, then Veghel and Cannon. The firebases follow a road cut out of the jungle, twisting its way along the sides of the mountains. The Eagles' Nest, the last firebase prior to entering the A Shau Valley, was opened earlier out of sequence to the other firebases due to the necessity of providing artillery support during our "island hopping" operations. Not quite on the rim of the valley, but with an imposing position perched on the eastern edge of the Valley, the Nest was an extremely valuable asset for our artillery. With an absolute height advantage we could not only "see" across the Valley but also well to the South.

On each of the LZ's that would ultimately become firebases, we had been meeting only sporadic resistance, i.e., ground fire. The air assault onto LZ Blaze was located on the Rao Nai River. The Rao Nai meandered down out of the mountains from the North. A gentle rise just below the bottom of the "U" of a quick horseshoe turn in the river was the point we would focus on for the landing zone. Northeast of the horseshoe was a valley from which the river flowed, and the surrounding four mountain ridges all funneled to a point that made the clearing below the horseshoe an obvious LZ. The horseshoe clearing may have been more than apparent to the bad guys also as an LZ. "Blaze" our next to final "stepping stone" would ultimately become the worst case scenario of resistance to our westward movement into the A Shau.

Our PZ was firebase Birmingham. It was a warm, nice mid-summer day. We were relaxed. We were confident. The grunts hopped aboard as the Huey sat at idle speed, rocking like a cradle on the uneven ground in an almost hypnotic motion. My upper body was shaded from the indirect angle of the warm sun, which washed over my legs and thighs. It was a therapeutic, heating pad, cozy feeling. My feet lay propped over the mini-gun can of ammo attached to my machine gun just like I was sitting in a recliner.

As the formation of Hueys came up to speed, I slowly reached up and dropped the dark visor on my helmet; partially to keep the sun and dirt out of my eyes, but more to keep alive the relaxing dreamy pulse I was feeling for a few more moments. I was in that state of being you lapse into just before you drift off to sleep. Pulling pitch off Birmingham, the cool rush of air brought me slowly back to an alertness that I still wasn't ready for.

It was a short ten minute ride to LZ Blaze. The quick succession of impacting rounds pummeled the entire LZ as we watched from a holding orbit south of the LZ. The quick flash of a blended mixture of reds, yellow, and orange fire could be missed in the blink of an eye; masked in the subsequent dirty black smoke, the heaving dirt and ensuing dust cloud of the exploding round. The Cobra gun ships followed in concert with the artillery barrage as they dove on the LZ, unleashing the 2.75 inch rockets by the dozens.

The first lifts of the Lancers are taking horrendous fire from the surrounding mountain sides. Too far away to see the action directly, the radio keeps us informed as we listen in vicariously to the battle. My recent nap is a matter of history as the adrenaline begins pumping through my body listening to the battle. We are cautiously anxious to get into the fight. It's a feeling like, been there done that, and you don't really want to do it again. But like a narcotic fix, the need to enter the fray is overpowering and you want to help your buddies however you can.

"Bravo six, Bravo six, taking heavy fire from hill 838, we gotta get there heads down over there....we're getting shot to pieces here!" "Lancer 22 taking heavy AA and fifty-one fire from hill eleven-twenty." A voice breaks radio protocol, "Ted...break off, break off... you're in a cross fire...turn left now...turn south..." Another voice, anonymous, obviously strained, "Man they've got us in cross-fires all over the river bed."

As suddenly as it has begun, the air assault is cancelled. Thor in the Command and Control bird was orbiting high over LZ Blaze. He has stopped the lift before we lose any more birds on the assault. "All elements, this is Thor. Continue orbiting, we are going to suppress that triple "A" fire coming from the hills...Stand-by."

As we fly in an elongated race track orbit, the camouflage cover of the grunt next to me has "Green Bay Wisconsin" written in black ink across the back of his helmet. I lean over and begin making small talk with him. I offer him a cigarette, which he accepts, and explain to him how I hail from the Upper Peninsula of Michigan. He is familiar with Crystal Falls, my hometown, having hunted deer near their on several occasions with his father. This guy is as close as I've been to home since arriving in Viet Nam, and we talk about home, deer hunting and of course the Packers.

The radio's silence crackles with clipped call signs and conversations that are almost business casual as our fast movers arrive on the scene. A forward air controller is talking with a flight of four F-105 Thunderchiefs "Thuds" that have come to our rescue. The Thud leaders' voice, a relaxed, twangy Southwestern drawl contradicts the undercurrent of battle that has already transpired today.

The Bird Dog begins weaving, looping, twisting and turning through the mountainous terrain along the river. Orbiting safely to the south of the river, we watch as streaks of heavy tracer fire and antiaircraft fire search out to touch the little Bird Dog intent on marking targets for the Thuds. "Holy shit" BJ says as we watch in disbelief as the Bird Dog explodes in a fireball just as a white phosphorous rocket leaps from its wings towards an intended target. Large flaming pieces of the "push-pull's" wings and twin tail boom twist and cartwheel onto the mountainside, unrecognizable as anything more than a confetti of smoke, flames and metal.

The Thud leaders' voice is the next thing we hear as he organizes his flight for the bomb run on the marked target. His voice is all business, nothing but business, as initially undetectable to us they make their bomb runs. The flight leader has already dropped his bombs, and I only know that because of the arcing climb away from the mountain terrain. There is a tinge of shiny aluminum as the sun reflects off the jet to mark his silent departure. I catch an illusion of almost dark, vaporous motion, only realizing in my mind what I have seen moments after the fact, as the five hundred pound bombs released by the flight leader rock the mountainside with multiple micro-second rippling shockwaves. Now that I know where the fighter bombers are coming from in the sky, I see a small black dot coming from the deep blue high above. Quickly the black dot metamorphoses into the form of a fighter, releasing his bombs as the pilot pulls off and away from the target, mimicking that same arching climb as his flight leader.

The third speck of darkness in the sky comes hurtling toward earth with its load of twenty-five hundred pounds of explosives. "Slingshot three to lead…I'm hit." Looking closely at the approaching darkness of the third fighter, its wings already taking shape, I look for any obvious signs of damage. There's no telltale smoke trail, no incoming tracers or flak, nothing that can be seen by the naked eye. “Three this is lead…break it off…RTB. We’ll be on your six all the way home.” “RTB” meant return to base, and they would follow him home. “Mike, I can’t get out. Just tell Julie I love her.” Once again radio protocol had broken down to a personal level of communication between two fellow warriors. “Kip, eject…eject…” The voice was almost pleading. “I can’t move, there’s no way” I could sense in his voice as it filled with emotion his great effort, stuck in the cockpit, struggling even as he spoke. The F-105 plunged earthward, rapidly becoming an image of despair as the radio remained silent but for the final communication between two friends. Once again the crippled pilot spoke, “Mike, just tell Julie I love her…Oh God.” With that, the jet is very close now; it’s closer than I have ever seen. The crippled pilot doing his job to the very end releases his bombs. It’s hard to explain which happened first, the plane disappearing in a huge mushroom cloud of flame and smoke, or the concussive blast of the plane’s bombs completely obliterating the crash and final flight of Slingshot three.

“Slingshot four, this is lead.” His voice was filled with a mixture of pain and pure evil. “Put those fucking bombs right....on…the…target.” “Roger, lead.” With that, the final fighter, already heading toward the target straight as an arrow, just like the others, streaked out of the dark blue sky and dropped his load on the smoldering mountain side. Rejoining his flight high above the mountains that had taken one of their own, Slingshot lead had a personal message for Thor, our battalion commander. “I don’t need an excuse to come back, and when we do, we’ll have enough ordinance and aircraft to reduce that mountain to an ant hill…Out.”

A new FAC has arrived over LZ Blaze and continues to mark targets on the surrounding mountains and river. The enemy fire has diminished only a little, as the thirty-seven and fifty-seven millimeter antiaircraft fire only seems to intensify. More F-105’s and F-4’s arrive to bomb and drop napalm across the mountain tops and ridges. Wave after wave of concussive blasts and napalm blanket the mountains. The mountain tops disappear in a cloud of grayish white smoke, and huge brown scars like acne pock mark the once verdant vegetation.

Somewhere a forward observer does his deadly work as the mountains and areas surrounding the LZ erupt with artillery fire of all types. It's a grand finale' Fourth of July multiplied a hundred times over. Hell has descended on this small spot of earth in the form of the might and power of the United States. It is breathtaking to watch, and I imagine even more frightening to be endured by our enemy.

We are all speechless. It has been an extremely expensive operation in terms of life, emotions and equipment, and our mission had just started. On the assault again, the radio chatter comes to life again as calls of taking fire ring out. Our aerial rocket artillery saturates the hillsides of the mountains with high explosive. Every call for help from the Huey slicks is responded to in kind, and brings the ARA to the rescue.

I take a moment as we begin our approach to turn to my new found friend from Green Bay. "Keep your head down out there, it's hotter than hell." He acknowledges my comment with a big smile and a thumbs up. I tap him on the helmet for luck. "Look me up when you get back to the World." He smiles again. "I'll do that. Be cool."

It's an easy wide open approach, one bounce and out. The grunts don't want to stay with us any longer than necessary, and we sure don't want to hang around either. We are still taking intense fire on the approach, but not from the big guns of an hour before. I concentrate my machine gun fire on every possible muzzle flash I can see, and when I can't find an obvious target, I provide a grazing fire knowing the grunts will need all the help they can get as they un-ass the bird. As BJ flares over the LZ and settles down on the grassy river bank, I shift my fire rearward. I feel the helicopter immediately get light on the skids in most part to the lack of weight of the grunts we have carried.

My peripheral vision picks up a blur of movement to my

right side. As I turn to look, my friend from Green Bay is just falling to the deck of our Huey. His weapon lies on the ground just outside the door of our helicopter as I look at him lying on the floor. His eyes are wide open; a look of total surprise on his face as his hands grasp at his chest. "Clear! Let's get the hell outta here BJ, we got wounded on board." Craig looks over from the gunner's position, as I leap around the pole that separates my seat from the cargo deck. "Clear right" Craig says as BJ has already pulled pitch and we thunder out of the LZ. "Shit" I'm freaking out. As I look at my friend lying on the floor, blood bubbles from his mouth as he begins coughing a frothy mess of misty blood.

Looking at his chest a small black spot has torn through his jungle fatigues. I unhook his web belt and gear and rip open the fatigue jacket. He's not wearing a tee shirt as I look at two ugly holes in the breast bone area of his muscular chest. Bright red blood is oozing from the holes as I tear his bandage from its pouch on his LBE. I have unplugged my helmet from the aircraft communication system. "Craig, get me a bandage from the first aid kit" I holler, pointing at the first aid kit, trying to be heard above the noise of the Huey's engine and rotors. Not hearing, even though he's looking right at me, Craig never the less understands what I want, and leaps to the pouch hanging on the bulkhead behind the pilots. Handing me the thick bandage I take Craig's hand still holding the bandage and push it down over the bullet hole on my buddy's chest. I lean over to Craig, my mouth inches from his helmeted ear. "Put your other hand on the other bandage and apply pressure, he has a sucking chest wound," as I point to the bubbling froth coming from his mouth. Craig looks me in the eye his lips a tight thin line, nodding his head understanding. He's doing well for a new guy, I think to myself. While Craig held the compress bandages on Dave's chest, I gently rolled him on his side looking for the exit wounds. The bullets had not been as kind exiting Dave's body. The jagged, torn exit wounds were the size of fifty cent pieces. Grabbing the rolled up rubber poncho on Dave's pack, I folded it into a twelve inch square and pressed it against his back. I slowly lower him back to the cargo deck, holding the poncho in place until I am sure his body pressure would keep it secure.

I reach back to my gunner's position for my microphone cord plugging it back into my helmet to apprise BJ of the situation. Plugging in I let him know how seriously the grunt is wounded as we headed for the closest MASH unit back at Phu Bai. Looking at the back of BJ's head, he shakes his head in the affirmative understanding what we need to do. Our peter pilot begins switching radio frequencies to alert the MASH unit we are inbound with a wounded trooper.

Looking down at Dave, the blood foaming from his mouth seemed to have diminished somewhat. I grabbed his left hand, kneeling at his side. "You got a good one Dave, you're going home. You lucked out. You got here after me and you're going home before me. Just save me a spot in the woods for deer season." On more occasions than I care to admit, we have lost a soldier to shock from non-life threatening wounds. Shock is an even greater silent killer than the injuries and wounds received during battle. Dave's wounds are definitely traumatic and serious, and I talk to him to try keeping him from going into deep shock. I didn't know if he could hear me or not but I kept up the small talk hoping it would help both of us. Fifteen minutes later we are on the helipad of the MASH hospital. Unconscious, Dave is loaded on a litter and quickly rushed through the sand bagged pierced steel planking blast wall surrounding the surgical hospital. I hope he makes it.

One week after the assault, the eight inch gun, the one-seven-fives and one-five-fives seemed like permanent fixtures on Blaze. Flying over or re-supplying the fire base during fire missions was an awesome experience. The guns firing their salvos looked like erect penis' belching flames and black or white smoke from their long barrels. Then like a penis expending its load, after the awesome blast, the barrel drops slowly into a flaccid state, only to be reamed and stroked again with another deadly load of shell and powder bags.

This piece of real estate had cost much more than it would

ever be worth to anybody in a lifetime, let alone the lives it had cost to take in the first place. What the hell is any no name piece of earth worth during war when the bad guys want it more than you; which I guess is the way it is in every war.

June 20, the road to the A Shau Valley from the plains of the South China Sea is now open. It winds through the lowlands and rice paddies into the valleys and on to the mountains. The road with its wide loops and hairpin turns makes its way past fire bases Birmingham, Bastogne, Veghel, Blaze, and Cannon. Carved out of the side of mountains, it snakes its way past the watchful eyes high atop the Eagle's Nest and on into the A Shau Valley. The road which took three months to build by the 27th Engineer Battalion of the 45th Group crosses the Ta Bat airstrip into fire base Currahee which occupies the middle of the A Shau Valley floor.

We are on hand for the ceremonial arrival of the first aircraft to land on the Ta Bat airstrip located in the middle of the A Shau Valley. A U.S. Air Force C7A Caribou loaded with water and C rations is the first to land here since the mid 50's. Providing security for the landing and ceremonies were tanks and APC's from elements of the 3rd Squadron 5th Cavalry of the Ninth Infantry Division that had just that day traveled up QL 547 marking its grand opening also. The 326th Engineer Battalion opened the valley floor in seven days and constructed the 1200 foot Ta Bat airstrip in just 56 hours.

The festivities over, we head back for the Haunted House. After landing on the west side of Camp Evans to refuel at the POL pad, BJ has our peter pilot jump out of the copilots seat and take my gun position in the rear of the helicopter. It is customary, but not within the allowed regulations for AC's to give their crew chiefs "stick time" on the fundamentals of flying a Huey, "just in case." I had never heard of a crew chief being required to fly a Huey due to pilot incapacitation, but the flight time was a real moral booster for me, and the peter pilots loved the opportunity when presented to shoot the machine gun, or just get a "MIB" Man in Back viewpoint of the ride.

BJ had previously given me practice in hovering and various take off sessions in the Huey out over the rice paddies. Today, I would practice repositioning the bird from the POL pad and land back at the Haunted House. As I smoothly lifted the collective to lift the Huey off the ground, I gently pulled back on the cyclic stick lifting the nose off prior to the heels of the skids coming unglued from the ground. A slightly less than text book lift off, but for me, it allowed a rolling take off versus a full fledged hover which I had not accomplished with any great manner of success to that time. Moving easily through translational lift I continued the climb to a thousand feet as BJ worked the radios talking with the Camp Evans control tower. After a short circle around Camp Evans, I began the descent to the Haunted House under BJ's watchful tutelage as he talked me through the approach. "Pull up slowly on your collective now, and keep your cyclic stick neutral or slight aft of center as we begin to bottom out on the approach" he said in that measured instructor's voice I had heard so often. We were centered between the two flight platoons revetments as the ground rushed up to meet us. BJ was telling me to pull up on the collective, but in a panic I pulled back on the cyclic. Not getting the desired response, I froze on the controls watching the ground rushing up to crush our fragile machine. "Collective, pull up on the collective" BJ shouts into my helmet earphones. But instead of collective, I pull further back on the cyclic stick as the Huey fast approaches a mid air stall. "I've got it" BJ says, just as the Huey breaks and stalls slightly to the left. BJ recovers smoothly from the stall and brings 644 to a low hover just to the side of our revetment. Nothing else is said as he easily slips the helicopter into our revetment and shuts down the engine. Smiling at me, he just shrugs his shoulders and say "We gotta work on that a little more Lot!"

We are into the middle of dinner chow as BJ and I make our way up out of the rice paddie swamp toward the mess hall. Coming down toward the flight line is Papa, our Commanding Officer. Catching BJ's eye Papa motions him over where we cross paths with him. "Say BJ..." Papa unsmiling, a question in his eyes and on his lips, "Who was flying that approach just now into the revetments?" he queries. BJ looks at Papa, and without so much as an afterthought or a hint of indecision lifts his right arm, thumb extended toward me and says "My chief was sir." As BJ continues to move his arm and thumb accusatorily in my direction, I just know it is all over for me and BJ now. Papa, not acting in the least bit surprised, or even bothered by BJ's arrogant declaration, says... "Oh, okay" as he continues his walk giving me barely a cursory glance even as I detect a slight hint of a smile. Just another everyday common occurrence at the Haunted House, home of the Ghost Riders.

Chapter Thirty Nine

Early July, lunch time, fire base Curahee, the middle of the A Shau Valley. To say it's hot would be an understatement. I have a hammock slung in the shade under the tail stinger and radio masts of the Huey waiting for the word to go. Today's assault will be on the very edge of the Laotian border. Intelligence reports at least an NVA Division building up and threatening Curahee and the surrounding Valley. We are lifting the 2/506th Infantry Battalion on the assault. Other elements stand by, but I guess we are going in just to see if they can make some form of contact with the gooks.

At 1300 there will be a B-52 Arc Light strike over the mountain and LZ area. Standing next to BJ, looking up, searching the sky for any sign of the big bombers, we make small talk. The azure blue sky is devoid of clouds, and we should be able to see the big jets' contrails if the atmospheric conditions are just right. I look at my watch, "It's 1300 BJ, where are they?" "Your watch must be fast, they'll be here at 1300." He responds. Two minutes later still searching the sky for the B-52's; the mountains to the West of Currahee begin to erupt. The mountains rumble, it's like an earthquake that just goes on and on and on, shaking the ground we stand on. Long columns of smoke and dust fill the air on the horizon as we mount up for the ensuing assault. There was never a hint of the giant Boeing B-52's above us. No jet noise, no contrails, it was eerie, almost unbelievable, had I not been there to experience it for myself.

We have a load of grunts on board, their feet characteristically dangling from the sides of our bird swinging back and forth like a bunch of children on park swings. Lifting off the pick up zone of Currahee, the mountains and LZ only five miles away are covered in a haze of dirt and smoke in an otherwise clear sky. As BJ lowers the nose of the ship accelerating to keep up with the Huey ahead of us, the ground drops away. A small, shallow river meanders to the south of the fire base. Its gravel sand bars are exposed now that the swelling rains of the monsoon season have ended. As we low level down the twisting river a hundred feet off the ground; there standing on one of these gravel islands in the middle of the river is a most magnificent buck. The deer watches as we pass close overhead, neither flinching nor obviously afraid. It is a beautiful reddish brown with a huge rack of mature antlers, and I can't believe how any animal could have lived so long in a valley dominated with so many booby traps, mines, artillery, and bombs. It moves me to think that a handsome animal such as this can exist in the insanity of the war we bring to its domain; and that some crazy fuck with a weapon on either side doesn't simply shoot it because he can. Or maybe it's because this animal does simply exist in this violence, we all have a reason to believe in something other than and something infinitely better than killing for the sake of killing.

Climbing out of the river bottom, making a long slow looping turn to the West toward the mountains, the radio is filled with the chatter of command and control as the assault begins. "Papa" our new commanding officer in the lead bird acknowledges taking fire on the approach. The "Redskins," "D" Company 158th Assault, in their Cobras, come along either side of our helicopter giving close air support on the approach, much the same as the F-4's had done on our assault of Dong Ap Bia. I watch them approach from my seven o'clock position level with our ship. We are close enough to each other I can almost tell you the color of the pilot's eyes as we look at each other. The Cobra pilot lowers the nose of his bird beginning his gun run. Watching the Cobra inch by us, the gunner leans over his gun sight.

With my machine gun extended, I hold my fire; we are still too far out from the Z. The Cobra begins to fire his rockets at the LZ. Six rockets sequentially shoot from the pods mounted on the side of the ship. Watching their trajectory by following the smoke trail, they impact on the trees and jungle canopy. Six more rockets spew from the sides of the helicopter, exploding closer to the LZ. I guide the belted machine gun ammo into the gun as I shoot in sustained fire following the rockets with my tracers. The last six rockets from the Cobra emit a red puff of smoke two thirds of the way into the target. That red puff means the rockets are opening up; they're shooting "nails," flechette rounds into the target.

The Cobra breaks off its gun run as another Cobra takes its place. All the slicks on the assault have been taking fire. Closer to the ground now, I am concentrating my fire on dark spots in the jungle that could be hiding the bad guys. I can clearly see the Cobras rockets hitting the trees just outside of the LZ. The grunts are fanning out in the grass and I wonder how long the Cobras can provide supporting fire so close to the LZ. We are taking fire, I can't see where it's coming from, but our Huey is definitely taking hits. A quick scan of the engine gauges reassures me that everything is fine for the moment. BJ can tell also, as his control of the aircraft is more precise and purposeful as we hit the LZ as smooth as I've ever felt while riding with him. Almost as an afterthought I say to BJ that we're taking fire. "Ya I know!" He responds gruffly. "Well, okay then"...

Landing back at Curahee while the grunts load up, I jump out and make a cursory scan of 644. The tail boom is dented and jagged rips have torn the aluminum. On closer inspection the jagged hole and tears in the skin of my bird had chunks of trees imbedded in it. Those son-of-a-bitch Cobras were taking this close air support a little too far. I told BJ about the hits on the tail boom, and he's pissed too. He immediately gets on the radio to tell Papa of the friendly fire damage. As it turned out, there was only sporadic contact with the NVA, and it seems all that hostile fire turned out to be coming from our own Cobras!

Chapter Forty

C.C.N., Command and Control North, the South Vietnamese are being trained to control their own destiny. They are calling it the Vietnamization of the war. As we leave the forward operating base of the Special Forces, three Vietnamese Air Force CH-34 helicopters call sign “King Bees” carry between them six green berets and twelve Montagnards, or “Yards” as the green berets call them. Our Huey is flying as the cover ship protecting American interests, our Special Forces. Today we are flying twenty-five kilometers, twenty five “kliks” into Laos. The insertion is to be quiet, only a “recon” a reconnaissance patrol. No noise, no artillery, no air strikes, just quiet. Sneaky Pete is what the “SF” the Special Forces call it. As we fly west, I look north to the A Shau. It has become an all too familiar valley for me, and a valley of death for many. The 101st takes liberty with the 23rd Psalm and changes it somewhat; “Yea though I walk through the Valley of the shadow of death, I shall fear no evil, because we’re the meanest sons of bitches in the Valley!” Yet knowing we are flying CCN operations, and all they entail, the “valley” is my security blanket. It’s a place I know and I’m comfortable with, like home.

It is a hot cloudless July day as we fly at four thousand

feet. The air is cooler up here, and I enjoy the solitude as I look out at forbidden and very hostile countryside. The Vietnamese CH-34's are a thousand feet lower and ahead of us about a mile. The LZ for today is a two thousand pound bomb crater. You could put your average middle class American house in a crater that size and never see the chimney.

As we approach the LZ, the King Bees set up for the approach, and one, two, three, drop their cargo of grunts. In and out, no sweat, we're on our way home. Ten minutes later as we approach the border we get a call from the SF lieutenant we just left back in Laos. "This is 'Mousetrap six'." "Go ahead Mousetrap six," BJ responds. "Ahhh....the bad guys know we're here, we have a Prairie Fire," this was a code word meaning they needed an emergency extraction, "Over." "Roger" BJ responds, "We're on our way." Immediately Rudder, our co-pilot, begins coordinating with the CH-34's and the SF base camp as BJ begins the turn back into Laos.

I look to the bomb crater LZ as the 34's once again set up for the approach. There is nothing to indicate that trouble is on the horizon. Purple smoke drifts lazily over the bomb crater LZ, all pretense of stealth gone. It still looks serene and peaceful. We're still at four thousand feet as I continue to watch the first "34" making his run to the crater. A ridgeline a hundred-seventy five yards to the West of the LZ erupts in tracer fire of incredible intensity. I have never, ever, seen ground fire of that magnitude. "Holy shit," I say. "Roger that" says our co-pilot. As we continue orbiting east of the LZ, the first helicopter hovers at the edge of the crater. I can just make out our guys jumping in as the loaded 34 lowers his nose and picks up speed and altitude successfully getting out of the Z. The second Vietnamese 34 is right on the tail of the first as the ground fire increases to an unimaginable level. Pieces of the H-34 are shedding like hair off a dog yet the Vietnamese pilot continues on to the crater. "Get the FAC guys on the horn, and tell him we need fast movers out here ASAP" BJ tells Rudder.

More guys are jumping on the second CH-34 as it

miraculously comes to a hover over the Z. As the helicopter sits hovering, tracer fire appears to be actually "absorbed" by the bird. One man jumping on is hit and falls back to the edge of the crater, and is lifted up by two Montagnards and literally thrown into the bird even as it begins to move away from the LZ. As the third CH-34 begins its approach to the Z, the ground fire hasn't diminished in intensity, and actually appears to be more concentrated on the ship. I don't like it at all. I can't believe one, let alone two; helicopters have flown through the maelstrom of fire and made it out.

As the third ship heads into the Z, the pilot starts screaming "rotor overspeed, rotor overspeed" and breaks off his approach to the LZ. A rotor overspeed will prohibit the pilot from taking another load because he doesn't know what the consequences of the overspeed have been, and any stress or load to the rotor system could result in complete rotor failure. It would be much the same as overstressing the wing of an aircraft, and then not knowing when the overstress would cause failure and loss of the wing. BJ, knowing the consequences of a rotor overspeed, immediately makes a tight turn for the LZ and pushes the nose down aiming straight for the LZ. "Everybody hot mike" I say as we come screaming out of the sky.

BJ is going full out for the LZ bomb crater as I start suppressing the ridgeline with my M-60. For a few seconds there is a lull in the incoming fire, as if we had taken them by surprise. The FM radio clicks in our ears, a sure sign the gooks have 57 millimeter radar controlled guns! Those damn guns have a range of three and a half miles! We're being tracked electronically. Then red and green tracers, everything but the kitchen sink is flying directly at us. Some of the incoming "tracer fire" keeps getting bigger and look like glowing orange and red basketballs that mysteriously arc away from us as they apparently lose their energy. The helicopter is exploding in bits and pieces all around us. With the clear visor on my helmet pulled down, pieces of instrument panel and glass pepper my chin and cheeks, stinging like a thousand hornets. I know I'm a dead man, but I keep shooting, focusing on one spot on the damn ridgeline I know has bad guys. I can see the damn gooks standing there firing at us, trying to kill us. So I'm trying to return the favor. I'm gonna kill em'! Fuck em'! I know I have target fixation, I should be raking the entire ridgeline with fire. I just can't break my concentration on the gooks in this particular area of brush and trees. I watch gratified as my tracers find their mark. I sweep the brush with machine gun fire, left to right, up and down as some tracers disappear in the foliage and others ricochet off the ground. Having lost all sense of time and spatial relation, the Huey shudders from retreating blade stall as BJ stands the Huey on its tail and pancakes down on the edge of the Z. The landing is so firm, that at first I think that we have been shot down. But a quick glance at the engine gauges, the ones still working, indicate we're still a viable flying machine.

Three Montagnards and one SF "buck" sergeant climb aboard turning to fire on the tree line as I holler "clear left." Turning to monitor the engine gauges I notice both windshields are cracked and holed from bullets. I think to myself, now how the hell did that happen. Craig and I had just cleaned them. We had left the SF compound with clean windshields! (I'm pissed because now I'll have to change the damn windshields when we get back). Then the reality of the situation hits me, and I realize what has happened in the preceding minute. I shake my head, bewildered that I couldn't understand at the moment, in a rational way, why the windshields had been shot up.

Pulling pitch the Huey comes to a smooth ten-foot rolling hover as BJ simultaneously pitches the nose over getting us out of Dodge City. The helicopter begins to shudder as if passing through translational lift. However the shudder is manifest by the engine making a grinding, growling noise followed by a complete compressor stall. Two of the Montagnards are simultaneously hit, as metal shavings and more pieces of my Huey fly through the air.

The Huey drops like an elevator in free fall, collapsing out of the sky nose first. We hit so hard, I can feel my spinal column compress like an accordion and I black out for a few seconds.

Although I can still hear, I can't see. Then, just as if somebody has turned the lights back on, I can see again.

BJ and Rudder, unharmed in the crash, are moving around, flipping switches and shutting down the aircraft, releasing their seat belt harness' getting ready to bail out. Rudder is talking to the Forward Air Controller giving him a situation report. The SF sergeant and Montagnards have been thrown against the back of the pilots' seats. One of the wounded Montagnards is dead or unconscious and the other is trying to sit up on the cargo deck. I rip off my flight helmet, jump out and open BJ's door, slide his bullet shield back, and pull my "sixty" off the gun mount. Craig is following suit on the right side of the helicopter. Pulling my ammo can out of the helicopter, I grab my M-203 and bandolier of ammo for the grenade launcher and pick the smoke and fragmentation grenades off the soundproofing like they're apples off a tree.

Setting up the sixty on the edge of the bomb crater, I noticed a rip-rap path of bamboo about two feet wide snaking neatly around the bomb crater disappearing into the elephant grass on either side of the bomb hole. We had found a vein of the "yellow brick road," the Ho Chi Minh Trail.

I aimed my machine gun down the closest avenue of approach and checked my M-203 to make sure I had a round in the chamber. It was a high explosive round. I figured in these close quarters a flechette round would be more effective, and threw one in the tube. A 40-millimeter flechette round has about a hundred, one-inch arrow like "nails" in them. When fired, the nails open in an expanding cone. It can be a very devastating round in close quarters like elephant grass; even better than the buckshot rounds I also carried.

The SF sergeant is giving Craig a field of fire on the other side of the bamboo trail, as the remaining Montagnard pulled the two wounded Yards from the helicopter and laid them on the slope of the bomb crater. Then he takes up a position on the far edge of the bomb crater facing away from us in the direction of the bad guys. We are all moving like mechanical robots, doing what survival dictates is immediate and necessary to endure the next few hours.

My heart is beating at a hundred miles a minute. I am gulping air, trying to catch my breath. The LZ is hot, maybe a hundred or a hundred and ten degrees. The air is permeated with the stink of smoke grenades, gunpowder and a talcum of dust and dirt from the bomb crater. Already I look like I've just stepped out of the shower. Sweat rolls down into my eyes, burning like hell. As I rub the sweat from my eyes, the powder of dust and dirt smears my face with mud and grit. My nomex flight suit has big sweaty spots, and the red dirt from the bomb crater is sticking to those wet spots like fly paper. God, I need a drink of water. I half-crawl, half-crouch run back to the helicopter. I grab my two-quart canteen looking at the C and LRRP rations under the seat. Yeah right, I smirk to myself, like I'm gonna have time to eat.

After catching my breath, taking stock of the situation, I knew it was all over. If we didn't get out quick, we never would. It was understood this was all volunteer. If we didn't make it back, Uncle Sam would deny we had ever been here. But I knew the Ghost Riders wouldn't let us down. They were probably already figuring out who's coming to get us. At least I hoped that's what was happening; just in case, I pulled a frag grenade closer to me. This one is for me I thought, I won't be a prisoner.

The shooting had almost stopped. In the high elephant grass, only the rotor mast of the Huey was visible to the gooks. The NVA could not see us, nor could we see them. It would only be a matter of time now. "What the hell have we got ourselves into" BJ asks the Special Forces sergeant. The sergeant looks over his shoulder from the edge of the crater at BJ, his face painted in shades of greens and brown camouflage, expressionless. He has an olive drab tourniquet wrapped around his forehead for a sweatband. About twenty-two or twenty-three years old, the sergeant rolls over on his back to face BJ. With a Midwest farm country accent, unexpectedly he smiles, his straight bright white teeth out of place to the features of camouflage paint. "What we got ourselves into Sir... is a world of shit!" We have a comic among us in the middle of hell! I start chuckling, I can't help it, it strikes me as so damn, scary, funny. I look over at BJ; he half shakes his head, a crooked, worried half grin on his face. Craig, listening as he keeps watch on the trail, pounds his fist into the ground "Shit, shit, shit."

The first mortar round impacts in the jungle grass about thirty yards to our right. "Damn they're good" the sergeant says, referring to the NVA gunners. As the second round explodes fifteen seconds later, it is ten yards closer to us. BJ's talking to the Forward Air Controller on the radio in the Huey. Rudder hollers to BJ, "BJ get the hell outta there." The helicopter is the perfect aiming point for the dinks. BJ, half in and out of the helicopter, slides down to the ground. "Six point seven minutes" BJ says. "What," Rudder looks at the Bridge not understanding. "We're gonna have close air, our fast movers, in six minutes" he repeats.

Slight whooshes, craaackboom, craaackboom, craaackboom, the NVA have zeroed their mortars on us. The shrapnel is slapping at the grass, peppering the skin of the Huey like Swiss cheese. I tuck into a fetal position, feeling exposed, naked and vulnerable. The depression of the bomb crater makes an excellent shelter from the mortar explosions unless one lands directly in the hole with us. Rounds continue to impact, ranging on the helicopter as the "bulls eye." The mortar rounds are now impacting on all sides of the crater. One round hitting very close to the edge of the crater lifts my body nine inches off the ground from the concussive affect of the blast. The over pressure from the blast deafens me and everything becomes quiet and muffled. The FAC pilot, knowing the dilemma we're in, tries to help us however he can as he launches his WP, the white phosphorous rockets at the enemy hilltop.

The sun is high overhead, bright and blazing, a hot white sunshine. Suddenly, blackness, like the eclipse of the sun, fills our LZ bomb crater shelter. Instinctively I duck down, and turning my head sideways, look up to see the overwhelming presence of a mottled gray belly of rivets, grease stained streaks of oil, bombs and canisters, and the beautiful fluted twin tail pipes of an F-4 Phantom. Following only seconds and close behind, offset to the side of the first F-4, another jet flashes by. The air is simultaneously ripped open with the roar of the jet fighters engines. The noise is beyond deafening even with my blown ear drums. With all this transpiring in a nanosecond, it was so frightening, I didn't know if I should throw up, lose my bladder and bowel control, or just flat out die. I had been concentrating so much on the incoming mortars; I was taken completely by surprise at the arrival of the fast movers. I could only imagine how the gooks felt. I wanted to stand up and shout, jump up and down, to wave the American flag, here comes the cavalry, go get 'em guys.

BJ jumps back out of the protection of the crater to the radio on the helicopter, exposing himself to the mortar fire. The FAC orbiting high overhead reassures BJ that all is well. "Pop smoke" BJ hollers as he twists his big frame looking down at me. I grab a red smoke grenade and throw it in the bottom of the bomb crater. The O-2 Bird Dog orbiting overhead rolls smoothly over onto his back pulling the nose of his aircraft earthward. As the FAC twists and turns leveling his wings, a rocket jumps from the wing of his aircraft. A small circular white ring of smoke marks the launch of the rocket as it streaks toward the hillside loaded with gooks. The "Willy Pete" the white phosphorus rocket explodes on the ridge, a perfect shot and a perfect marker for the F-4's bombs. As I look to the sky for some sign of our friends, BJ yells at us to get down as he leaps from the toe plate of the Huey's skid. Explosions rip the sides of our bomb crater LZ as I hear a loud cry and look up to see BJ spinning through the air in an exaggerated slow motion like a lazy windmill. Landing shoulders first in a heap near Rudder, BJ's body lays half in and half out of the crater. Rudder grabs him by the back of his nomex shirt and quickly pulls him into the crater with us. Sliding down further into the hole, I hear the shriek of the first jet and moments later the thunderous explosions of bombs. The shock wave ripples across the ground, hitting like a hammer, as the earth shakes from side to side.

Half sliding and pulling at the loose dirt in the bomb crater I make my way over to BJ's unconscious body. Rudder lays uphill next to the Bridge's side, his finger tips pressing at the throat checking for a pulse. "How is he Rudder?" I ask. Rudder just looks at me shaking his head slowly side to side. "Shit" is all I can think to say as I look at the mangled lower torso of my aircraft commander. I don't know where to start helping Rudder as we simultaneously reach for the torn and shredded nomex flight pants. Sand, blood and pieces of nomex pants mix together filling his wound as we gingerly try to clean it and see how bad it is. Huge chunks of flesh are missing from his right inner thigh, but we can discern no arterial bleeding as we rip the pants away from his wounds. Pulling at a piece of his nomex flight suit sticking in the wound causes BJ to awaken with a loud moan. Rudder and I each say together "take it easy BJ we got you," "you're gonna be fine" I hasten to say. He's obviously in shock as his open eyes just stare up at the sky. I lean over his face with my body protecting his eyes from the sun. There is no sign of recognition in the eyes that stare back at me. We need the medical first aid kit on the helicopter for BJ and the wounded Yards in the crater with us.

I climb to the edge of the crater just in time to see the second fighter release four more bombs. The five hundred pound bombs ripple off the wings, one off the left wing, followed moments later by one off the right wing, then the left wing and again the right. I watch as the fins extend out from the bombs creating drag to slow the bombs fall. The lead jet is just a glint of light in the sky, as the sun reflects off its canopy. I duck down below the edge of the crater knowing the concussive affect from the blast can take my head off. The jets loop around high overhead, each making another pass, dropping their bombs.

After the second bomb run it is deathly quiet. The ridge where the bad guys have been is blackened earth and twisted, torn stumps of trees. As I look up, I locate the fighters by their engine noise, black specks high in the afternoon sky. They extend out at the top of their loop, disappearing from my view. The gray of the aircraft makes it almost impossible to follow them in the brilliant blue sky. As I continue to watch, hoping to catch one more glimpse of them, listening to the noise of the engines fade away, I quickly say a prayer of thanks. I know they have been quite literally our salvation.

I scramble for the first aid kit on the Huey, not knowing if there are any bad guys left, I keep my body doubled over. Snatching the kit off the bulkhead; with one big leap I jump back into the LZ bomb crater rolling in a cloud of sand and dust as my momentum propels me down to BJ's side. The Bridge rolls his head from side to side coming out of shock. "Hey man" he says casually to me, "what happened?" "Ya dumb ass, you got hit by a mortar." I say in a scolding tone of voice, forgetting he's probably still out of it mentally. Bridge pushes his chin to his chest trying to look down the length of his body. Unable to see much, he begins pushing himself up to get a better view. "Whoa' there Boss," as I lay a hand on BJ's chest, "just lay back and take it easy so we can get ya patched up, OK?" Opening the kit, Rudder talks to BJ as he helps me with the compress bandages. We place the big cotton compress bandages on the exposed wounds of BJ's legs and tie them tight. Both his leather combat boots are mangled and torn. His right foot is more damaged than the left with half of his boot at the toes completely blown away. Not much we can do about that I think to myself. Boy I sure hope we get some help fast. The bandages we have put on BJ are already soaked and dripping blood.

Far to the West, where the jets had disappeared, I see the glint of sunlight like a sliver of glass, reflect once, then twice. As I continue to stare I can barely make out the dark specks of the fighters as they wing over and head back in on a flat trajectory. I am elated, maybe they're coming back to do a victory roll! One behind the other they come in fast and silent. They are traveling so fast, the roar of the engines is well behind them. As they get closer, the air crackles with an eerie sucking vacuum noise building into a crescendo of doom. A thin, wispy, grayish black trail of smoke streaking straight from the tail of the Phantoms is the only clue that this aircraft is hurtling along with enormous speed and power. Unlike the bombs, the napalm canisters they're dropping now are released twinkling, tumbling like glitter, twisting like confetti. The napalm splashes in a sheet of white hot, purplish blue and yellow flame across the defoliated and splintered tree line on the ridge. The napalm igniting so close, I feel the heat, the air rushing to fill the vacuum created by the sticky jellied flames.

Four tons of bombs and a thousand gallons of jellied gas has been dropped in less than five minutes on a ridge not bigger than two football fields.

Chapter Forty One

"Wow, what an air show, blow it into firewood, then burn it" the sergeant says as he cups his hands behind his head. He's lying on the side of the crater, head tilted back "catching a few rays." He continues, eyes closed "that's one of the best I ever seen, whatdaya think, Hham" as he directs his question to the Montagnard sitting on the edge of the crater next to him. Hham just smiles, nodding his head.

Bridge and the two wounded Yards lay quietly near the top edge of the bomb crater. The FAC droned high over head, providing some small comfort to us by his mere presence. Sitting in the crater, more assured we would get out, we have patched up and taken care of the wounded the best we can, as we sit and wait for our ride home. Still vigilant, watching the bamboo trail, I hear the throbbing wop of Huey rotor blades approaching long before they arrive. I hope they get here before I see someone I don't want to see coming down this trail, I think to myself. Damn, I'm ready to go home.

First to arrive is Ridge, my hooch mate and R&R buddy. As I looked up at him hovering twenty feet in the air, Preacher, Ridge's aircraft commander slides the Huey in close to the crater.

Flying in a high orbit overhead, keeping an eye on things is "Goober," Granger and Greg Distoné's bird.

As we load BJ and the wounded Yards into the Huey, Rudder, Craig and I clean out 644. The time involved to secure and attempt a recovery operation for 644 is too risky. Rudder has received authorization to destroy our bird in place. As we get the thumbs up from Ridge that they're loaded and ready to go I'm bumming out at having to leave 644 behind, let alone destroy it. "Let's do it," Rudder says. I grab the thermite grenade we carry just for this occasion; pulling the pin I shove it into the fuel tank of my bird. I give the side of my Huey a final pat on the engine cowling and run for Ridge's bird.

The heavy black smoke from the burning JP-4 jet fuel on my Huey billows straight up into the afternoon sky, as the helicopter burns quickly. The Preacher does a low orbit over it, the magnesium of the Huey burning with a white hot glow. The SF sergeant displays no show of emotion concerning our morning frolic in the jungle. Sitting at the door, one leg dangling out in the slipstream, he takes a long drink of water from his canteen. "So what the hell was out there," I finally ask him. "I have never seen so much ground fire in my life." He shrugs, but seeming more relaxed and conversational, he responds, "We ran into the 90th NVA Regiment I think, or elements of it. That's who we were going out to recon. They musta' moved on us during the night...I don't know. Close to three thousand NVA regulars out there I'd guess." As he continues, "Your pilot needed to know for his report, and the FAC guy needed it for those Marine F-4's that did the buzz job. They really kicked the shit outta them. Boy you guys really know how to live," he said, a hint of sarcasm in his voice. Luck was on our side, yeah, we really knew how to live. We had just wasted, crispy crittered, zapped, some percentage of a regiment of almost three thousand bad guys. This guy is way too cool for me. And that's the way it worked flying CCN's. Back to candy land. Damn, it was good to be going home.

Leaving BJ, my Boss, at the MASH hospital in Phu Bai was one of the most difficult things I have ever done. We had grown close as friends and warriors and I would miss him and his great flying skills immensely. Coupled with BJ being hit, Greg Distoné has had his fill of Sergeant Kaiser. Unknown to any of us in the flight platoon, he has requested a transfer to the infantry! His orders have arrived; it took only five days for the whole transfer to take place.

In our hooch that evening, he has given us the good news, bad news scenario. "What the hell is wrong with you Greg?" I ask. "I couldn't take Kaisers' shit anymore." We are numb. "Man you're fuckin' crazy." Ridge says. "You're going to get your ass wasted out there in the boonies." Greg just continues to make jokes. We are all feeling really bad...Like sick to our stomach bad and he's telling us jokes! I ask Greg "What do you got Greg, seven plus months to Deros?"..."Yeah." "What the hell Granger...did you know?" Granger just sits on his cot head hung low. He's as shocked as the rest of us. "That fucking Kaiser, he's gonna get his." I say. "Greg you know what you got yourself into?" Ridge asks. For the first time in a serious tone, Greg turns and faces all of us. "All I know is that I'm outta here tomorrow, no more Kaiser, no more bullshit. I'm going to miss you guys, but not the bullshit." "You're always gonna have the bullshit Greg, in one form or another. It's part and parcel to life." I say. He nods his head knowing I'm right...Unfortunately it's too late to change things now. The damage is done.

No aircraft to fly and time on my hands...not a good thing in Viet Nam. Sixty eight days and a wake up!

Chapter Forty Two

I have a new "H" model Huey and Beastie as my aircraft commander. I'm still leading a charmed life. "Better him than me, somebody else is gonna get it (hit, wounded, KIA) not me." I still hold onto that teenage belief of invincibility. I'm going to make it through this thing…No problem…

Went back to visit BJ the day after the excitement and they had already evacuated him to Japan. The mangled foot was the real problem. I'm bumming because we didn't even get to say an appropriate goodbye or exchange addresses, and Lord knows I probably would never see him again.

Returning after an easy day of flying I get the buzz that Greg Distoné has returned and is up in the company area. It's been only three weeks since Greg has left for his infantry company, but I'm excited to see him, and find out what's been going on.

Entering my hooch, Greg is laying on Grangers' bed like he's king of the hill. "Well look at the big ol' fat ugly dog the cat dragged in." I said. Actually it looked like Greg had lost twenty or thirty pounds off his large heavy frame. So I felt compelled to correct myself, and acknowledge the weight loss, Greg looked the picture of healthy living. "Well maybe not fat anymore, but you are sure still butt ugly!" "Sticks and stones" Greg says as he gives me one of his big smiles. Rolling out of the cot, he stands and gives me a warm hand shake followed with a big bear hug. Looking him in the eye I say "What's goin' on, you miss us so much, they let you come back and slum with us?" Sitting back on the cot, others from the flight platoon begin arriving to say their hello's and catch up with Greg too. Smiling and shaking hands with everyone, Greg says he's returned back to the rear for a maintenance stand down. Still giving Greg a hard line of good natured ribbing I say, "You've been gone like what, three weeks, and you're already taking a break! Man, that's like banker's hours. Show me where to sign up for the infantry." Greg responds as usual with a quick retort "Well we have plenty of room in my platoon now." With that, the story telling turns to a more serious note and all the joking stops as Greg tells of his time spent so far with his new unit. His head hangs down as he stares at the floor, his voice drifts to a monotone. He begins telling the story of his most recent action leading up to and returning back to "Evans" for the maintenance stand down.

"Five days ago we were doing a recon out in the hills near the Valley. Nothing big deal happened during the first day on the move. No contact, not even a hint that the bad guys were near. That night we set up in a night defensive position on a small hill. My platoon was at full strength, thirty two guys. They took out our 'LP's' first, our Listening Posts. Four guys 'wasted' man, no shit, 'gone', 'zapped'. That freaked us all out. Especially me, this would be my first contact, maybe even a firefight. Hell I was ready to have a continuous run of diarrhea." He tried to make a joke that none of us believed was meant to be funny. "We went on full alert. Then later during the night we got hit by a large NVA main force unit. We kicked their ass, we kicked their ass real bad." Greg says this in an almost detached manner. The story has just started, and we all just stand and listen, knowing that there's something else that's coming far more sinister than a fire fight with the gooks. "Well, the fog rolled in on us, and we couldn't get any support for the next three days. I don't know if you guys remember how the weather was out there?" He looked at us for some affirmation remembering the weather. Some of the guys shook their heads remembering how stinko the weather was in small pockets out in the mountains. "Well anyway, we couldn't get any direct support because they couldn't see or find us. They hit us for three days. They overran our position four times and we made em' pay real bad for that every time. But they got a lot of my guys." Once again Greg is detached, somewhere far away from our hooch and his flying friends, somewhere far away on a hill. "Yeah, we made them pay… but they made us pay too. Nine of us came out when we were extracted." As a group, we were speechless. I was stunned. And all this time Greg has been holding it in, making jokes.

"Hey, I made sergeant! I never get any respect around here; show a sergeant a little respect would ya!" We all kind of laughed and snickered, knowing Greg, still the jokester, was talking about and imitating Sergeant Kaiser. "They gave us the Silver Star, and I got a Purple Heart." Greg says. Granger says to Greg, "You mean you all got the Silver Star. All the guys left on the hill?" "Well no, really just me and another guy." Greg says, almost like he's embarrassed to mention it. This is the nation's third highest honor a soldier can receive for heroism, and he's embarrassed! Half the guys shout at the same time, "What did you do to get it?" "Nuthin' much, just kept my ass alive for four days." He obviously was not going to say anymore about it. "Where were you wounded?" I asked trying to change the subject for his benefit. "In my private area, and no, you cannot see it, or touch it" Greg says. The old Greg is back, fluttering his eyes in a come hither look. The blue mood has passed, and we deluge him with question upon question about life in the boonies, a hero in our midst. Greg spends two more days with us and leaves vowing to return again soon.

Chapter Forty Three

Flying North of Salt and Pepper on a resupply mission we get a call for an emergency extraction of a Marine Recon squad that is on the run from an NVA force of indeterminate size. The Marine grunts are being supported by a couple of Marine "C" model "Hog" gun ships. The Recon team is on the move in the tall elephant grass as we search for them. As we "low level" along the large undulating valley I notice movement on a small rise that is mostly a granite type of rock. Confirming the Recon teams' approximate position with Beastie, and realizing this could be the bad guys and not the team we are searching for, I immediately begin suppressing the rocks. As the tracers from my M-60 smack and ricochet off the rocks, I hold the machine gun level with our line of flight, letting Beastie do the deflection work for my machine gun as he banks and turns the helicopter. Tracer fire snaps at us from every position of the clock as Beastie weaves and "S" turns our bird. Just as we pass through level flight from one of Beastie's evasive moves, a gook stands up from his hiding place behind a large rock. His RPD 60 machine gun is leveled at our ship. Seeing the gook raising up, I have no time to adjust my aim to bring suppressive fire on the NVA soldier. The timing of the gook standing up is matched with Beastie's jinking. Following the track of my tracers spitting from my gun, the rounds are attracted like an iron to a magnet as they rip into the gooks chest and stomach. Looking into his eyes, he is looking at me, staring straight at me. I see a quick look of surprise on his face, his mouth open as his body snaps backwards, disappearing like a target hit on the rifle range. The haunting look of his eyes stays with me. As we go zooming by him, the machine gun he held slowly slides backward off the rock. It had all happened so fast that the only confirmation that it did happen was the gook RPD machine gun sliding ever so slowly backward off the rock.

Beastie talks with the Marine Recon lieutenant trying to find their location in the tall jungle grass, even as he flies evasive maneuvers with the Huey. I can hear the heavy labored breathing of the Marine LT, as they are continuously on the move evading the NVA. The lieutenant gives Beastie left and right directions until finally he tells Beastie to look for the waving flag of a tee shirt. One soldier sitting on the shoulders of another grunt sticks his M-16 above the jungle grass, tee shirt tied to the barrel waving it frantically. Jesse spots the flag as Beastie flies the Huey sideways toward the embattled grunts.

I feel my stomach flip flop as the floor falls away beneath me as Beastie unexpectedly dumps the collective and the Huey drops like a pancake into the lush jungle grass just to the side of the recon team. The rotor blades rip at the top of the jungle grass as the rotor wash turns the area into a hurricane of green turmoil.

The Marine grunts dive in belly first, or jump in like Olympic hurdlers all ass holes and elbows; any thought or semblance of an organized, disciplined extraction completely nonexistent. "We're good to go!" shouts the lieutenant as he surveys his team and simultaneously gives me the thumbs up. The look on his face as he twists to look back out the door of the Huey, his weapon pointed and ready to fire is enough to cause me to stare out the door myself. At that point it wouldn't have surprised me to expect North Vietnamese gooks to magically appear pushing through the maelstrom of flying grass and dust. Half out of my own fear of exactly that happening, and half out of instinct, I push down on the trigger of my M-60 and sweep the grass with fire from nose to tail. My right boot always rests reassuringly against the floor mic as I lift the toe of my boot and with a slight twist of my ankle key the mic; "We're clear, let's go Beast" I say excitedly. We can't get out of here too soon, as a cold shiver courses through my body that causes me to shake my shoulders involuntarily; death is walking on my grave.

It is a hot summer afternoon, and my Huey, with its load of Marines, struggles into the air. Our aircraft performance is degraded by the weight of bodies and jungle heat as Beastie struggles with the ship to lift and accelerate away from the demons fast approaching. As we break through the top of the jungle grass, ground fire erupts from below us. Blinks of light, the muzzle flashes of AK's, SKS's and RPD's dot the grass as the soldiers behind the weapons are indistinguishable, almost invisible forms, as the moving jungle grass sweeps over them like a surging ocean. Shifting my fire to suppress the now distinct threat, I feel bullets "thwacking" at the fuselage and floor boards of our bird.

The Marine gun ships are not very effective with their covering rocket fire. Our co-pilot, a FNG, is screaming at the Marine gun ships for more fire support. Not really paying any attention to the conversation but hearing it nonetheless, it is a distorted and broken communication. I hear him yelling, almost shrieking like a woman, unrecognizable as the same man who only minutes before had a richly timbered pitch to his voice. I am annoyed by his lack of control regardless of the situation we're in.

This doesn't look or feel good to me. The panic that surrounds me is contagious, and I fight back the knot of fear twisting in my aching stomach. Bullets continue to hit the aircraft and the cabin as the Marines we have just rescued are bucking and jumping as they are hit by shrapnel and incoming ground fire.

Craig and I had earlier in the month adapted Cobra mini-gun ammo cans to hold almost eight thousand runs of 7.62 millimeter ammunition loosely folded into a can that normally holds ten thousand rounds. The standard issue ammo can held only two hundred rounds, and when we were in heavy contact, it was a pain in the ass to change ammo cans in the middle of a firefight. It had proven to be a very easy and utilitarian concept, along with the minigun can affording us some limited protection for our lower legs from shrapnel. It gave me some small comfort now to be shooting almost nonstop without worry of running out of ammo. I had been shooting continuously for over five minutes, and had gone through at least three thousand rounds during that time.

We have traveled no more than a mile, unable to get through the translational lift. The "hits" on the helicopter are taking a toll on engine performance. The Huey, unable to carry the load of grunts, settles back gently into the grass.

While jumping out of the Huey to get Beastie's bullet shield and door opened, my right leg collapses under me. No pain, it's like I've slipped in wet grass. Looking down to see what I've slipped on, my pants are soaked in blood. "Shit" is all I can think to say as I struggle awkwardly to stand; one of the Marines lifts me up like a rag doll and sets me on the floor of the Huey. "Pop his door for me would ya'" nodding my head in the direction of Beastie as I start surveying my wounded leg. The jar head opens Beastie's door as I tell him how to slide Beastie's bullet shield back.

Beastie jumps out quickly and begins to survey the situation, not realizing I've been hit. As I lift my leg and pull the bloused trouser from my boot Beastie does a double take. In mid-stride going in the opposite direction he turns and rushes to my side. "You hit Lot?" I can see the immediate concern on his face, and hear the worry in his voice. "Yeah I think so" I say stupidly. I mean after all, there's a lot of blood on my pant's leg. But it doesn't hurt at all. I have a copper metallic taste in my mouth as I impatiently yank at my nomex trousers to pull the pants up to see the damage; I feel the pants drag across something like a big sliver. "Yow, ow, now that hurts" as I unwillingly utter a yelp of both pain and surprise. Again Beastie standing there bends over talking to me trying to minister my wound. "I'm okay, I'm okay" as I push his hands away from the flesh wound on my leg. I'm embarrassed by the attention Beastie is giving to me. "Really Beastie, I'm okay," not really knowing in my heart of hearts if I am or not.

Ignoring me, Beastie grabs the first aid kit, wiping the blood away from my leg while constantly hitting the sliver of metal that's stuck in my leg. "Stop Beast, there's something in my leg; I've been hit by shrapnel from something." Sliding my fingers pensively down my leg to the big metal sliver, I wiggle it slowly side to side and think about best/worse case outcome for two seconds. Then I think "what the hell," before I grasp the edge and yank it out with a quick pull. Blood bubbles from the open wound as Beastie jams the compress bandage over the jagged cut tying the bandage securely over the wound. Although my leg is sore as hell, there appears to be no serious damage done. Compress bandage in place, I hobble around getting my gun off the mount and setting it up.

It is deathly quiet, unlike only moments before, when the staccato hammering of gunfire and aerial rockets had permeated the area surrounding the crash site. A stiff breeze blows over the jungle grass bending it in a rhythmic, undulating motion. Almost like the ebb and tide of the ocean, captivating if you could just concentrate on the peacefulness of the setting, which under the current circumstances would be impossible. Very little of the breeze reached ground level as the heat and humidity of the day drenched my flight nomex with perspiration, turning it into a soaking rag that clung to my body trapping more heat rather than dissipating it.

The only disturbance to our silence is the Marine gun ships orbiting high overhead making occasional rocket and gun runs around our position. The Marines had established a defensive perimeter around our Huey. Claymores were set, fields of fire established and rules of engagement to contact agreed upon. I was scared shitless. We are at the Alamo. No surrender here. Shit! The only comforting thought is that we have Marine gun cover, such as it was, and help in the form of a Ghost Rider certainly on the way. We listen. The ears acutely attuned to the slightest difference in the noise of our surroundings. Time passes. Craig comes low crawling under the belly of the Huey to my position. His earpiece for his transistor radio shoved in his ear. Getting up close to me, personally a little too close for my liking, he whispers “They’re walking on the moon.” “No shit” I whisper back to him. He gives me a big smile.

Great! I’m going to die today. No doubt about it in my mind. I have that fragmentation grenade by my side again. The only thing is, my parents will remember and struggle with this meaningful day the rest of their lives. Craig keeps on smiling. I don’t tell him what I’m thinking… What for? He’s happy, I guess. “Cool…get back to your gun.” Another smile and he low crawls back to his machine gun.

The word is…no shooting, unless we have a visible target. That works for me I think to myself. My leg is throbbing now, the pain slowly intensifying, black and blue surrounds the deep purple of the calf muscle. A disturbance in the grass that is somewhat distinguishably different from the soft rustling of the grass in the wind catches my ear. Ahhh….I’m just nervous, hearing things….But the Marines on either side of me have heard something too. Everyone is very alert now. I can feel that old adrenaline rush pumping into my body…a feeling that is discernible from any other I’ve ever felt. And I have only felt it a few times, all of them in the Republic of Viet Nam…Voices now, soft and muffled. Gooks! The grunts say you can smell them before you see them. Well I beg to differ, I heard them, and then I smelled them. Wow…..

The gooks are at my twelve o’clock and moving towards us. The Marine gun ships continue to orbit high above, oblivious to our plight. Why don’t they see them? Why don’t they fire those dink asses up? A flurry of hand and arm signals is quickly exchanged between the Marines in our hastily set defensive perimeter surrounding the helicopter. The exchange of signals between the recon grunts is quick and succinct. Not a word is spoken, but a simple plan of action is communicated and understood by the small Marine recon team. It's like watching deaf people communicate. The Gyrene on either side of me pulls a frag grenade holding it high at arms length. The Marines all around the Huey are doing the same thing. I watch in fascination if not in total horror, as they move their arms in unison. One potato, two potato, three potato and they throw the grenades in an exaggerated arcing motion to their front. I go to a prone position counting…three….four….wham, wham, wham blasts all around the Huey as the fragmentation grenades do their nasty work.

Quiet. Real quiet now. The dinks know we're close, but where? The lieutenant sends out two men with K-bars to find out where they are. Thirty minutes has elapsed since the grenade toss. Where the hell are the Ghost Riders? Then the rhythmic thump in my chest, not my heart, but the throbbing of those lovely, dear Hueys. I detect it as if a doctor listening to the heart of a patient. Sensitive to the mildest of vibrations, help is coming. I detect the high speed rotor noise of Cobras! Alright! I am physically and emotionally drained. I lay my head on the feed cover of my M-60. No more today, please Lord. I say a silent prayer of thanks.

A purple smoke grenade envelops the crash site as the Cobras "box" my downed Huey with rockets, 40 millimeter grenades and mini gun fire. The Marines each throw two more grenades into their field of fire. As the Cobras make strafing passes over the crash site, the Ghost Riders are there to make our extraction. Lifting out and away from my Huey, it appears like its ready to fly. I am sad that I have to leave another bird in the jungle. For the short time I had it, she performed admirably for me and our crew.

Chapter Forty Four

A couple of days rest for my leg wound had rejuvenated my soul and spirit. It's blazing hot, and my three fans are unable to keep up with the heat in our hooch. My Huey unbeknownst to me had been "hooked" back to the Haunted House and repaired almost as good as new. So I was right back in the thick of things and loving it, because that meant I could fly in the wild blue cooool again!! Forty four days and a wake up!

The bullet holes on my bird are giving it that "lived in" look. I walk around the Huey getting reacquainted. We haven't flown my ship since our attempted extraction of the Marine patrol. I notice four bullet holes in the mini-gun can that holds my ammunition for the machine gun. That was where the shrapnel from my leg wound must have come from I muse. When the bullets fly it was always a mystery as to where those rounds would or could go.

Doing a post-flight inspection of my bird, I see Granger walking up to the flight line from the company area. He must have had an early day. The machine guns are off the mounts and the doors are closed on his bird. As he approaches I give him a big smile that quickly evaporates. The look on his face is one

I've seen before on other faces bearing bad news. Not comprehending what it could be, I wait for him to speak. He looks at me, his facial expression a mask of pain. "What?" I ask. Still just staring at me, he's on the verge of tears. "What Jim?" I say again. "Greg" is all he can whisper, forced from his choked up throat. "What…what about Greg?" My heart is pounding out of my chest…"Come on man, what's wrong, what's happened?" I raise my hands up, grasping for understanding, my hands open and close. I feel like forcibly shaking whatever information he has to say out of him. I holler, "Dammit Jim…what happened… tell me…?" "He's dead" is all he can say. Greg's been gone less than two weeks, after spending three days with us on his maintenance stand down. Granger's body heaves a big sigh like he's unable to catch his breath, followed by a moaning, as he tries to hold back the tears…putting my arm around his neck, I comfort him while in my own misery I can't catch my breath. My throat hurts choking back tears and overwhelming emotion. My arm wrapped around his neck, a hard knot of pain in my stomach, I feel like I am going to be physically sick. I wonder how, why, when...does it all end.

Standing in silence by the Huey, Granger finally says "He was watching an artillery shoot; he was sitting on a bunker watching a fucking artillery barrage. He was killed by a short round." I can't believe what I'm hearing. What a waste of human life. Killed by friendly fire; he wouldn't have been there had it not been for that prick Kaiser forcing him, harassing him to make an irrational decision like joining the infantry. Kaiser was gonna get his. What goes around comes around. I'd make sure of that.

Only days after Greg's death, we suffer another loss close to home. And in some mysterious way, the unfolding chain of events makes retribution for Greg's death possible. Earlier that same week, one of our Ghost Riders was shot down over by the Eagle's Nest during a re-supply log mission. The Huey had crashed in an LZ that was quite steep, reminiscent of hill 937. The hydraulic reservoir had been hit and the helicopter had lost hydraulic pressure resulting in a loss of control and ultimate crash. Staff Sergeant Gilmoyers' helicopter was dispatched from

Camp Evans with a spare hydraulic reservoir to replace the damaged one, and hopefully the downed bird could be flown out instead of having a Chinook hook it out. Gilmoyers' bird landed at the crash site facing uphill. In his haste to get to the downed helicopter, Sergeant Gillmoyer ran forward thru the arc of the Huey's main rotor blade. He was instantly decapitated at the shoulders. The news of his death and the way in which it happened really disturbed the company and more directly our flight platoon. It was such a waste. A careless lapse of situational awareness and Murphy's Law came into play. "If anything can go wrong, it will."

Having the most time in grade as an E-5, I am made assistant flight platoon sergeant under Sergeant Kaiser. A sadistic streak runs through me, this is going to be fun in a real bad way! Kaiser and I working together, what a concept! He knows I hate him, yet is unable to do anything about it now that I'm assistant platoon sergeant. Not joking, I remind him how I'll get his stripe if he gets wasted. I really want your stripe, I tell him. I will wear that bloody rocker on my arm with pride, 'cuz that means you'll be dead. Please don't come back anytime soon either! It's been over a week since Greg was killed; we miss him and his humor. I hold the payback position for Greg, and paybacks are a bitch, Kaiser!

Lying in my cot one morning, catching up on some much needed rest, I'm on a maintenance stand down. My serene atmosphere is suddenly disrupted by Sergeant Kaiser. Kaisers arm is holding up my parachute privacy curtain, his body half in, half out of my area. He screams at me "What da' yre' doin' in the rack sergeant?" Rolling over on my side facing Kaiser, I blink my eyes trying to orient myself and shake the sleep from my brain. "What" I say. Kaiser explodes; "What the hell…get outta bed. What kind of example are you setting for your men? You're sleeping, your helicopter is filthy, some assistant platoon sergeant you make. I wanna see you on the flight line in ten minutes." With that, Kaiser drops my parachute covering and stomps from the hooch the screen door slamming with a hard bang behind him. "What the hell is his problem?" Rubbing my eyes with the palms of my hands, I try to understand what has just happened. I am on maintenance stand down. I can sleep if I want to, that's what standing down is all about. I pull on a pair of cut off jungle fatigues; throw on a sleeveless tee shirt, slip on my Ho Chi Minh rubber sandals and walk over to flight operations. Walking into the darkened flight operations hooch, the air conditioning feels great. "Hey sarge" I say to Sergeant Dassell, flight operations NCOIC. "Hey Lot" he says as he turns his head from a pile of paperwork he's sifting through. "Just confirm …I am on maintenance stand down today and tomorrow right?" Looking at the schedule board he nods "Yup, you sure are. Why don't you go catch some more sleep?" he says. "Too bad your bird wasn't scheduled today" he smiles. "Yah isn't it. Hey…thanks a lot." I give Dassell a wave of my arm as I exit the operations hooch heading for the flight line.

Coming up from the rice paddy swamp I can see Kaiser up on the roof of my helicopter. He's moving the scissors up and down, bending over looking at something. My blood is starting to boil; who the hell does he think he is screwing with my bird. Still more than twenty yards from my bird I shout at him, with loathing oozing in my voice "What's your problem?" "You're my problem" he says with disgust in his voice. "Look here" he says, pointing to the gimble ring as I vault up to the roof, barely feeling for the hidden kick steps on the copilots side of the fuselage. My emotions were launching me up the side of the helicopter. I am on the verge of throwing his ass off the deck, barely able to contain the hatred I feel for him. "What" I say again. Without answering, Kaiser runs his small finger under and around the inside of the gimble ring. Pulling his finger out with a nickel size gob of grease on his finger nail, he says, "Look at this." "Yeah, what about it?" Without giving him a chance to respond, understanding the game he wants to play, I say "Are you kidding me? You got me outta bed for that! I sure hope you found some grease under there. I don't think I'd be flying this crate if it wasn't lubricated." With that I jumped from the roof of the helicopter to the ground. My ankles hurt like hell hitting the ground, but that pain was feeling pretty good right about then. I could hear Kaiser ferociously kicking the face plates on the hidden fuselage steps as he came off the top of the helicopter. Hollering behind me "You're going to get this bird in shape, or I'll have your stripes" he says as I feel him close behind me. "Oh yeah!" I continue to walk away from him, back towards the swamp and company area, "Well if you want that shit cleaned off, do it yourself asshole.... I'll be in my rack, enjoying my maintenance stand down!" As far as I was concerned, Kaiser had been warned. But Kaiser is unrelenting, his bully attitude sureness that he has the upper hand, just like all the other times he's played mind games with the junior members in his charge. But this time will be different I think to myself, I've had it up to my ears with him. Half running to catch up to me, Kaiser grabs my left shoulder with his hand, slowing me and turning me in the same motion. That was all it took to end this argument as I spun in front of him. My close, dearly departed friend Greg Distoné is clearly on my mind and it was time for a little payback. A look of startled surprise on his face quickly changed to a look of object fear as my eyes met his. My unmasked revulsion and hatred for him caused him to pull his hand away from me in an instinctive, almost defensive motion. As he loosened the grip on my shoulder, the turning momentum of my body with all the force and hatred transferred to my right shoulder and clenched fist met squarely under his jaw. Hitting him with a savage upper cut, behind the punch is all the energy and emotion of four months of bullshit and harassment that like a festering wound, needs to be tended to. I hit Kaiser so hard, I hear his teeth click and crack as the force of the punch lifts him off the ground. His eyes roll into the back of his head like a capsizing boat as his unconscious body, his legs buckling under him, hits the ground like a limp rag doll. I stand over him, fists clenched at my sides. "You're the one that should be dead you son-of-a-bitch." I say over his motionless body. My body is shaking and quivering with rage hoping he will get up so I can hit him again. Finally I turn, some of my anger vented, I walk back to my hooch.

It didn't take long for the shit to hit the fan... Forty-five minutes later an orderly from Company headquarters was pushing my parachute aside giving me the follow me hand motion. "The C.O. wants to see you." He said. Here we go, I thought.

Walking into the orderly room the first shirt looks at me and shakes his head. Unable to read his body language, I just figure it's gonna be what it will be. Top wouldn't look me in the eye as he got up from his desk, knocked on the wall to the C.O.'s office and disappears behind the curtain hanging in the doorway. The silent treatment is not a good sign I think to myself. Can they send me to LBJ? Christ, I hadn't thought about that!

Top pulls back the curtain separating the orderly room from the C.O.'s office and motions for me to enter. Standing at attention, I snap the C.O. a crisp, by the book salute. "Sergeant Lahti reporting as ordered sir." The C.O. "Papa" is not wasting any time as he looks me up and down, leaning back in his chair. "What's your side of the story sergeant?" "What am I being charged with sir?" The C.O., who was a good man, narrows his eyes looking at me, his arms rest on the arms of his chair. "Are you playing a game with me sonny?" "No Sir!" I respond. "Well at the moment, you're not being charged with anything. I just want to know what the hell happened." A slight agitation in his voice now. I proceed to tell him the story, rhyme and verse, on everything that had transpired since Kaiser had stormed into my hooch. On occasion Papa will stop me to clarify a point and then motion for me to carry on. I also tell him that I was defending myself, as Sergeant Kaiser had approached from behind and had assaulted me while I was walking away from the helicopter. When I mentioned the assault on my person, the C.O.'s head snapped up, leaning forward in his chair, looking at me, eyes narrowed to slits. Behind clenched teeth he said "So you're saying this is self defense?" "Yes sir, I believe that's my position. I would not have struck the sergeant had he not surprised me by grabbing my shoulder." I didn't see why I should make it easier for them to hang me. "I see" he responds, as he sits back in the chair. The first sergeant hasn't moved during the entire discourse of our conversation. Looking up at Top the C.O. asks "Do you have any questions for Sergeant Lahti?" "Only one sir; Lahti do you realize how much trouble you can be in, if we find you guilty of assaulting a senior officer?" "Yes sergeant, I realize that."

“Okay, you’re dismissed Sergeant Lahti.” The C.O. says. “Yes sir, thank you sir.” Giving the C.O. another crisp salute, I turn on my heel catching Top’s eye as I turn. He shakes his head again slowly as he looks at me and then turns to look at the C.O.

Later that same afternoon I am once again called to the orderly room. Sergeant Kaiser is sitting in a chair conversing with Top but stops immediately as I walk in. I look hard at Kaiser, assessing the damage I may have done to his jaw. It looks real sore. It’s going to definitely be a beautiful black and blue face for a while. He returns my stare, glaring at me. I smile, as I slowly walk past him to an empty chair. I turn my head so only he can hear as I slowly settle in the chair next to him “Fuck you shit bird.” Kaiser immediately jumps to his feet as I sit down looking only at Top or the orderly who is desperately trying to ignore the whole tense atmosphere. Kaiser, not knowing how to bring this new charge of insolence to Top without looking like he’s grinding his axe on me sits back down.

As I sit down, Top gets up once again, and goes through the motions of knocking and entering the C.O.’s office. Without ever fully entering the inner office, he turns and motions for both me and Kaiser to enter. My anger is slowly beginning to swell up in me as I feel my blood heading for the boiling point again. The mere sight of this puke next to me rubs me the wrong way. Not caring about courtesy, rank or feelings I walk in ahead of Kaiser before he can stand and go ahead of me into the C.O.’s office. I see him smirk, like the cat that ate the canary, as I return the look with one of my own.

Entering the office, Magnet Ass, my platoon leader stands at the side of the desk next to the C.O. Well this doesn’t look very good, I think to myself. Kaiser, following close behind me, stands next to me as we simultaneously salute Papa. “Sergeant Lahti, we have heard both sides of the altercation between you and Sergeant Kaiser.” “Yes sir” I respond. He continues, “We feel that in the interest of fairness, to both you and Sergeant Kaiser, based on the facts and circumstances presented, that if you would make a formal apology to Sergeant Kaiser, we can forgive this unfortunate incident and carry on." Catching a side long glance at Kaiser, I can tell this is not what he had expected at all. His mouth drooped open, a hint of a chipped tooth, and then quickly closes as his cheek twitches from a nervous tick. Good, I think. Screw you asshole. I guess going to jail isn't an option they want to put on the table for me. Pausing for a minute to think and phrase my answer, I carefully and slowly respond so the full impact of what I'm going to say is not lost in translation. "Sir, based on my feelings pertaining to Sergeant Kaiser, and the circumstances surrounding not only this attack on my person, but the constant verbal and mental harassment placed on other members of my flight platoon, I respectfully decline your offer to make any form of apology ever to Sergeant Kaiser." Not pausing to let them respond, I half turn and look at Kaiser, a smug look pasted on his face as he realizes that I won't apologize. As I continue, "Furthermore Sir, I wouldn't let Sergeant Kaiser lick the sweat off my balls if I met this scumbag dying of thirst in the middle of the Sahara Desert...Sir!" Kaiser's mouth dropped open again, smug look gone from his face as his jaw and lips moved, forming unintelligible garble. That pretty much put the lid on any easy way out for them to shove the whole affair under the carpet so to speak...

I guess they were all stunned by my pronouncement, as a full thirty seconds lapsed before the Major dismissed Magnet Ass and Kaiser from his office. "Sergeant Lahti, you give me no choice but to find you guilty under Article 15 for misdeeds pertaining to your comments and actions resulting in the assault on Sergeant Kaiser." "Yes sir" I respond. "If I may make a comment sir." The Major nods, "Keep it clean sergeant." I smile, "Yes sir." "Sergeant Kaiser has unduly harassed, hassled, belittled and browbeat the flight crews of first platoon. His character is Napoleonic. He is unintelligent, unable and unfit to run a flight platoon. He commands neither the respect nor the following of the soldiers under his command. He is also directly responsible for Specialist Distoné requesting a transfer to the infantry from our company over a month ago, and indirectly his death in the field. What man in his right mind would volunteer to go from an aviation unit to an infantry line unit if there wasn't more to it than meets the eye? What more can I say about an individual who disrupts the flow of the green machine by his mere presence." "What about Distoné? What haven't I heard?" The C.O. asks. "I had brought the matter to the attention of Cracker Jack several months ago Sir, and I feel it was being handled through him and Sergeant Gilmoyer. But since Cracker Jack was killed back on 937, and more recently the death of Sergeant Gilmoyer; I don't believe Magnet Ass has been aware of the conflict Sergeant Kaiser is creating in the flight platoon." "I see" Papa says "Okay, you are no longer assistant flight platoon sergeant, but you retain your rank as a Specialist Five, three months deduction of pay, and if one more thing happens with you around here, I'll bust you to Private E nothing and ship YOUR ass to the infantry! Are we understood?" "Yes sir" "Then get outta here" as he waves his hand at me, shooing me away like a bothersome fly.

Relieved as I walk from the orderly room, I feel justice has somehow been served for Greg, and someone in power is now aware of the Little Hitler running first flight platoon. Within two weeks of the fight on the flight line Sergeant Kaiser is transferred out of the 158th Aviation Battalion. Jerry Hollandale is justifiably promoted to Staff Sergeant in charge of first flight platoon. In some meager way justice may have been served. But somewhere, somehow, Kaiser would someday get his in spades. Of that I was sure. Thirty-two days and a wake up to go.

Chapter Forty Five

Another CA, another combat assault. Our S-2, our intelligence section at Battalion H.Q. forecast it to be hot according to Beastie. Hot meaning we can expect to take fire on the way in, and on the ground. They have information indicating definite signs of bunkers, and activity on high speed trails. The months of late spring and summer have run together. Flying endless assaults, some ass and trash, there's no more bullshit. Principally, we are taking the war to the bad guys. It has been emotionally trying, and downright scary more often than I care to think about. Unlike my first days and months with the Ghost Riders, when we went looking for trouble, we see action in some form every day. Whether we are taking fire, doing an emergency med-evac, carrying body bags or prisoners out of the field, we are always closely in touch with war and death.

August 20, 1969, I am a "two digit midget," as the shortimers say. Twenty days and a wake up, and I'm outta here. Back to the world, and round eyes. I'm trying to figure out when I'll quit crewing my bird. People buy the farm, get killed in action, "KIA," generally in the first month they arrive in country. They get hit either because they're too stupid, or they're too ignorant of how easy it is to die, how cheap life really is. Or, generally you get it in the last month because you're too cautious or hesitant, and don't move or get out of the way fast enough. I've made it past that first month, almost a year ago now. And I'm definitely trying to stay in the groove, be cool, and not become a statistic myself by being overly cautious. I mentally prepare myself for the assault. It's a fine day to die, but somebody else, not me. "Better him than me," this has become the mantra that I live by. It's just another day, but nonetheless, I steel myself and my emotions for the worst case scenario, and hope for the best case outcome.

The machine guns, seasoned and well used, are cleaned and oiled, ready for action. No more worries about rusty ammunition, we're shooting all the time now. My M-203 tucked behind my left shoulder, on the seat with me, locked and loaded, is easy to reach in one fluid motion, and always ready at a moment's notice should my M-60 jam up.

Beastie has become an excellent aircraft commander, as I knew he would be. His technical skills are flawless, and he exudes a confidence that always allows me to feel safe and secure, knowing he'll make the right decisions.

We are number two in formation behind the Magician, Magnet Ass. Our load of five grunts, on board with full gear, look as if they've been around the block a couple of times. We all know the game plan. The assault, a couple of "kliks" east of the Laotian border is south of the A Shau Valley on gently rolling terrain. Interspersed with not quite mountains or escarpments are these ridges of rock outcropping. Our LZ is a natural grassy field on the side of a rock outcropping flanked on three sides by jungle. The approach will be made flying into the open end of the three sided box of jungle. This is a free fire zone, and after dropping the grunts, we'll fly straight out, suppressing the area with machine gun fire as we go. It seems like a straight forward CA.

Looking back at our platoon formation, I feel like I'm in the groove. Our company is a seasoned "Slick" company now. We have all had in some way or another our trial by fire and as a team, all the flight crews work exceptionally well.

Our Cobras from Delta Company, the "Redskins" our "gun company" are forward of the initial assault bringing doom and gloom to the LZ and surrounding country side with 2.75 inch high explosive rockets. Some are equipped with 7.62 mm mini-guns blazing; others suppress the area with 40 millimeter grenade launchers. It is good close fire support, and being a two digit midget I really appreciate it.

Turning to look forward, my dark visor dropped down against the glare of the sun in my eyes, I see Hollandale pull his M-60 out and begin to suppress forward into the LZ and surrounding jungle. We are flying thirty second intervals. From the moment the Magician pulls out of the LZ, we will be touching down thirty seconds later. This will get our entire infantry company on the ground in the shortest amount of time.

Following Jerry Hollandale's lead, I begin to suppress the jungle fixating on the white hot gasses squirting from the flash suppressor on the end of the machine gun barrel. Instead of just random shooting however, I shoot at likely areas that could hide an enemy bunker, a machine gun, or a soldier lying prone in the rolling grass. Like a child picking at his food, I selectively put a ten round burst of 7.62 millimeter on this knoll that tree line, or that hummock of grass. Waiting for that blink of light, puff of smoke or dust, or a streaking tracer indicating return fire, I pick away at the jungle.

"The LZ is cold," Magnet Ass announces as I look forward watching the infantry grunts fan away on two sides from his helicopter. Both Craig and I simultaneously cease firing upon hearing Magnet Ass' pronouncement of a cold LZ.

The grunts move out twenty yards from the LZ, taking a knee as they face out and away from the LZ, weapons at the ready, alert and waiting for guidance from their platoon leader. I swing my M-60 towards the rear of our bird as I watch the platoon leader with his "RTO" his radio telephone operator; kneel in the knee high grass. I notice the RTO's whip antenna is characteristically tucked into his LBE so as not to get chopped up by the approaching Huey's rotor blades. Thinking about that whip antenna, I look up at my rotor blades and then to ground level assuring that we will have sufficient rotor clearance in the Z.

Just as Magnet Ass pulls out of the LZ, Craig says "We're taking fire….." as his machine gun fires three or four rounds and then falls silent. I feel, more than hear the rounds impacting the helicopter. "What the hell!" I automatically squeeze the trigger on my M-60. I'm not following the trail of tracer rounds spewing from my gun, but more instinctively shooting for survival, as an immediate sense of foreboding comes over me.

Looking towards the jungle edge, I spot everything I had been looking for only a moment earlier. Hidden bunkers become visible as muzzle flashes from automatic weapons and tracer fire is erupting up and down the tree line. I return fire, twenty or thirty rounds at each muzzle flash I can see, shifting fire without let up, a thousand rounds jump from my gun trying to give Beastie some protection.

Continuing to suppress the jungle with machine gun fire, in my periphery I see the three grunts sitting on my side of the cargo bay, their legs dangling out of the cargo door are agitated. They are shifting on their butts, their shoulders moving side to side as they drag their rucksacks across the helicopter deck, scooting closer to the edge of the cargo bay, ready to jump. I know that the infantry guys hate riding on helicopters. They feel vulnerable and exposed, with nowhere to hide, nowhere to go. I understand their concern, but we are still a hundred feet off the ground, moving at sixty miles an hour!

Putting suppressive fire on individual targets, I simultaneously turn to reassure the grunts sitting next to me to wait a few more seconds before jumping. What has been initially a drizzle of hostile fire turns into a torrential down pour of enemy ground fire. As I open my mouth to speak, the entire instrument panel of my bird explodes into a thousand pieces of glass and metal. The windshields are systematically holed and splintered with incoming fire. Pee Wee our co-pilot is the first to get hit as his back arches and he pitches forward in his armored seat. Beastie instinctively ducks his head trying to make himself as small a target as possible. I watch his body shudder as enemy fire also hits him.

Then, as if in slow motion, Beastie, unconscious and slouching to the left in his seat, drags the cyclic stick to the left. The Huey pitches slowly up into a nose high attitude simultaneously rolling to the left. The grunts are jumping and falling from the helicopter even as we begin to roll.

As I watch us roll to the left, the only thing I focus on is the swaying yellowish green grass. Time is beginning to stand still. Looking straight at the grass, the chopper has rolled over ninety degrees, the ground is close and rushing up to meet me. I am falling from the helicopter as I try to grab and brace myself for the inevitable. I think of my parents, my brothers and sister, knowing it's all over. I see each of them sequentially framed in special moments in time, like watching a slide show. And the only pervasive thought I have is how I won't get a chance to say good-bye to them. It is a very sad feeling.....

Chapter Forty Six

The turbine engine is screaming. It reminds me of pushing the gas pedal to the floor on a parked car, and listening to the engine shriek. Only this is much louder, and from the sound of it, it's ready to come unglued, it's ready to explode.

I am disoriented. I try opening my eyes, but they're full of dirt, and I squint back the tears as the dirt scratches my eyes. As I try to move my hand, all I can feel is the dirt and grass in my hands. I can feel my arm is still attached to my body, so I walk my fingers like a crab along the ground or whatever is in front of my face to my helmeted head. I grab the edge of my plexiglas shaded visor and push it up. As I wriggle my fingers between my helmet and forehead, I sweep my eyes clear, blink, and tear my eyes clean.

The engine's noise is ear-piercing, as I desperately try to figure out what has happened. Squinting through the tears and dirt, I turn my head more to the side as I see a sliver of bright light to my right. The Huey has crashed on the left side and I am face down in the earth still strapped into my seat. My M-60 is crushed beneath me. As I become more aware of my surroundings, the pistol grip of the machine gun has crushed my chicken plate. The cracked pieces of chest protector pressed into my chest makes me painfully aware that I must get out of there. The cargo deck of the Huey is almost perpendicular to the ground. Understanding now what is up and down, I do a push up on my knees, as I lean up against the twisted tubing of my seat.

Looking up and over my right shoulder, Pee Wee our co-pilot has been thrown through the Plexiglas windshield of the Huey. His shoulder strap inertia reel has obviously failed, and his feet rest on the radio console of the ship. As I wiggle through the collapsed space between my seat and the cargo deck, I see the arms, legs and torso of a grunt crushed under the helicopter. As I stand, I try to not step on the body, but there is so very little space that it is impossible not to.

Craig's upper torso is leaning out of his seat into the cargo deck; his arm hangs down resting on what was the aft bulkhead of the Huey. "Craig" I holler his name. I push myself up actually standing level with his head. Craig's clear visor is down, his eyes are closed. He actually appears to be sleeping. Just where the visor retracts into the helmet is a spider web crack with a hole in the center of the web. Even now a bubble of blood is filling the hole, threatening to spill from it. There is nothing I can do for him.

Beastie had been held in his seat by the seat belt and shoulder harness. Not knowing if he is still alive, I cannot reach around to him because of the wreckage and the way the helicopter is positioned. I break the safety wire on the red quick release handles behind his seat and pull the seat rearward toward me. As the seat tilts backward, Beastie groans softly and I'm elated he's still alive.

Carefully I put two fingers on Beastie's neck checking his pulse "Beastie, it's Lot, can you hear me?" Beastie's head moves slightly to the left as his eyes flutter under closed lids. "Just take it easy…, relax…, I've got ya now guy. You're going to be okay." I try to comfort him, to reassure him we'll make it out of this, not really believing that we'll even make it through the next few seconds. I don't want Beastie to shock out on me. His pulse is weak but steady, as I look at his wounds. It appears Beastie has been hit by two rounds each in the right arm and leg and one round through his left foot. The bleeding is manageable as I grab the emergency first aid kit hanging on the bulkhead. I hurriedly bandage him as best I can, the engine still screaming.

Fearing the complete disintegration of the engine and possible fire, I leave Beastie, knowing he'll be alright for the time being. The crashed helicopter is positioned in a manner that will afford him protection for the moment from any further hostile gun fire.

I pull myself up and kick out the remaining Plexiglas in the windshield of the Huey. Jumping headfirst through the hole in the windshield I'm immediately engaged by fire from further up the hill. Incoming fire is zipping through the air. I am protected momentarily by the nose and belly of the Huey as it lies on its side. I low crawl under and around the nose of the ship, peeking around, I continue to crawl to the downhill side of the Huey for protection.

The rotor blades of the Huey have sheared off, and mere stumps of the blades are all that is left on the rotor hub. The Huey's turbine engine, "unloaded" of the huge rotor blades mass, screams in agony. Threatening to explode at any second, in a panic, I can't remember how to shut the engine down.

Two grunts protected by the angle of the hillside are shooting at the unseen enemy below. As I crawl along the roof of the Huey which is now the downhill side of the ship, I pick up an M-16 lying in the grass. The engine compartment cowling has been torn open exposing the two-inch stainless steel mesh fuel line. Two more grunts lay contorted and unmoving just aft of the sheared off tail rotor. I recognize one of them who had been riding on my side of the ship. From five feet I empty the M-16 magazine into the fuel line. Jet fuel spews from the line as the engine runs out of fuel, and what's left of the rotor blades spool down and grind to a halt like a big ceiling fan.

Chapter Forty Seven

The assault helicopters have stopped coming in, due to my chopper plugging up the LZ. Usually there is only room for one bird at a time in the LZ, and that is the situation today.

Making my way back to the uphill side of the helicopter, I search for the lieutenant I had seen only minutes before on the approach. He and his RTO are behind a small rock outcropping to my left firing selectively up into the jungle and rocky ridge. I whistle to get his attention. As he rolls to his side looking at me, I holler “Do we have a medic?” “No” he responds, “he was on the next lift in.”

The Cobra gun ships are laying down a heavy barrage of high explosive all around us, the mini-guns slicing through the jungle. But the gooks are too close to us to bring effective fire from the Cobras without also hitting us. Just over the uphill side of the ridge, artillery fire is pounding the jungle into kindling and firewood. It seems as if the gooks are going to stand and fight. The incoming fire is increasing in intensity as I low crawl back around the side of the ship to get Craig’s’ M-60. There is a grunt to my right firing full auto, protecting the uphill side of the ship. To his right is a grenadier, a “thumper man,” putting high explosive on the rocky outcropping overhead. The thumper man generally carries sixty to eighty rounds of mostly high explosives with them. Occasionally they will also carry a few buckshot and flechette rounds depending on their mission. This guy is firing his M-79 like he has a vested interest in the company that makes and sells this ammunition to the military. He's firing just like a machine on automatic.

Enemy fire is cracking and whipping all around us as the seven grunts and I that are left on the LZ engage in a non-stop fire fight. The lieutenant, hunched over, helmet pushed askew with the radio mashed up against his ear shouts and points where he wants my M-60 set up, facing up slope. I shove and push Craig's mini-gun can of ammo in my right hand and drag the "sixty" by the carrying handle in my left hand. As I set the gun up, dirt from small arms fire is smacking the ground around me stinging my face and hands from fragments of dirt and rock. I realize immediately that we are at a distinct disadvantage to the unseen enemy fire coming from above us. Finally the gun is set up and I get a sense of satisfaction as I shoot long bursts of grazing fire into the rock and jungle. The lieutenant shouts another command and motions with a hand signal to his grenadier. Normal voice communication is almost impossible, and we communicate more through hand and arm signals than anything else. The grenadier is loaded with a vest full of 40 millimeter grenades. Cradling his M-79 grenade launcher, he rolls and low crawls to a small tuft of grass and rock to my right. The grenadier rises up on an elbow looking up to the escarpment. He rolls over on his back and with a sideways motion of his body, half rolls and elevates the short barreled thumper. Over the din of gunfire the M-79 emits a hollow "poop" followed by the impact of his round near the jungle's edge. Like a machine he breaks the gun open, pulls another round from his bandolier, loads, and in one smooth motion fires again. The grenadier shoots accurate and effective high explosive rounds up on the NVA. As the gooks shift positions looking for cover, I begin to snap small bursts of fire at them. The grunt and I develop a routine of his searching fire followed by my killing fire as the NVA move to escape.

Feeling a tug on my sleeve, I look thinking it's the grenadier wanting to get my attention. But the grenadier, still three feet away, is focused on the terrain above. Bewildered as to who tugged at my arm, I look at my shoulder, lift my arm slightly, and there on my forearm is a jagged tear in my nomex flight suit. As I continue to stare, another round cracks just over the right side of my head. Instinctively I grab the M-60, tuck it to my chest and roll to my left as I scoot back a couple of feet. The machine gun ammo ratchets out of the can as I become enmeshed in belts of my own ammo from the roll. I thrash about thinking how stupid I am. I've just created my own web and encased myself in it.

Another round spanks the earth in front of my gun. Now I'm pissed. I twist and break the linked belted ammunition and shoot eighty to a hundred rounds to get clear of the confining ammo belt. As I straighten out a length of the machine gun ammo belt, I lift my head carefully and look along the edge of the ridge and escarpment for any target of opportunity. A hunched movement in the grassy brush above and to my left takes the full fury of my M-60 as I fire at least two hundred rounds at the spot. "Fuck you, you fuckin' gook" I holler, unable to contain my frustration and emotions any longer.

I look at the grenadier who is looking back at me. He looks at me wide eyed, like I've lost it, then with the realization I really am okay, he smiles and says "Aw right man, fire 'em lil' gook bastards up." "Airborne" I respond. "All the way" the grenadier responds, giving me a clenched fist "Black power" sign. We are brothers to the end, bonded together for all eternity. I've got your back, you've got mine.

Twenty and a wake up to go, short timers get zapped in the last month! Somebody else, not me! I've been here before, I will get outta this, I just gotta keep cool. Everything becomes brilliantly clear and focused as I move in an exaggerated slow motion. Although I know my body is moving at light speed, I feel a calmness surging through my body. The adrenaline rush clarifies my thought process. My hearing can isolate and separate unique and individual sounds of the battle. I can hear the gooks up on the hillside hollering now, talking in an excited manner. The "LT" talking to his "six" on the radio, a rifleman changing magazines, listening as he ejects, then taps the fresh magazine on his helmet, the grenadier breaking open the breach of his M-79 and the click of the round sliding into the chamber.

With an exaggerated clarity on how to reposition myself and my gun, I slide effortlessly in synch with myself and move again to my right. A small depression allows me to get a few inches lower to the ground. It feels just like the Grand Canyon to me. Another bullet cracks just over the left side of my head. I come to the realization that some dink has got target fixation on me! What's that all about, I ask myself? Why me? What did I do to him? I just want to get the hell out of here.

I pull more ammo out of the can and loop it in a pile at my side. I look at the grenadier, and wave my hand to get his attention. "Give me something to shoot at." He nods as I point uphill to my left where I can see the heaviest fire is coming from. The grenadier begins shooting so fast, I wonder if he's on the same rushing train I am. I watch in amazement at how fluid his motions are loading, firing, reloading. He puts high explosive rounds in the trees, on the trees, near the trees, in the rocks, and finally I get movement. Lots of movement now, like we've stirred the hornets nest! I begin firing. I twist the machine gun in a mad frenzy trying to concentrate fire on pockets of NVA as they rise from their hidden positions. The barrel of my gun is overheating, turning a powder white. I'm taking a toll of my own now on the exposed NVA troops. Empty shell casings begin to pile up, the spent brass burning my wrist, my arm. At least thirty NVA emerge from the jungle at the top of the hill, running at us in a full charge. We don't have the fire power to defend our position; we're going to be overrun! As the main body of troops clear the trees, one of our Cobras drops from the sky and literally comes to a hundred foot hover. Like an eagle waiting high in the sky, waiting and watching, its next meal now in sight, the grim reaper has come to harvest his crop. The Cobra gunner, bent over his gun sight, unloads in one awesome salvo all thirty-eight of his rockets on the tree line and escarpment aiming for the now concentrated troops. Instinctively I duck my head and flatten like a pancake as shrapnel; dirt, rock, body parts and smoke envelop the LZ.

Even as the rock, dirt and dust continue to shower us, I lift my head. NVA bodies litter the grass and tree line. The few remaining NVA, wounded, dismembered, bloody, and dazed, stagger and struggle back towards the protection of the jungle. I lift the pistol grips of my machine gun and begin firing into the wounded stragglers, cutting them down without remorse or pity. The Cobra gun ship that had come to our rescue joins in, twisting and pivoting, firing its mini-gun in two second bursts completing the carnage until there are no targets left to shoot.

The LZ is quiet. It's all over just as quickly as it had begun. Only the wop of Huey rotor blades in the distance and high speed rotor noise of the Cobras circling the LZ like sharks moving in for the kill disturbs the now still and quiet jungle. The NVA have vanished just as quickly as they appeared. The "LT", radio handset still crushed to his ear, calls in artillery as a follow on to securing the area. The artillery brackets all four sides of the LZ. The surrounding jungle turns into a massive kill zone. The rushing whoosh of the heavy artillery close overhead, joins with the now familiar sharp crack of "105" rounds. I can feel in my chest the heavy "whump" of 155's or eight inch rounds, as the thunderous impacting rounds gently heave and shake the earth I lay on.

The adrenaline rush leaves me shaking uncontrollably, my knees knock together. The grenadier crawls over to me and sticks out a dirty and calloused hand. "Name's Larry" he says. "Frank, Frank Lahti, ahh…Lot" I reply as I grab his hand and squeeze it firmly. Larry smiles. "Ya did some awful nice shootin' Larry. How long ya been in country?" It's then I notice Larry's black ace of spades and the short timer calendar on his helmet as he points to it. "Twenty and a wake up man" he says. I stare at Larry. Not believing the coincidence I ask, "When did you get in country?" "September eleven" he responds, looking at me like he wants to say, "Eat your heart out sucker." "Me too" I say. Now it's

Larry who's doing the staring. "Capital Airlines out of Oakland?" Larry says again, "Yeah man, I think so." "That's way too cool man."

We had come to Viet Nam together on the same plane. Now with some optimism, we would be going home together. Two short timers had made it through hopefully the last battle of their lives. No bad omens here. Words can't convey the emotions Larry and I feel. Without further thought I know it's time for me to quit flying...

Chapter Forty Eight

The flying war is over for me. Less than three weeks left in country, and I'm too short to stand in line for chow anymore. I'm so short; the guys would step on me while I was waiting to eat. My first sergeant has graciously put me on permanent charge of quarters or "CQ" duty. On my return from R & R I had my "talk" with Top about that prick Avionics guy, and the injustice of seniority and time in country. I think I was getting a little pay back from Top.

I go to work at six p.m., answer the company telephones, and do limited administrative "secretary" work until seven a.m. the following morning. It is great duty.

One night as I sit on the sandbags outside the headquarters hooch, far off to the east towards the sea, lighting dances across the horizon, followed by the rumble of thunder. It is not customary to expect thunderstorms at that time of year. But as I continue to sit and look to the East, to the ocean, I hear the elongated hollow "woof," "woof," "woof" of what I now recognize must be naval artillery shells passing overhead. They must be from the battleship New Jersey, or maybe the light cruiser Oklahoma City I speculate. Nah, that's not the shell from a cruiser, they fire six inch shells. Only a one ton shell like the "Jerseys' sixteen inchers" could make that kind of noise. With a range of over twenty miles, they could be hitting a target in the mountains. As I watch and wait looking to the West, to the mountains, I see the resulting "lighting" confirming my earlier speculation.

I had noticed in my travels through Japan, Hong Kong, and Viet Nam that Asian artists' were predisposed to painting moon rises and moon scapes over mountains. As I stand outside one evening, I watch the moon rise out of the South China Sea. I had seen moon rises through out the year in Viet Nam. But with an uncluttered and relaxed mind I could now appreciate it for the natural thing it was. It is one of the most breathtaking and beautiful settings I can ever remember seeing. The moon fills the entire horizon with its glow as it slowly ascends into the heavens. Later, not to be outdone, the moon setting over and slowly disappearing behind the mountains to the west makes me understand why those artists try in vain to capture the elusive splendor of the moon in all its glory.

Will I make it home? Now I know my mortality is an absolute surety. I knew it was all over for me when we crashed near the escarpment on the grassy plateau two weeks earlier. I learned that I don't want to leave this earth, nor the people that are closest to me, with any doubts or misrepresentation as to whom I was, or how I felt about them. I am compelled to say everything that needs to be said to anybody that touches my life in a personal way. There will never be a doubt as to where they stand with me. No misconceptions, no lies, this is who I am, and this is how I feel about you.

Always there is a need to find closure with traumatic events. I look to the past and search for understanding as to why things happened as they did. But no explanation can, nor ever will exist to explain fate, chance, luck or maybe divine intervention. Call it what you want, it's what memories are made of, both the good and bad. This is a facet to war that creates the internal stress to understand, to affirm, to know why? It is a fruitless effort. It will drive you crazy, if you think it's logical, war is anything but logical.

Love and friendship, however, have become synonymous. I have never felt so thankful for the special understanding of life I have been given to live and experience. I am wrapped in a cocoon of self-fulfillment, satisfied that I have experienced war for the most part unscathed and with all my faculties. I have no melancholy or sad feelings anymore about home or Viet Nam. I am going home God willing. My next full moon will be enjoyed with a new appreciation for my home, for my family and my girlfriend.

You look to the past, from the rise and fall of the Roman Empire, the Ancient Greeks and the Trojan War, all the way to the Korean War, in any armed conflict, one common thread exits between fighting men and the man standing on either side of them during battle. We dearly protect our compatriots not for God, the American way of life, or Mom's apple pie. We fight only to protect each others back and to simply stay alive. So we can go home.

"All the way to the sky" was a meaningful phrase that Craig and I "collaborated" on one starry night after a particularly grueling, stressful, and deadly day flying an emergency extraction out in the mountains. The phrase "all the way to the sky" simply meant, "without end." As profound as the distance is to the sky, the stars, the endless universe, it was our way of saying in a philosophical manner "eternally." We would always be there for our guys, and each other, right to the bitter end. An infantry platoon had been ambushed early that morning, and was in continuous contact fighting their way to a hastily contrived mountain pinnacle landing zone. Being an emergency, any resources that could respond were compelled to react as rapidly as possible to provide aid and assistance. At the moment we were one of three helicopters closest to their position. The pinnacle was so small that BJ could only rest the left skid of 644 on the edge of the mountain top. The right side of the Huey hung hundreds of feet over the edge. The grunts, through the running battle, had carried their dead and wounded with them. Firebase Airborne was the closest suitable drop off point, and we shuttled the dead and wounded as fast as we could possibly go. The trip from Airborne to the LZ and back was not more than a ten minute flight allowing us to quickly evacuate the men from a very precarious position. However, in the time it took to get back, there were more wounded and dead, and the number of troopers left in the fight was quickly diminishing to almost nonexistent. Artillery had joined with Cobra gun ships to slow the advance of the NVA and provide cover fire on the approach for our birds. But by then, the NVA made almost no attempt to conceal themselves from our approach as they obviously smelled death and defeat of our sky soldiers close at hand. The killing was almost maniacal on both sides, as we fought quite literally for our lives and the men waiting to be extracted. Anybody would have been proud to serve with these men, as the airborne soldiers firing their weapons all the way into the Huey were bolstered by Craig firing his M-16 out the side of my door with the supporting fire of my M-60. It all seemed very inaffective in halting or slowing the progress of the advancing NVA. Pulling the last lift of grunts off the mountain and exiting with a stomach heaving dive was nothing short of miraculous as BJ nosed the helicopter over, literally falling off the edge of the precipice. The artillery rounds for the LZ where already on the way as "TOT" or "time on target." Our Peter Pilot had coordinated with the big guns on Currahee to shield our departure on the last lift exiting the LZ. The timing of the deadly eruptions could not have been better as the incoming 105 howitzer shells saturated the jungle LZ with lethal shrapnel. It was over, great teamwork and coordination, all the way to the sky, we'll always take care of our own. We talked about how the true depth and significance of life beyond family and loved ones had little value or meaning to the rest of the world. The immediate and intimate concern of our families was insignificant in comparison to the cares of the rest of the world. The only people able to feel the anguish of war, or the true depth of loss, of misery, of pain, would be those on the front lines pulling the trigger, and the people immediately connected to those soldiers so far away. To give it meaning so others would understand would also be pointless. But on occasion it would pass our lips coupled with a knowing look, as punctuation for something akin to eternity. For what we have shared, like family, I am your "brother," "all the way to the sky"--and maybe even a little farther than that.

"Brat" Bradley L. Kirstman was a door gunner in second flight platoon. He was the last person I personally knew to become a casualty of the war before I left Viet Nam. Sitting near the griddle in the mess tent at breakfast, I saw him cajoling the cooks for an extra pancake, and he was killed later that morning on an ass and trash flight. I don't miss that feeling of excitement at the possibility of contact, or going in harms way. If there are any lingering feelings, if any thoughts haunt me, it is those of my close friends who have died here. I think of them often. "Better him than me" just doesn't work for me anymore. The only way I can accept their death and press on is to keep them in my heart and memories. I will never forget them. And as long as I keep them in my thoughts, they are truly not dead. When a person dies, that container that we call a body is nothing more than a hunk of flesh. I have come to think of it in that way. The vessel that carried the spirit or soul of that individual is broken, and can't be fixed. The brain that body held is the true spirit of who that person was. And now the soul of that person, the brain, no longer functions, gone with the broken vessel. But I will remember their mannerisms, their laughs, the smiles, the pranks, all the good, and some of the bad, of my friends. And as long as I live, they will not be dead, because I remember.

Chapter Forty Nine

Only eight days and a wake up to go. Ho Chi Minh died today. We are put on full alert at Camp Evans to expect some nastiness from the gooks. But it is a quiet night with nothing more than an occasional artillery shoot, and maybe somewhat more than the usual illumination around the perimeter. Falling into the easy routine of administration makes my remaining time pass quickly. Generally I will do paperwork until midnight, interspersed with communications from the sergeant of the guard for the bunkers, or the "O.D." - the officer of the day. The O.D. and the sergeant of the guard are rotating positions, changing personnel every night. So I get to chat with a new officer and sergeant every night and it sure breaks up the monotony of the night. They are responsible for the orderly running of the company while the "first shirt" and C.O. are away from company headquarters.

A few days later at about three in the morning, I go outside for a smoke. The closeness of the company headquarters hooch has left me warm and clammy. The air is cool for an early September morning, and I shiver as the sweat quickly evaporates from my body. The parade ground is well lit with mercury vapor lamps, the generators powering them hum in the distance. As I stand there enjoying the quiet and solitude of the night, I casually survey the surroundings knowing in little more than a week this will all be only a memory.

Standing there thinking about home and my future, I catch movement to my left. The steel Conexes are located there, forming the west boundary of our company area. Shielding my eyes from the bright glow of light within the parade ground, I scan the area where I had noticed the movement. My eyes are still adjusting to the dark as I make out a figure lying prone on the top of a Conex container with a weapon! The barrel of the weapon protrudes from the top of the container as I try to see who is up there. Moving ever so slowly along the sandbagged path of the company hooch I can make out that it is definitely a G.I. with an M-16. As I get closer, I recognize him as a relatively new gunner attached to the second flight platoon. "Marsak" had extended his Viet Nam tour by six months to get out of the infantry and become a door gunner in an aviation unit.

"Hey, Marsak." "Hey Lot." Marsaks' response is barely a whisper. "What da ya doin?" I ask. "Keep away man, it's either him or me" a slight panic in his voice. Not wanting to do anything to alarm Marsak, but wanting to understand what the heck was going on, I asked him "You don't have a round in the chamber do you?" "Oh no." he responded almost immediately. "We're not supposed to lock and load in the company area." Well okay, I thought; at least he has the presence of mind to not have a loaded weapon. He was after all an experienced infantryman. "Who's out there?" I glanced around the well lit company area, a little nervous myself, peering into the shadows, looking for anything out of the ordinary. I crouched down on a knee, I was actually getting a little anxious that maybe I should have a weapon myself if he really had seen something. "Stay back; it's either him or me." he repeated. With the tone of his voice, I sensed that Marsak wasn't all there at the moment.

Marsak had spent eight months with the infantry prior to extending his tour to get a door gunners slot. He was a quiet young man who did his job well with the Ghost Riders. He had been with our company for a little over two months after his thirty day leave spent stateside.

"Who's out there?" I asked Marsak again. "Charlie....man, it's Charlie." His exasperated response was almost a hiss, "It's either him or me" he repeated again. "Where is he?" Still not understanding if this was real or imagined. "Out there man." Marsak points with the barrel of his weapon into the darkness. I could see in his eyes and understood that Marsak was possibly on the verge of flipping out. "Stay here man; I'm going to get us some help." "It's either him or me," Marsak said in an almost pleading voice obviously very concerned for my safety. Back in the company hooch, I call the Officer of the Day and advise him as to what was transpiring. Going back out to keep an eye on Marsak, and wait for the O.D., Marsak had left the steel Conex and is nowhere to be seen. I move about the area cautiously looking for Marsak, hoping at the same time the O.D. would show up.

A few minutes later the O.D. shows up with two guys from the perimeter guard as I explain what has happened. We split up and begin to scour the company area and surrounding hooch's looking for Marsak. After twenty minutes of fruitless searching, I make a swing through his hooch, hoping that maybe he has returned. There's Marsak on his cot, sleeping, curled up with his M-16 still cradled in his arms. I slowly take the M-16 from his hands and let him sleep.

Returning to the C.Q., the O.D. has left one of our guys to keep a watch on Marsak. The following morning, Marsak is shipped out, in a straight jacket.

Later that day after Marsak has departed; I'm relating the evening's events to "Booger," Marsak's crew chief. Booger told me that Marsak had been having nightmares and telling stories about this very event. Sometime after Marsak had gone on his extension leave, his infantry platoon had been caught in a "daisy chain" ambush. All of the men in Marsak's squad had been either killed or seriously wounded. Marsak "believed" that Charlie knew they had missed him in the kill zone. And in Marsaks' mind,

Charlie was coming after him, the missing squad member, to finish the job. We all had issues here, I had been down the crazy road myself, but it had gotten to Marsak.

Chapter Fifty

Arriving from Viet Nam at Oakland California, the Army terminal, the place I had left just one long year ago was an unfamiliar place now. The place was jammed with returning 'Nam vets. Without at first consciously realizing it, I was analyzing my physical being, wondering if anything had really changed. I walked the same, and I talked the same for the most part. Maybe I had a little more of the "salty" language than I had before. I definitely talked the language of an experienced head, a dope smoker. Oh yeah, I definitely liked dew, grass, Mary Jane, Wacky tobaccee. Grass may very well have kept me sane those last three or four months. It had provided an outlet, an escape, just like booze did for the "rednecks" and hillbillies. Only thing is, I was in the states now. The land of McDonalds, movies, girls, cars and anything your heart desired. No more need to escape with smoke, I wanted to live now. I wanted to taste and experience all that life and the United States have to offer, without being clouded over, stupefied and diminished in the brain.

But I still felt basically the same. One year hadn't changed a thing. When I became aware that I was challenging myself to prove I had changed or not, I realized that that, in and of itself, was a change. But not so dramatic that I could say definitively,

"Frank, you've changed."

Everybody coming back was welcomed with a steak dinner, cooked to order. All I wanted was to get the hell out of anything military or green. To that end, I skipped the steak and went straight for the showers and a new "class A" uniform for traveling.

Turning on the shower, the hot water misting from the flow of water felt great. Our mode of showering in Viet Nam had been accomplished with "drop tanks" painted black, laid over a tall wood structure. Drop tanks were the spare fuel tanks the aircraft jettisoned from our fighters, the "fast movers" that went up North. They littered the beach and country side, and made excellent water storage tanks when cleaned out. Solar power from the sun and the heat of the day provided limited warm water to be enjoyed. Gravity fed the shower heads, and canvas provided some privacy.

But now the hot water splashing and misting at my feet felt wonderful as I moved face first into the shower. The water pressure from the shower head stung my face as I instinctively turned my back to relieve the stinging sensation. Turning my face away from the water exposed my butt to the shower and with a yelp; I jumped out of the shower spray. Surprised that I had been stung unexpectedly by the force of the water, I laughed realizing I had missed that water pressure in the last year. Then it came to me, if I had forgotten or missed something as simple as water pressure, what subtle emotions or feelings could have changed within me?

It seems like I've been gone five years, but it's only been twelve months. I keep telling myself that nothing much has really changed. I've been home for three days, no great shakes there. It's a twelve hour time difference and a world apart from Viet Nam. It's as if it never was, just a great daytime nightmare, just like my daytime nightmare I experienced in Viet Nam. People go to work, they go shopping, Friday night games, dates, the hangout, cruisin' the strip, a daily routine, it's all the same, and nothing has changed.

I'm standing on the sidelines at a Friday night football game talking with Ken, a Marine 'Nam vet from my hometown who was at Khe San. As we watch the game and talk quietly, a siren sounds in the distance. It's the 10 P.M. curfew siren for school kids. For me it's the siren announcing incoming rockets and artillery. I am locked in place, frozen to the very ground I stand on, unable to move. Only my eyes move as if in an epileptic state, darting about, seeking cover, somewhere to hide from the incoming. No one but Ken notices the look on my face and without sarcasm says in a quiet voice, "The siren gotcha', didn't it?" For three seconds, I'm back in Viet Nam, my heart in my throat. Yeah I think...maybe I have changed, I might have a war story to tell.

Epilogue

"Mustering" out of Viet Nam, back in Bien Hoa, division rear of the 101st Airborne, I look for Larry, my thumper man. After leaving the LZ that we were shot down in, I want to see Larry again, to assure that we indeed had fought our last battle together. I have a special bond with that man, but I will never see Larry again. I remain in Bien Hoa for three days clearing up all the final paper work, waiting for my "Freedom Bird" home.

Tonight sitting in the EM Club, I sing the same songs I had heard while going through the final "P" training test maze one year earlier. I wonder if guys are still going through their initial training just as I did, even as I sit there knowing it's all over for me. It is a time I begin to reflect on the past year. It had seemed like forever, but none the less, it was over in the blink of an eye. I worry in those last days about getting zapped by an errant mortar round fired haphazardly by the gooks. It would really piss me off to get "it" in that manner while defenseless and waiting to go home. After constantly carrying a rifle and pistol for nearly a year, I truly feel naked not having any kind of weapon near me.

Returning to the States I meet up with my buddy Scotty back in Savannah Georgia. He never did fly while in Viet Nam, more through choice than desire. He is all in one piece and it is good to see him again. Scotty and I get a house off base with two other Viet Nam returnees and party hearty every night we can. After leaving the Army I exchange letters with Scotty only once, and it is a bitter sweet ending. He explains that he does not wish to remember that period in his life nor the people that he associated with during that time.

BJ to my surprise, refusing by his count four attempts by the military to medically discharge him, stays in the Army. He is adamant about returning to flying status as a Warrant Officer. My first reunion with him is on Thanksgiving morning at Hunter Army Air Field two months after my return from Viet Nam. As I sleep off a Holiday hangover, I am rudely awakened, pulled from the bed and pushed to the floor with my mattress on top of me. Someone

(BJ) is jumping up and down on top of me! It is a reunion of the greatest magnitude. After my discharge from the Army it will be thirty six years before I reconnect with him, and it's like we've never been more than a day away from each other. That's brotherhood!! He finally accepts his discharge and now flies and rebuilds airplanes for fun. He has two great sons, grandchildren, and his wife Susan, who has been with him as his new bride even before BJ's tour to Viet Nam.

My new found friend Dave from Green Bay, who I had struck a quick friendship with on the assault into LZ Blaze; after years of searching for him did not make it. Like Greg and so many others, he will always be with me in spirit, remembering those deer hunts in the great North woods of the Upper Peninsula of Michigan. After many years of hunting as a youth, I am unable and unwilling to pull the trigger anymore. If that is my worst fate of war, I accept it gladly!

After Viet Nam, I finally aspired to something I had always wanted, I became a professional pilot. I am now in control of my own destiny, instead of leaving it in the hands of other pilots. I will catch myself occasionally wondering if I had the "SISU," the guts, the determination, or simply the ability to fly the hostile LZ's we so often went into along with those other great pilots. I certainly would like to think so...